The Cakes of Wrath

"Skillful writing in this lighthearted mystery featuring ov[er]-the-top characters and fun dialogue . . . Readers should exp[ect] the zaniness that seems prevalent in the beautiful, historic[,] absurd New Orleans." —*Kings River Life Magaz[ine]*

"Another great addition to the Piece of Cake [Mysterie[s]. The author's good plotting keeps you turning those page[s]. Love the characters and always look forward to stopping [by] and seeing what is going on at Zydeco Cakes."
—*MyShelf.com*

"A joy to read from start to finish. The descriptions are vivid. The prose is smart, snarky, and possesses as much character and charm as New Orleans itself." —*The Season*

Arsenic and Old Cake

"[It] wrapped me up in a delectable mystery right from the first page. With a cast of unsavory characters at the B and B, I was having a hard time trying to figure out who the murderer was. Jacklyn Brady kept me on my toes, and I didn't manage to solve the mystery before Rita." —*Cozy Mystery Book Reviews*

"This is my favorite book in this series! The quirky characters, residents of the B and B, are fantastic and funny, and full of secrets, some deadly secrets . . . The romantic tension jumped up a notch in the edition as well . . . I highly recommend this story and this series. They are full of mystery, mayhem, and way too many delectable treats."
—*Escape with Dollycas into a Good Book*

continued . . .

Cake on a Hot Tin Roof

"A fast-paced delightful amateur-sleuth tale starring a feisty independent pastry chef . . . *Cake on a Hot Tin Roof* is an interesting whodunit." —*The Mystery Gazette*

"The setting and atmosphere in *Cake on a Hot Tin Roof* are very appealing . . . Rita is a very appealing character with loads of energy and a lot to deal with . . . All done with aplomb." —*The Mystery Reader*

"The New Orleans setting keeps the book lively, and I loved the rich details and ambiance the author conveys . . . Jacklyn Brady has mixed up the perfect concoction of suspects, motives, means, and opportunity. True-to-real-life characters and situations that could be ripped from the headlines of any major city news outlet make *Cake on a Hot Tin Roof* a sequel that fans of this series will not want to miss!" —*MyShelf.com*

"A truly excellent read. While one doesn't regularly connect the fun and frivolity of Mardi Gras with the darkness of murder, this is something the author balanced well." —*Fresh Fiction*

A Sheetcake Named Desire

"A tasty treat for mystery lovers, combining all the right ingredients in a perfectly prepared story that's sure to satisfy." —B. B. Haywood, national bestselling author of *Town in a Strawberry Swirl*

"A decadent new series with a Big Easy attitude." —Paige Shelton, national bestselling author of *If Catfish Had Nine Lives*

Rebel
Without a Cake

Jacklyn Brady

BERKLEY PRIME CRIME, NEW YORK

THE BERKLEY PUBLISHING GROUP
Published by the Penguin Group
Penguin Group (USA) LLC
375 Hudson Street, New York, New York 10014

USA • Canada • UK • Ireland • Australia • New Zealand • India • South Africa • China

penguin.com

A Penguin Random House Company

REBEL WITHOUT A CAKE

A Berkley Prime Crime Book / published by arrangement with the author

Berkley Prime Crime Books are published by The Berkley Publishing Group.
BERKLEY® PRIME CRIME and the PRIME CRIME logo are trademarks of
Penguin Group (USA) LLC.

For information, address: The Berkley Publishing Group,
a division of Penguin Group (USA) LLC,
375 Hudson Street, New York, New York 10014.

ISBN: 978-0-425-25827-9

PUBLISHING HISTORY
Berkley Prime Crime mass-market edition / September 2014

PRINTED IN THE UNITED STATES OF AMERICA

10 9 8 7 6 5 4 3 2 1

Cover illustration by Chris Lyons.
Cover design by Diana Kolsky.
Interior text design by Laura K. Corless.

To the women of the amazing weekend in Pigeon Forge.
Linda, LJ, Connie, Gayle, Alison, Jill, Nic, and Geralyn.
You filled me up with friendship, laughter,
and writing talk right when I needed it most.

One

"*You need to tell her,*" the voice inside my head whispered. It's an annoying voice, so despite the fact that my aunt had raised me to listen when my conscience voiced an opinion, I did my best to ignore it. It isn't *always* right, and besides, I was pretty sure Aunt Yolanda hadn't counted on me having to deliver bad news to Frances Mae Renier when she gave me that advice.

Frances Mae, known by most as Miss Frankie, is my mother-in-law (which explains why Aunt Yolanda didn't know about her when I was a kid). She's also my business partner. Together we run Zydeco Cakes, a high-end bakery near New Orleans's Garden District. Actually, I do much of the running. Miss Frankie is my mostly silent partner who does behind-the-scenes stuff like writing checks and nudging high-profile clients our way.

My name is Rita Lucero, and I want to say up front that, despite my hesitation to come clean with Miss Frankie,

I am *not* a coward. I *am* a trained pastry chef who moved from Albuquerque to New Orleans just like *that* last summer when Miss Frankie offered me the chance to take over the day-to-day operations at Zydeco after the death of her son, Philippe, my almost-ex-husband. I'd had to stand up to Uncle Nestor to do it, too. Believe me, that took courage.

My complicated relationship with Miss Frankie is why I was parking the Mercedes I'd inherited from Philippe's estate in her driveway on a Friday night. I should have been joining the rest of Zydeco's staff for a birthday party at the Dizzy Duke, our favorite after-hours hangout. But Miss Frankie had summoned me, so here I was. I didn't know what she wanted, but that wasn't unusual. Still, I was feeling a little resentful as I climbed the front steps and rang her doorbell.

A stiff wind tossed the branches of the massive trees that lined the street. Their shadows did a macabre dance suitable for the Halloween season on Miss Frankie's sweeping front lawn, and I smiled as I watched them shift and bend.

Halloween is one of my favorite holidays. Not because I'm overly fond of ghosts and goblins, but because I have sweet memories of trick-or-treating with my parents when I was young. They died in a car accident the year I turned twelve. I've lost too many memories of them over the years so I cling to the ones I've managed to keep. Losing them flipped my world upside down for a while, so I knew how much losing her only child had rocked Miss Frankie's. I do my best to be gentle with her, which is why I was hesitating over telling her that I'd be going to Albuquerque for Christmas. We'd limped through the holidays last year, mostly ignoring the festivities and staying home rather than joining others. She tries hard not to be clingy where I'm concerned, and some days she succeeds. Others, she hangs on to me like a good-quality plastic wrap.

Miss Frankie was well aware that I had missed home since I'd moved to New Orleans. She knew that, with the exception of one brief visit from Aunt Yolanda and Uncle Nestor, I hadn't seen my family in over a year. I'd left my familiar Hispanic culture behind and stepped into the very different world of New Orleans, and sometimes homesickness hit hard. Surely Miss Frankie would understand why I wanted to go back for Christmas. At least she'd try to.

I heard footsteps on the other side of the door, and an instant later it flew open. Miss Frankie greeted me with a warm hug and a glimmer of excitement in her golden brown eyes. In spite of the late hour, she looked ready to begin her day. Her auburn hair was teased and sprayed, a whiff of Shalimar noticeable as she wrapped her arms around me. She wore a pair of wide-legged pants and a loose-fitting tunic made of silky rust-colored fabric. A pair of off-white sandals revealed toenails painted a deep pumpkin color to match her fingernails.

"Thanks for coming, sugar. Let's talk in the kitchen. I've got everything in there."

I wondered what "everything" was, but I knew there was only one way to find out. After closing the door behind me, I followed her to the back of the house. "I can't stay long," I warned as we walked. "I'm meeting the rest of the staff at the Duke in half an hour to celebrate Dwight's birthday."

Dwight is one of Zydeco's best cake artists and an old friend from pastry school. He'd come to New Orleans to work for Philippe, but he'd been supportive of me since Philippe died and I took over at Zydeco. I wanted to show him that I could be a good friend, too.

I was even looking forward to the party, which I considered progress since I'm not much of a partier. When Philippe and I were married, I was much more likely to be found balancing the books while he entertained our friends. Since stepping into his shoes at Zydeco, I'd been making an effort to loosen up.

Miss Frankie glanced back at me. "Is that tonight? I guess I plumb forgot about it. But don't worry. This won't take but a minute." She stopped just inside the kitchen and motioned me toward the table, which was piled with magazines, recipe books, newspaper clippings, and a large three-ring binder—the kind she used whenever she coordinated a social event. It's her favorite thing to do.

"It looks like you've been busy," I said. "Are you planning a party?"

She grinned and headed for the coffeemaker. "Not exactly." She turned back to me and linked her hands together over her chest. "Oh, sugar, isn't it exciting? I decided to take Pearl Lee's advice."

I knew right then that we were in for trouble. Pearl Lee Gates is Miss Frankie's cousin, five foot nothing of "Let's see how much I can get away with." She's a few years younger than Miss Frankie, which puts her somewhere in her late fifties or early sixties, I think. Talking to her is dangerous enough. Taking her advice could be a disaster. You'd think Miss Frankie would know that by now.

"What advice is that?" I asked. I thought I sounded remarkably calm, considering.

"Well, about Christmas, of course. It's only two months away."

Uh-oh. I got a squidgy feeling in my stomach, and my conscience gave me a sharp poke. This was the perfect time to tell Miss Frankie about my plans. And I probably would have if she hadn't kept talking.

"I was thinking about giving it a miss again this year. The thought of sitting around while people talk about Philippe—and you know they will—is just too much. It's barely been more than a year since he died and people think I should be through grieving. But we both know it doesn't ever really end."

We'd just stepped onto uneven ground so I thought about my response before I spoke. I didn't have any experience with losing a child, but I did know how easy it was to get stuck in the moment of a loved one's death. I didn't want that for Miss Frankie, and I knew Philippe wouldn't have wanted it either. "It doesn't end," I agreed cautiously, "but it does change with time. I still miss my parents, but the thought of them doesn't hurt like it used to."

My conscience flicked me again, but Miss Frankie was staring at me with eyes that were too bright and a smile that looked too brittle. She tried so hard to cope with the death of her only child but I could tell that she was on the edge of tears, so I swallowed my news and smiled instead. "So does this mean you're going to join your family this year?" I said. "I think that's wonderful."

"It's better than that," she said, waving me toward a chair. "We're *hosting* this year."

I think I gasped. I was all for Miss Frankie taking a step forward this year, but hosting? What was she thinking?

"You're doing what?" I squeaked.

"Hosting the family. They'll all come here this year."

If Pearl Lee had been in the room, I might have throttled her right then and there. In Miss Frankie–speak, *family* meant a dozen cousins from the Dumond family line along with their spouses and any children or grandchildren who had no other plans. Throw in a couple of ancient aunts and uncles and a Renier relative or two at loose ends, and she could be looking at fifty mouths or more to feed.

"That's a huge job," I pointed out in case she'd failed to do the math. "Are you sure that's what you want?"

"Well, of course, it's far too big a job to do alone. That's why I'm counting on your help. I'll admit that when Pearl Lee first suggested it, I thought it would be too, *too* much, but then she pointed out that by inviting everyone here, we'll be able to set the tone for the holiday week and maintain some kind of control over the events. It's my turn anyway, so I really should just jump in and do it."

"But I—" I sank into the closest chair and tried not to sound angry. That wasn't easy. Miss Frankie has a habit of volunteering me for things without talking to me first. It's one of the few downsides of our relationship. "I'm sure everyone would understand if you wanted to wait another year."

"But I don't want to wait. That's the point."

I knew that Pearl Lee was responsible for Miss Frankie's attitude, and that irritated me big-time. Pearl Lee has her fair share of problems, but Miss Frankie is fiercely loyal. I'd learned not to bad-mouth her cousin in front of her, so again I went with a careful answer. "Pearl Lee might have a point," I said with caution. "But wouldn't you rather put your heads together and do this with her?"

Miss Frankie waved a dismissive hand. "Pearl Lee is useless when it comes to things like this. I need your head, sugar. I've been thinking that if you make some amazing cake for the family, they'll see that the bakery is in good hands and we'll be able to focus on the future instead of the past."

"Yes, but—" Hearing her talk about moving on was a good sign, even if her chosen method for doing it was questionable. I took another deep breath to steady my nerves. "You can't keep making commitments for me without talking to me first. What if I had other plans?" Okay, so it wasn't the direct approach, but it was the best I could do with the threat of my mother-in-law's tears so close to the surface.

When it comes to Miss Frankie, it's more effective to steal a few bases at a time than to try for a home run right off.

Her expression fell, but she looked concerned for only a moment. "*Have* you made plans? Gracious! I never even thought. Well, that's no problem. You'll just invite whoever it is to join us here. After all, the more the merrier. Is it one of your young men?"

By that, she meant Liam Sullivan, a detective with the New Orleans PD's Homicide Division, and Gabriel Broussard, part-owner of the Dizzy Duke. I'd been seeing both of them over the past year—all open and aboveboard—but neither relationship had progressed to the "spend holidays together" stage.

I screwed up my courage, ready to tell Miss Frankie about Albuquerque, but she didn't wait for an answer. She waved a hand at the mess on the table. "We can work all of that out later. That isn't what I wanted to talk to you about anyway. I have the most wonderful news for Zydeco, and I simply couldn't wait to tell you. How would you feel about making a cake for the Crescent City Vintage Clothing Society Belle Lune Ball?"

Every thought inside my head froze and my heart began to thump. The Crescent City Vintage Clothing Society was one of the most prestigious groups in New Orleans. The Belle Lune Ball, held each January, was a premiere social event. The moneyed set shelled out staggering amounts of cash for tickets every year, and the silent auction brought in a whopping total that was used to help disadvantaged women around the world.

"Are you kidding me?" I asked. "We actually have a shot?"

Miss Frankie smiled slyly. "You like the idea?"

"Um . . . *yeah!* It's only one of the biggest events in the whole city. Do you know what a coup like that would do for our reputation?"

"I have a good idea. That's why, when I heard that the

society had an opening, I invited Evangeline Delahunt to lunch. She's eager to find someone quickly. For an event that size, time is running out. I saw an opportunity to get your work in front of the right people and I took it."

Uuurch! My excitement ground to a screeching halt. "Wait a minute. You're not talking about *this* year's ball? The one just three months away . . . are you? With the holidays and everything, it's going to be tough to come up with a design, coordinate everything, and put together the kind of cake they'd want."

"Well . . . it's a little more than just the cake, sugar. Actually, she needs a caterer for the entire event." Miss Frankie flicked her wrist as if catering dinner for a few hundred people would add barely any extra work. "Don't worry, though. I have faith in you."

"But Zydeco doesn't *do* catering," I pointed out in what I hoped was a reasonable tone. "We've never done catering."

"That doesn't mean you can't do it. You've had training, and I know Ox and Dwight have, too. Really, Rita, I'm offering you the chance of a lifetime. But if you really don't want to do it, I'll call Evangeline and tell her to look for someone else. She'll be disappointed, but I'm sure she won't hold it against you."

I kneaded my forehead and tried to pull my thoughts together. "Why did she wait so long to find a caterer? Surely she knows what a huge job this is."

Miss Frankie waved her hand again. "Well, of course she knows. She's been in charge of planning the ball for at least a decade. This is a great opportunity for Zydeco and for everyone who works there. There will be press coverage of the event, and there's a very good chance you'll be interviewed yourself."

"But we don't *do* catering," I reminded her again. "I don't want Zydeco to gain a reputation as a caterer. I want it to be known as New Orleans's premiere bakery for high-end cakes."

"And it will be, after you do this job." Miss Frankie gave me a look that clearly said she thought I was being a bit slow on the uptake. "Philippe tried more than once to get his foot in the door with Evangeline Delahunt. He never could do it."

That made my ears perk up. Philippe and I had met in pastry school, and at least in the beginning, we'd indulged in what I thought was a healthy and harmless competition, pitting our cake decorating and business skills against each other whenever the occasion arose. Looking back, I could see now that before we'd separated, the competition had become less healthy, but I hadn't realized it at the time.

Hearing about Philippe's failure to land the contract I'd just been handed made my competitive side yawn and stretch like a cat waking up after a long nap. I tried again to get an answer to my question. "If working for Evangeline Delahunt is such a *coup de grâce,* why is she looking for a caterer at this late date?"

Miss Frankie's gaze flickered ever so slightly, which set off a warning bell in my head. "She had to let the first one go. Something about them failing to produce an appropriate design and menu. I could have told her she'd be dissatisfied with her original choice if she'd only asked my advice. Anyway, she'll be coming to see you tomorrow morning at ten. I hope that works with your schedule."

"Wait a minute," I said. "I haven't agreed to this yet. Who was her original choice?"

My mother-in-law gave me an enigmatic smile. "Gâteaux."

I could almost hear the sound of her reeling me in. Gâteaux was Zydeco's stiffest competition, and Dmitri Wolff, Gâteaux's owner, was a complete snake in the grass.

He'd not only tried to lure away my staff, but also indulged in a little industrial sabotage before trying to buy Zydeco from Miss Frankie after Philippe died. I smiled slowly. "Wolff couldn't make her happy?"

"Apparently not."

Just like that, every one of my objections disappeared. Like I said, I have a competitive nature. So what if Gâteaux had had months to come up with a winning plan? The important thing was that I had a chance to succeed where Dmitri Wolff had failed.

I had an amazing staff made up of the most talented cake artists around. About half of us had formal training in the kitchen, and the others were talented artists who'd learned on the job. We worked together like a well-oiled machine. Most of the time anyway. If anybody could do this, I thought to myself, we could. And besides, it would be morally irresponsible to leave such a well-publicized and popular event without a caterer. Or, considerably worse, with substandard food for their event.

I swallowed all of my concerns and smiled. "I'll make it work."

"Good. Now, about Christmas—"

The abrupt change of subject caught me off guard, and before I could shift gears, I heard the sound of Miss Frankie's back garden gate open and close, followed by rapid footsteps tapping toward the kitchen door. A moment later someone banged on the door urgently.

Mild concern hit me at once, but relief at the interruption was the stronger emotion. After all, I thought, nothing bad ever happens in Miss Frankie's neighborhood. Yep, I actually thought that. And yeah, I was wrong.

Two

"Goodness, what a racket!" Miss Frankie said, waving me back to the seat I'd risen from. She peeked out the window and glanced at me with a scowl. "Well, for heaven's sake, it's Bernice. Honestly, Bernice! There's no need to break down the door," Miss Frankie scolded.

She opened the door and her next-door neighbor, Bernice Dudley, stumbled inside. The two women have been friends and neighbors for much longer than I've been around. I'm pretty sure they're roughly the same age but they wear the years very differently. Miss Frankie is tall, thin, and angular with short hair that's not only kept teased and heavily sprayed by her stylist, but tinted an unnatural shade of auburn for a woman her age.

Bernice is shorter, rounder, and generally fluffier. But not today. It took only one look for me to see that something was wrong. She clutched a Bible to her chest and her face was as white as the cloud of softly curling hair on her head. She blinked back tears as she staggered through the door. After fumbling with the knob for a moment, she looked up in frustration. "How do I lock this thing?"

Miss Frankie gently nudged her out of the way and turned the lock. "Why, Bernice, you're shaking like a leaf. What's wrong?"

Bernice tightened her grip on the Bible. "I just saw someone outside my window. It about scared me to death."

Concern suddenly trumped the relief I'd been feeling over the interruption. Bernice is a sweet woman, and I didn't like thinking that something had frightened her.

Miss Frankie just looked confused. "What do you mean, you saw someone?"

"I mean, I *saw* someone," Bernice snapped. "A man. Right outside my kitchen window."

That got me on my feet in a hurry. I looked out the large back window, hoping I wouldn't see anything—or anyone— out there. The two women live in an affluent neighborhood with a low crime rate, but it is part of New Orleans and bad things can happen anywhere. Better to be safe than sorry.

The dense trees separating one property from the next would make it easy for someone to hide in the shadows, but I couldn't see any men, strange or otherwise, skulking around the backyard. That made me feel a little better. "Are you sure you saw a man?"

Bernice gave her eyes an impatient roll. "As sure as I'm standing here. He was right outside my window, staring inside. At *me!*" A shudder racked her body and she collapsed onto the chair I'd vacated.

I turned back for a second look. I could see Miss Frankie's reflection as she sat beside Bernice and patted her hand.

"I'm sure it's not anything to worry about," Miss Frankie said. "It was probably one of the neighbors."

"It was *not* a neighbor," Bernice informed us tersely. Her attitude surprised me. I'd never seen her like this, and it worried me. "I know all my neighbors," she insisted. "This was not one of them."

"You didn't recognize him, then?" I asked.

Bernice took a shaky breath and her gaze fell to the Bible on her chest. "I thought I did for a minute. He looked like . . . like someone. But it wasn't him. That I know for sure."

"Try not to let it upset you," Miss Frankie said in a soothing tone. "It's almost Halloween. Kids are out playing tricks. One of them just wandered into your yard, probably trying to spook you. It's understandable that you were startled, but let's not overreact."

Bernice's cheeks turned a deep shade of pink. "I am *not* overreacting. I know what I saw, Frances. That was no child playing tricks. And don't you look at me that way. I know you think I'm seeing things, but I wasn't."

I checked the window for a third time, craning to see into all the corners of Miss Frankie's yard. The trees were still doing their dance in the wind, and shadowy shapes flitted here and there in the moonlight. "Maybe it was a trick of the wind," I suggested. "You know . . . a shadow or something."

"It was *not* a shadow. I saw a man clear as day. I saw his *face*. He was as close to me as I am to you. Just, thank God, on the other side of the window."

Miss Frankie glanced at me briefly. I could see the doubt in her eyes. "In that case," she said to Bernice, "why did you leave the house? Something horrible might have happened to you."

Bernice put one trembling hand into her pocket. "Well,

I couldn't stay there by myself, could I? I had my Bible and I said the Lord's Prayer over and over while I was running over here. And besides, I had this with me." With a flourish, sweet little Bernice pulled out a small handgun.

I gasped in surprise. "You have a gun?"

"Well, of course I do. Don't tell me you don't carry protection."

"No, I don't. Is it loaded?"

She gave me a *duh!* look. "There wouldn't be much point in carrying it if it wasn't."

I guess she had a point there. But still . . . "Do you know how to use it?"

"Rita, honey, I've been shooting since I was knee-high to a grasshopper. Daddy taught all us kids."

My own father and I had skipped that particular bonding ritual, but I didn't mind. Leaving my post at the window, I joined the other two women at the table and jerked my head toward the gun in Bernice's shaky hand. "Did you know she had that thing?" I asked Miss Frankie.

She shrugged casually. "Of course I did. I have one myself."

Whoa! *What?* "You do? Where?"

Miss Frankie transferred her patting hand from Bernice to me. "Oh, sugar, just about everybody I know carries a gun. It's not something you need to worry about."

I wanted to believe her, but it was hard to relax. "Bernice is obviously upset. She's shaking like a leaf. The last thing she should be doing is running around the neighborhood with a loaded gun." Turning to Bernice, I added, "What you should have done was call the police. In fact, that's what we'll do right now."

I reached for my bag, intending to find my cell phone.

Bernice grabbed my wrist with a surprisingly strong grip. "No! No police."

"But if there's someone dangerous in the neighborhood—" I began.

Bernice shook her head so firmly, a couple of white curls bobbed out of place. "I know you mean well, but I can't let you call the police. Polly Ebersol, the church music director, lives just down the block. She's a sweet woman, but she does love to talk. If she sees the police at my house, everybody at church will know about it before morning. Come Sunday, I won't be able to show my face in the sanctuary."

Now *there* was a good reason to take a safety risk. "I understand that you don't want people talking, but what if something happens to you? Or what if this guy moves on and robs one of your neighbors?" *Or worse.* "You'd never forgive yourself if he hurt a friend."

Bernice's eyes flew wide and the hand at her throat fluttered. "Oh! Do you think . . . But I—" She turned to Miss Frankie. "You don't suppose she's right, do you?"

Miss Frankie went back to patting Bernice's shoulder. "If you're sure you saw someone, it might be a good idea to call the authorities. Just in case. But I really think it was just kids pulling a prank."

Bernice tilted her head to one side and gave that some thought. "But he looked so *real*. Then again, it's been a while since I saw him. Maybe I was mistaken."

I stared at her. "Are you saying that you recognized the man? I thought you said you didn't know him. So who was he?"

Bernice slipped the gun back into her pocket and put both hands on her Bible. "I don't believe I said that I didn't know him. I said it couldn't possibly be him." She closed her eyes for a moment, and I wondered if she was offering up another round of the Lord's Prayer. "I can't believe I'm going to tell you this," she said when she opened her eyes again. "And

I'll only tell you if you both promise not to say a word. Not one single word. To anybody."

She waited until Miss Frankie and I had vowed utter silence.

"The man I saw tonight looked exactly like Uncle Cooch. He had long gray hair and a beard hanging halfway down his chest."

"This is Louisiana," Miss Frankie reminded her. "There are plenty of men who look like that."

"Not all of them have a lazy eye," Bernice argued. "Or a birthmark on their cheek." She pointed to a spot just below her eye. "Right here. It's in the shape of a football but very distinctive. I guess you could say it's a family mark, but it doesn't show up more than once or twice in a generation. My granddaddy had it, too,"

I counted to ten, drawing on all my patience. Though I'd never known Bernice to be overly emotional, there's a first time for everything. But it was beginning to look as if I'd miss Dwight's birthday party completely, and that wasn't okay with me. "If it was your uncle coming to see you, he's probably still out there. Why don't I go look for him?"

Bernice sat straight up in her chair and shook her head firmly. "Abso*lute*ly not. You'll stay right here. We all will. You did bolt the door when I came in, didn't you, Frances?"

Miss Frankie nodded. "I did, but I don't think we need to worry. If your uncle stopped by for a visit—"

"I said that he *looked* like Uncle Cooch," Bernice said, cutting Miss Frankie off. "But it wasn't him."

"You can't possibly know that for sure," I said. "Obviously seeing him outside the window startled you, and you came right over here. I know you didn't really get a good look at him, but it all sounds innocent enough."

Bernice put both hands on the table and split a glare

between Miss Frankie and me. "Will you both stop talking for a minute? I swear, with the two of you yapping like a couple of hounds, I can't even finish a thought."

We both fell silent, startled by Bernice's uncharacteristic outburst.

Seemingly satisfied by our obedience, Bernice brushed a lock of snowy white hair from her forehead, took a deep breath, and lifted her chin as if defying us to utter another word. "That's better. I do wish you'd pay more attention, Frances. I've told you about Uncle Cooch before."

Miss Frankie lowered her eyes and tried to look sheepish, but the smile playing on her lips gave her away. "Of course you have," she said. "But in my defense, you do come from a large family. It's difficult to keep them all straight."

"Uncle Cooch was my father's youngest brother. He's just ten years older than me. You remember I told you about the still he had out in the middle of the swamp. Everybody knew about it, but nobody could ever find it. The location was passed down the Percifield line from father to son for generations. Nobody else ever knew where it was. Uncle Cooch had quite a business. Made a small fortune and hid a whole lot of it somewhere out there in the woods."

This was a side of Bernice that I would never have guessed at in a million years. I leaned up, chin in hand, eager for the rest of the story. "Your uncle is a moonshiner?"

"Among other things," Bernice said. "He hunted. Trapped. Fished. Even caught alligators for a while."

"He sounds like quite a character," I said with a laugh. "I'd like to meet him."

"That's not going to happen," Bernice said. "Uncle Cooch went missing out in the swamp fifteen years ago. Nobody's laid eyes on him since . . . until tonight."

Three

Bernice's words landed with a dull thud in the silence. Miss Frankie shot me a "do not encourage her" look, but I couldn't stop myself.

"So you're saying you saw . . . a ghost?" I asked.

"It certainly seemed like it," Bernice said with a soul-deep sigh. "We always thought an alligator got him. They found his boat a few days after he disappeared along with signs that there'd been a large gator in the area. His gun was on the bank of the swamp so everyone reckoned that he got out of the boat to catch a gator on dry land. That's extremely risky. Gators are much faster than humans on land. Anyway, that's what the police said, and we didn't have any reason not to believe them."

I stole a quick peek at the clock and decided I could afford to stick around a few minutes longer. I might miss most of Dwight's party, but I was fascinated by Bernice's story. "But no one ever found his body?"

Bernice shook her head. "We never found any other sign of him, but that wasn't surprising. Considering where he was when he went missing, nobody really expected to find his . . . remains."

"Then he's still alive," Miss Frankie said in a tone that brooked no argument. "It's the only possible explanation for what you saw tonight."

Bernice flashed a glance at the door and argued anyway. "I guess there's a chance you're right, but it seems unlikely. He loved his life. He adored Aunt Margaret and his kids. There's no way he would have just walked away from them without a word—especially not from Aunt Margaret. The Percifield men are loyal."

Maybe so, but he wouldn't have been the first person to run out on the family everyone thought he loved. But it seemed kinder not to point that out so I said, "Is there any chance he's been in contact with your aunt in secret? Maybe she knows where he is but she just hasn't told the rest of you," I suggested.

"I'm sure she hasn't heard from him," Bernice insisted. "Aunt Margaret would never lie. So you see, it just couldn't have been Uncle Cooch. That's what frightened me so badly."

Miss Frankie tried to look supportive. "Well, it's a puzzle for sure. Let me get you some coffee and cookies. What about you, Rita? What would you like?"

Offering food in times of crisis is what Miss Frankie does. I'm a bona fide foodie, but I wasn't sure coffee and cookies would work a miracle cure for poor Bernice. "Nothing for me, thanks. I'm sure there's a reasonable explanation for what you saw tonight, Bernice. If it wasn't your uncle, maybe it was some kid in a *Swamp People* or *Duck Dynasty* costume out for a few laughs. When you saw him in the window, you just thought it was your uncle Cooch."

Bernice gave me a sad-eyed look, and I could tell she was tired of arguing. "I suppose that was it. But I was so sure . . ." She laughed softly and put both hands on her Bible. "Silly of me, wasn't it?"

"Not at all," I assured her. "Anybody would have had the same reaction."

My cell phone rang and I recognized the ring tone as Edie Bryce, the office manager at Zydeco, no doubt calling to find out where I was. I stood and grabbed my purse from the back of the chair. "I'm sorry, ladies, but I can't stay. The others are waiting for me at the Dizzy Duke and I'm already late. I hate to leave the two of you alone, though. Why don't you come with me?"

Miss Frankie cut a glance at me over her shoulder. "Don't be silly. We'll be just fine—won't we, Bernice?"

Bernice nodded. "I feel much better now. Besides, I wouldn't want to intrude."

"You wouldn't be intruding," I assured her. "We're just having a drink to celebrate Dwight's birthday. If you come along, Miss Frankie, you can tell the staff about the meeting with Evangeline Delahunt."

Miss Frankie wore a pleased smiled as she carried the coffeepot to the table. She'd reeled me in once again, but at least she didn't gloat when she bent to kiss my cheek. "You can tell them, sugar. I won't mind at all. I'll stay here with Bernice and make sure all is well. Now go. Don't you worry about us for a minute."

Even with their assurances, I felt a twinge of guilt about leaving them alone. I told myself that even though Miss Frankie didn't believe Bernice had seen an intruder—or an uncle—she'd still keep the doors locked to be on the safe side. Frankly, now that I knew both of them were packing heat, I probably should be more concerned about that poor kid running around the neighborhood in costume.

I kept an eye out for anyone skulking around as I left the neighborhood, but everything looked peaceful. So I promised myself that I'd check with Miss Frankie on my way home, then pushed the worry to the back of my mind. I wanted to give all my focus to Dwight's party.

Luck was with me. Traffic was light so I made good time. I even found a parking space less than a block from the Dizzy Duke, which was a minor miracle on a Friday night. The neighborhood had donned its Halloween attire—orange lights glowing from darkened storefronts, flyers advertising haunted tours and numerous ghoulish parties scheduled to take place over the next week or so.

I felt a rush of pride when I saw an ornate banner of black and gold advertising the Belle Lune Ball. Anticipation buzzed along my skin, making me feel like a kid on Christmas morning. *This was going to be great*, I thought. *Everyone will be so impressed!*

As I hurried inside, I spared a brief wave for Gabriel Broussard behind the bar. He looked great with his thick brown hair, his deep brown bedroom eyes, and his sexy Cajun grin. My heart did a little flippy thing, which was almost enough to make me forget about Dwight's birthday and belly up to the bar instead. I showed a remarkable amount of self-control and kept moving forward. What can I say? I've always been responsible.

The house jazz band was onstage, and I found my staff gathered at our usual table near the bandstand. Everyone seemed in high spirits, and I felt a little giddy when I anticipated their reactions to my news.

Ox, known in other circles as Wyndham Oxford III, is

my second-in-command. He's another old friend from pastry school, usually thoughtful and always highly creative. I've often thought that he resembles an African-American Mr. Clean, but tonight, as he sat with one arm slung across his girlfriend Isabeau's shoulders and a toothpick dangling from his mouth, there was a dash of Vin Diesel tossed in as well.

Isabeau Pope is more than just Ox's girlfriend. She's also a talented cake artist. She's about fifteen years younger than Ox, twenty-something to his late thirties, and where he's dark and intense, she's blond and perkier than anyone has a right to be. But they've been together awhile now, and so far their differences don't seem to matter. Even though I would never have thought to pair the two of them, they seem truly happy together and I was glad for them.

Next to Isabeau, Sparkle Starr stared morosely into a glass filled with a strawberry daiquiri. At first glance, that drink seemed like an odd fit for Sparkle, who lives to contradict her name. Her long hair is dyed pitch black, and her lips and nails are painted to match. She rims her eyes with thick black liner and keeps her complexion ghostly pale. When I first came to New Orleans, I'd found Sparkle's goth appearance a bit unsettling, but time has mellowed my reaction so that tonight I barely even noticed the spiked dog collar on her neck or the gossamer black fabric of her bat-wing sleeves.

Next to Sparkle sat Edie Bryce, who is not only Zydeco's office manager but another former classmate from pastry school. Unlike the rest of us, Edie hadn't finished her schooling. She'd dropped out early after learning that her skills in the kitchen left something to be desired. She's midthirties and petite with chin-length dark hair and features that hint at her Chinese-American heritage. She's also eight months pregnant—a real success since her doctor had ruled hers a high-risk pregnancy at around the five-month mark. We'd all been walking on eggshells around her delicate emotions since the spring. Everyone at the bakery was ready for the baby to make its appearance.

Estelle Jergens, Zydeco's oldest employee, sat across from Edie. Sprigs of bright red hair poked out from beneath a kerchief she hadn't removed since leaving work, and her round face was flushed an almost identical shade of red—proof that she'd already had at least one birthday cocktail.

Finally, there was Dwight Sonntag, the birthday boy. He sat next to Estelle, slouched down in his chair in a way that I was sure added more wrinkles to his already rumpled clothing. If you judged his book by its cover, you'd come away thinking Dwight was scruffy, lazy, and dirty—none of which is true. Well, except for the scruffy part. His shaggy brown hair may look as if he'd been running his fingers through it and whiskers may always be sprouting all over his cheeks and chin, but he's one of the hardest workers at Zydeco—and also one of the most talented.

He saw me coming and gave a little chin jerk greeting.

"Sorry I'm late," I said as I claimed an empty seat next to Dwight. "Miss Frankie asked me to stop by and it took longer than I expected."

Ox scowled across the table at me. "Trouble?"

"No! In fact, she had some good news for us."

"For all of us?" Isabeau asked.

"Yeah. A great opportunity for Zydeco. But let's talk about that later." I placed my drink order, choosing a virgin margarita. Gabriel is a master of the craft and his salt-to-rim ratio is spot-on. The virgin variety isn't my favorite, but I was driving so I settled for the responsible choice.

"You should have brought Miss Frankie with you," Estelle said as our waitress walked away.

"Actually, I invited her, but she opted to stay home. Her

neighbor was having a rough night, and Miss Frankie didn't want to leave her alone."

"Nothing serious, I hope," Estelle said.

"No, just . . ." I hesitated for a moment, unsure how much I should share about Bernice's imaginary prowler. But nobody at Zydeco really knew Bernice, so I didn't see the harm. "She just thought she saw someone outside her window. Miss Frankie thinks it may have been kids pulling Halloween pranks."

Sparkle studied my face carefully. "You don't think so, do you?"

I turned the coaster the waitress had placed in front of me around on the table. "I don't know. She said it looked like her uncle, but he's been missing for the past fifteen years or so. Get this—the whole family thinks he was eaten by an alligator."

"She saw a ghost?" Isabeau asked, her blue eyes wide. "For real?"

"No! Not for real," I said with a laugh. "For one thing, there's no such thing. If she did see her uncle, it just means he didn't die in the swamp all those years ago."

Isabeau leaned toward me. "I know a way we could find out."

Ox barked a harsh laugh. "Oh no. No, no, no. I know what you're thinking and you are *not* going there."

"Going where?" I thought my question was innocent enough, but Ox seemed annoyed by it.

"Don't ask," he warned and shook a finger in Isabeau's face. "I mean it, Isabeau. Not another word."

If he wanted me to drop the subject, he was going about it the wrong way. What can I say? Curiosity has always been a weakness of mine. I would have pursued it, but at that moment the waitress arrived with my drink and Estelle pronounced the birthday party started. I swallowed my curiosity and concentrated on Dwight.

Ox offered a toast and then we brought out the presents: a DVD of some horror show that was his current favorite from Estelle; a pair of black bikini briefs with an orange flame—apparently an inside joke—from Edie; a bottle of expensive Scotch from Ox and Isabeau; and an ornate and extremely heavy German beer stein from Sparkle. I'd thought long and hard about what to get him and finally settled on a hand-knit beanie cap with a bright design for those times when someone forced him to dress up. By coincidence, the hat's colors matched the bikini briefs. Yay.

Once he'd opened all his gifts, Dwight cut his cake: two tiers of milk chocolate cake covered with buttercream. Ox had carved the cake in the shape of a Jack Daniels bottle. Sparkle and Estelle had done a great job with the gum paste label and the added touches of edible paint. Isabeau had experimented until she had a whisper of Jack Daniels flavor in the buttercream. They'd all stayed late to work on the cake, and Dwight was suitably impressed.

After a while the birthday celebration wound down and the band took a break. In the sudden quiet, Ox tapped his fingers on the table to get my attention. "Okay, so what's the big news? What did Miss Frankie want?"

I stood so everyone could hear me, and smiled around the table. "You're not going to believe this, but this afternoon Miss Frankie had lunch with Evangeline Delahunt from the Crescent City Vintage Clothing Society. Ms. Delahunt is coming in tomorrow morning to discuss hiring us for their ball."

I paused for their reactions, which naturally I expected to be positive. Instead, Edie struggled to her feet and waddled off to the ladies' room (which she did roughly every five minutes), leaving me looking at a set of glum faces.

Maybe they hadn't heard me right. "I know it's short notice, but I'm sure I don't have to tell you what a big deal this is for Zydeco. It's a great opportunity for us to get our name in front of hundreds of potential clients. Not to mention the society page and blogs." *Taa-daa!*

I waited through another uneasy silence until, finally, Estelle spoke up. "What's the big deal, y'all? Three months is more than enough time to make a cake."

Their unenthusiastic reception of the news made me proceed with caution. "Actually, it's a bit more than just the cake. She's looking for us to cater the whole event."

"Then you'd better be talking about next season's ball," Dwight said, apparently forgetting how happy he'd been with my birthday beanie. "Nobody in their right mind would take on a job like that with just three months to plan."

Okay, that reaction just irked me. "Actually, I *am* talking about the ball in three months, but what's the problem? We're the best around. This will give us an amazing opportunity to show people what we're made of."

Ox gave me a scowl. "Just how did this opportunity come up?"

"The first bakery the society contracted with failed to produce a design and a menu that Mrs. Delahunt could approve," I said carefully. "She had no choice but to end that relationship and look for a company that could do the job right. Thanks to Miss Frankie, we are that company."

Ox slowly put his glass on the table, and every head at the table swiveled to look at him, which double-irked me. Ox had always been closer to Philippe than to me. After Philippe and I separated, Ox was one of several friends—including Dwight—who'd come to New Orleans to help Philippe open Zydeco. I hadn't been aware that any of my old friends were working with Philippe until I showed up here. The fact that none of them had thought to mention it,

even on Facebook, had stirred up a lot of old feelings of
inadequacy.

It hadn't helped, either, that when I came to New Orleans
to get Philippe's signature on the divorce papers he'd been
ignoring for two years, I'd found that he'd used my ideas to
start Zydeco. Discovering that had felt like a shot in the heart
and was nearly as painful as the day I'd watched him walk
out on our marriage.

When Philippe died, Ox had expected to take over. He
hadn't been thrilled when Miss Frankie offered me the part-
nership instead, and although we'd made peace with our
roles, he still sometimes tried to show that he would have
been a better choice to run the operation. So when all of *my*
employees looked to Ox, every nerve in my body tingled—
and not in a pleasant way.

"Maybe you didn't hear Dwight," Ox said. "The ball is
less than three months away, and you're talking about a huge
amount of work."

"Not only did I hear him," I said, "I don't need either of
you to tell me that. Look," I said to the whole group, "don't
let the short time frame discourage you. We're the best in
New Orleans. We can do this and do it right."

"Or we can fail miserably, and publicly," Sparkle said in
her usual dour tone. "We're not caterers, you know."

"That doesn't mean we can't handle this. Come on! We
have plenty of time to pull it off. And yes, maybe we'll all
have to put in some extra hours and step outside our comfort
zones, but just think of how much it will mean to all of us
when we succeed. Everybody who's anybody in New Orleans
will be at the Belle Lune Ball that night. This won't just put
Zydeco on the map, it will put all of our names in front of
hundreds of potential clients."

Ox leaned back in his chair and folded his arms over his chest. "You don't know Evangeline Delahunt, do you?"

I wasn't sure what that had to do with anything, so I saw no harm in answering the question. "I've never met her."

"Then you also don't know that she's a pain in the ass. You won't be able to please her no matter what you do."

"Thanks for the vote of confidence. And keep your voice down, okay? We don't want someone to overhear you."

Ox laughed. "You think she hangs out with people who come here? Think again."

I wasn't so sure. People everywhere can hide the most interesting secrets, and that's especially true in New Orleans. Case in point: Gabriel had turned out to be not just a sexy Cajun bartender, but part owner of the Dizzy Duke with unexpected connections to the upper crust. There was no telling who might think the Dizzy Duke was a great place to come relax, and we didn't need word to get back to Mrs. Delahunt that one of us had been talking smack about her.

Isabeau's gaze bounced from my face to Ox's a few times but she didn't say anything. Sparkle linked her black-tipped fingers together and rested her chin on them.

Ox leaned forward in his chair. "This is a mistake, Rita. You should have talked to me first."

Talk to *him* first? Oh, now he'd done it. I was so angry, blood rushed into my face. I didn't want to make a scene, however, so I tried to keep my voice level. "First of all, I didn't talk to Evangeline Delahunt. Miss Frankie did. And second, where do you get off saying that we're making a mistake? I happen to know that Philippe tried to get this gig but never could. Now we have a chance to do what he always wanted to."

Ox shook his head but kept his eyes locked on mine. "Philippe never wanted that job. He knew Evangeline

Delahunt too well. His mother tried to push him into it, but he wouldn't do it."

His words hit me like a fist to the stomach. I wanted to argue with him, but I knew Miss Frankie well enough to know that Ox was probably telling the truth. But it was too late now. The only thing I could say was, "Even so, she and I are the partners at Zydeco. It's our decision, not yours."

Ox's expression turned to stone, but I was too furious to care.

Edie came back from the restroom and sank into her chair. "What's going on?"

I waved away the question, intending to fill her in later. Estelle bounced up out of her seat and scurried over to Ox. "Now, let's not ruin Dwight's birthday by arguing over something that's already done," she said soothingly.

Apparently, Ox wasn't in the mood to listen to her. He lurched to his feet and leaned across the table to get right in my face. "I hope you're happy. The two of you probably just signed Zydeco's death warrant." He shoved his chair out of the way and growled at Isabeau, "Come on. Let's get out of here."

His reaction left me almost speechless. And by almost, I mean that the only words I could think of were ones I didn't want to shout in public as he walked away. He made me furious, but I needed him at Zydeco, and even though he was pigheaded and nearly as competitive as Philippe had been, he was still a friend . . . I hoped.

"Hey!" Edie said, a bit louder. "Somebody tell me what you're all so upset about."

"Just wait," I told her. "This isn't the time."

Ox put a couple of tables between us and finally Isabeau hopped up from her seat. She gave Dwight a quick hug and mouthed, "I'll talk to him," at me before skipping after him.

Convinced that our argument had ruined Dwight's night, I started to apologize, but at that moment Edie let out a yowl that sounded like a feral cat. It was so loud even Ox turned back to see what was wrong.

"Edie?" I said, the argument forgotten for the moment. "What's wrong?"

She closed her eyes and slumped down in her chair, both hands on her belly. "I think my water just broke!"

Four

"Where's River?" Edie shouted from the backseat of my Mercedes a few minutes later. "Has anybody been able to reach him yet?" She was supposed to be lying down on Sparkle's lap, but I could see half of her face in the rearview mirror.

I maneuvered around a couple of slow-moving cars and prayed that I'd get Edie and her baby to the hospital safely. The possibility of delivering the baby on my own, with only Sparkle to help, did not fill me with confidence. Traffic was a bit heavier than it had been early in the evening, and it was taking all my concentration just to keep myself from panicking and causing a wreck.

Sparkle said something, but I couldn't make out what it was. It must have made Edie feel better, though, because she stopped screeching for a second.

Edie's relationship with her baby's daddy was new, complicated, and fragile. They'd met at the Dizzy Duke on the night Edie's younger sister announced her engagement—a piece of news that had sent Edie into an emotional tailspin and right into the arms of a handsome stranger. A contractor for a company doing business in the Middle East, he'd flown to Afghanistan the following day. She'd been five months pregnant when he came back to New Orleans to visit his little sister, who—*surprise!*—turned out to be Sparkle. Until that day, Edie hadn't even known his name.

Over the past three months, they'd been trying to figure out how they felt and what each of them wanted. Or maybe I should say that Edie had been trying to figure out what *she* wanted. River had thrown himself into the idea of fatherhood with gusto, even changing jobs to ensure he wouldn't have to leave the country again. Still, Edie kept him at arm's length and regarded him with suspicion. Which wasn't surprising. Edie doesn't trust easily.

River's willingness to step up and take responsibility made me like him, but it was freaking Edie out. She still hadn't decided whether she wanted River to be a major part of her life or not, and her indecision was driving Sparkle nuts. The only thing Sparkle wanted more than another tattoo or piercing was a family.

The two women were getting along for the moment, though, and right now that was all that mattered. I glanced at my cell phone to make sure I hadn't missed a call and tried to reassure Edie. "I've left two messages. River must be busy."

Edie locked eyes with me in the mirror. "Busy? He *said* he wanted to be there when the baby was born."

"I'm sure he'll meet us at the hospital," I assured her. "Like I said, I've left a couple of messages."

"And so have I," Sparkle said. She looked out the back window and frowned. "I don't see Ox's truck. Have we lost them?"

"I'm not all that concerned with creating a caravan," I

said as I shot through an intersection on a yellow light. "They know where the hospital is. My main concern is getting Edie there before the baby arrives."

Sparkle shifted so that she was facing front again, which caused Edie to let out a low moan. "If River doesn't call me back, I'm going to kill him," Sparkle muttered. "He knows how important this is."

The last thing River needed was both women turning against him, so I tried to stick up for him. "Hey, give the guy a break. It's not as if he knew the baby was going to come tonight."

"No, but he should keep his cell phone on," Sparkle said. "I told him at least a hundred times not to go anywhere without it."

Edie shifted around in the backseat, trying to get comfortable. "It's fine," she said in a tone that clearly said it wasn't fine at all. "If he doesn't make it, I'll know exactly how he feels."

I said a silent prayer for River to check his phone before Edie got the wrong idea. I didn't know him well, but what I did know convinced me that he was a genuinely good guy who just wanted to be a part of his child's life. He'd even gone along with Edie's refusal to find out the baby's sex before it was born, which I thought was pretty cool of him.

I tried again to reason with Edie, but she cut me off after just a few words. "Obviously, I can't count on River," she whined. "And the baby can't either. It needs a godmother. Somebody it can turn to and rely on. Somebody steady."

"River's steady," Sparkle said, apparently forgetting that she'd been threatening to kill him only a few minutes earlier. "He's real steady."

"Yeah. Until he takes off again for who knows where."

"He's not going to do that," Sparkle insisted. "Just give him a chance."

"I *have* given him a chance," Edie assured us. "I'm telling you, if he doesn't show up tonight, it's game over."

Sparkle was getting nowhere, so I gave it a try. "First of all," I said in my most reasonable tone, "this isn't a game. Second, you're in pain and you're nervous about going through labor and becoming a mother. I don't blame you. I'd be freaking out myself if I were in your shoes. Which makes this a really bad time to make big decisions. I think you should wait until the baby's here and the dust settles."

"But I don't want the baby born with just me there for it. I *don't.* I thought I could handle it, but I was wrong. Please, Rita. Say you'll do it."

I was so startled I swerved and almost hit the car in the next lane. I got the Mercedes under control and met Edie's plaintive gaze in the mirror. "Do what, exactly?"

"Be the baby's godmother, of course. What have we just been talking about?"

Had she forgotten that I had baby issues? That I knew nothing about kids? "You want *me* to be the baby's godmother?"

"Well, that figures," Sparkle grumbled. "I should have known you wouldn't ask me."

"You're the baby's aunt," Edie said impatiently. "Of course you'll be there for it, but you're part of River's family. The baby needs someone who doesn't come into the relationship with loyalties to one side or the other. Please, Rita? I need you to do this for me. I can't ask anyone in my family. We're speaking again, but I don't want one of them to do the whole guilt thing on the baby like my mother does with me."

She had a point about her mother. Lin Bryce had been determined to get her daughter respectably married, which had created a rift that only Miss Frankie's intervention had resolved. Like Edie said, they were speaking again but that didn't mean Lin had stopped pushing her agenda on her daughter. I was worried about the way Edie had already divided the two families into opposing sides, which did make me want to say yes, for the baby's sake. But being a godmother meant a whole lot more than buying birthday and Christmas presents every year. At least, it meant more to me, and I wasn't sure I was ready for it. Aunt Yolanda was my godmother, which was partially how I'd landed on her doorstep when my parents died. And even though I'd been seriously pissed at God for taking my parents, Aunt Yolanda had dragged me to church until I was old enough to make my own choices. So I knew all the religious requirements for being a suitable godparent. If I said yes, I'd be agreeing to make sure the baby had the "proper" spiritual training, whatever that was. It was a huge responsibility, one I wasn't sure I wanted.

And then there were my own baby issues on top of it; specifically, that I'd always wanted kids but had never even come close to having one of my own. Envy was another factor to consider. Could I give myself wholeheartedly to this baby, or would my feelings get in the way? It wouldn't be fair to say yes if I couldn't do the job right.

"Wow," I said over my shoulder. "Thank you, but that's huge. Can I think about it for a day or two?"

"Think about it?" Edie reared up so far, I could only see her eyes in the mirror. "Are you kidding me? This baby will be here any time. It needs a godmother *now*!"

Personally, I couldn't see any harm in waiting a day or two, but I'd heard that labor makes some women crazy and apparently Edie was one of them. Every instinct I had urged me to be cautious, but the wild-looking woman howling in my backseat convinced me to take a risk.

"Okay. Okay. I'll do it. Just lie down, all right? Don't get any more worked up. I'll be the godmother. But I draw the line at delivering the baby on the side of the road."

Edie grumbled under her breath, but she did disappear from the mirror so I figured she'd taken my advice. We were less than two blocks from the hospital by then, so I let myself relax a bit. If the baby hadn't made an appearance by now and if Edie stopped wigging out, we just might make it in time.

A few minutes later, I pulled into a parking lot and scanned the signs for directions to the emergency room. Half a dozen buildings were scattered about the medical complex, but I couldn't see an emergency room anywhere. "Where is it? Where is it?" I mumbled.

Edie popped up into the mirror again. "It's over there," she said and shoved her arm under my nose so she could point the way. "And just so you know, it's quicker to come in off the service street. Next time, you should go that way."

Her cell phone rang and she sat up in the seat to answer. "*Finally!* Where the hell have you been? If I was really in labor, I probably would have been bearing down by now."

Usually I'm not the kind of person who interrupts someone else's phone call, but six little words had set my ears ringing. I slammed on the brakes, threw the car into park, and scooted around to look at Edie. "What do you mean, 'if you were really in labor'?"

Edie waved me off, still talking on the phone. "Seriously, River, this is unacceptable."

I glanced at Sparkle, whose face registered as much shock as I felt. "She's not in labor?" I asked.

Sparkle cut a sharp look at Edie. "Apparently not."

I heard the screech of tires as Ox's truck barreled into the parking lot going much too fast. He pulled to a stop behind me and jumped out of the truck's cab, speed-walking to my window. "What's wrong? What's going on?"

The passenger's side door of his truck opened and Isabeau

and Estelle spilled out to join us. I didn't see Dwight, and figured he'd opted to stay behind at the Dizzy Duke.

"Nothing's wrong," I said as the two women reached my window. "That's the problem. Apparently, this was a trial run."

Ox's expression went from concern to outrage in a heartbeat. "What do you mean, 'a trial run'?"

"A test," I said, my words clipped. "A trial run. And apparently, we all failed."

Everyone started talking at once, which meant that I couldn't really understand anyone. I picked up a word or two here or there from each of them, and it was enough to let me know how they felt.

Sparkle: ". . . absolutely unbelievable . . ."

Estelle: "I was scared to death . . ."

Edie: "Will you *please* be quiet?"

Ox: ". . . ought to wring her neck . . ."

Isabeau: "Are you sure she's not . . ."

In the face of their outrage, I thought surely Edie would apologize, but she just flapped her hand again. "Hey! I'm on the phone here. Keep it down, okay? *Sheesh!*"

Estelle's mouth fell open and Ox's thinned to nothing but a line in his face. And now even Isabeau looked angry, which almost never happened.

Oops. Yeah, I was angry but I didn't want to turn the whole staff against Edie. I tried to diffuse the situation. "I'm sure it was just a false alarm. She probably thought she really was in labor. Let's let her finish her call and she'll clear up all the confusion."

Estelle leaned down to look in the car. Apparently she felt the need to give Edie the stink eye. "She said that her water broke. Was that a lie?"

"I don't—"

Ox tried to jerk open the back door. Luckily for Edie, the

safety locks had triggered as I drove. The car rocked a little but the door didn't open. I knew Ox would never have hurt her. He just isn't that kind of man. But he would've gotten right in her face and nobody needs to experience that.

He glared at me as if he suspected me of aiding and abetting. "Open the door, Rita."

"Not while you're this angry," I said. "Let's all calm down and talk this out."

Not surprisingly, Isabeau backed him. "That was a dirty trick and you know it."

I held up both hands. "You'll get no argument from me, but let's not do something we'll regret, okay?"

Estelle looked torn, but she took Ox's side. "She owes us an apology. Every one of us would have agreed to make a trial run if she'd asked us."

I knew she was right, but I didn't get a chance to say so. Edie broke away from her conversation with River to dig the hole a little deeper. "If I'd asked," she snipped, "you'd all have known it was a trial run. The results would have been skewed."

I sent her an exasperated look. "You're not making this better, you know."

Ox experienced an abrupt change of mind about talking to Edie. He shouted a few choice words at her and stormed back to his truck. I thought he'd been in a bad mood before, but that was nothing compared to this. I had a feeling it would take a while for him to cool down.

The weight of the world landed squarely on my shoulders. Ox wasn't the only one on my staff who looked ready to commit murder. The last thing I needed right now, with the biggest contract of my career on the line, was a civil war. I needed them all to pull together and get along. But if the stone-cold expressions on all their faces were any indication, the hostilities had already begun.

Five

I was frustrated and exhausted when I pulled back onto Miss Frankie's street an hour later. I'd done my best to negotiate peace with the staff, but I'd failed. Ox had continued to give Edie another very loud, very angry piece of his mind, and Isabeau had done the same. Neither of them had seemed to care that Edie wasn't really listening.

Estelle had sympathized with Edie one moment, then joined the outrage brigade the next. Sparkle had glowered at Edie while alternately chewing her fingernails to nubs and defending her brother.

River had shown up a few minutes after the others left, and that was when things got really hairy. Edie had read him the riot act for failing to show up for her phony labor. River had done his best to explain that he'd been in a meeting, but Edie hadn't stopped talking long enough for him to get out a whole sentence.

I wondered what kind of meeting River had been in late on a Friday night. I liked him, but he was still a mystery. The middle of the hospital parking lot didn't seem like the right place to satisfy my curiosity, though.

Eventually, River had convinced Edie to go with him to talk things out, and Sparkle had tagged along, leaving me on my own to think about what had just happened. I wasn't looking forward to going to work tomorrow morning. My staff members are all eccentric and mulish, and I had no idea how to get them to move forward as a team after Edie's ill-advised trial run. I just knew that the bad feelings from tonight would spill over into the workplace—just in time for Evangeline Delahunt to pick up on them.

Still pondering options for soothing ruffled feathers, I drew up in front of Bernice's dark house. I turned off the car and sat there for a moment, trying to mentally switch gears. I was annoyed with Miss Frankie for lying to me about the Vintage Clothing Society contract situation, but I was also concerned about Bernice. It wasn't her fault that Miss Frankie had manipulated me.

I'd called Miss Frankie on my way from the hospital. She'd assured me that they were both safe and sound. Bernice was still at her house and the two of them were having cocoa and watching TV.

Maybe I should have been satisfied with that, but Bernice had seemed so certain that she'd seen a man outside her window. Her fright had been real. If I could find evidence of a prowler, maybe it would help calm her down. At least she'd know that she'd seen a live human being, even if she didn't know who he was.

Now that I knew both women were carrying guns, I was a little nervous about skulking around in the dark without letting them know I was there, but I decided to take the chance. If I told them what I was planning, they'd probably decide to join me. I didn't think that would help. Besides, if there was any evidence there, three people searching together could easily obliterate it.

Grabbing the flashlight from the glove box, I climbed out into the night. The wind had died down a bit, and the temperature had dropped by several degrees. Cool temperatures and low humidity. It was the best kind of night if you ask me. To me this was T-shirt weather, but here in New Orleans many people bundled up on nights like this to ward off the frigid temperatures. It's all a matter of perspective, I guess.

I checked to make sure the coast was clear, then hurried up Bernice's driveway and lifted the latch on her back gate. Thankfully, I'd been here a few times, so her yard wasn't completely unfamiliar to me.

I waited until I was inside the yard with the gate closed before I turned on the flashlight. It gave enough light for me to see my shoes, but not enough to see more than a few inches in front of my face. Maybe this was a bad idea. It would take forever to go over the whole backyard, but I reasoned that if someone had been looking in Bernice's window, I could confine my search to the area closest to the house.

Walking slowly and carefully, I made my way around one of Bernice's many flower gardens. I kept the flashlight trained on the ground and looked for footprints in the soft dirt or any place where the grass might be matted down. Maybe Miss Frankie was right about neighborhood kids out for a good time. Or maybe Bernice's visitor had a more criminal reason for prowling around her house. Whatever the answer, I was sure it wasn't the spirit of Bernice's dearly departed uncle, and I wanted to prove that to her.

Bernice's house sits on a slight hill, making it one story

in the front and two in the back. I swept the flashlight across the first-story windows and the lower deck. To my relief, I didn't see any broken glass or other signs of a break-in on the ground floor.

I played the light over the deck steps to make sure they were clear then started climbing. The planks creaked beneath my feet, and I wondered if the noise was loud enough for someone inside the house to hear. Probably not, I decided, especially if Bernice had the TV or radio on.

From somewhere nearby a dog barked, startling me, and I almost lost my grip on the flashlight. I didn't want the neighbors to see me snooping around and call the authorities (or come after me with guns) so I turned off the flashlight and relied on the moon to guide my steps.

Without the light, I felt unprotected and vulnerable. A branch scratched against the side of the house, and a chill raced up my spine. I was being fanciful. There's no such thing as ghosts. But for a moment, I understood why Bernice had been so frightened earlier.

As I reached the upper deck, a cloud drifted across the moon and I lost my bearings in the darkness. My foot hit something solid and I lost my balance. I windmilled my arms, trying to stay on my feet, but I landed with a *whomp*, half of me on the top step, the other half sprawled on the deck. The flashlight flew out of my hand, hit the deck, and rolled.

I wasn't seriously hurt, but I was majorly annoyed. I didn't want to leave the flashlight behind. I'd need it once I got back on the ground. After falling, I was leery of going back down the stairs in the dark, and walking around on the deck was sure to be risky. Bernice was an avid gardener. Every time I'd been here, I'd seen gardening tools, plastic flats emptied of their flowers, and other gardening implements spread out over her deck, never in the same place twice. I didn't want to trip over something while I looked for the flashlight.

I had no idea which direction the flashlight had gone, so I slowly crawled around and felt my way. I picked up a splinter in my palm, swore under my breath, and changed direction. My fingers brushed up against something solid . . . and hairy.

My heart leaped into my throat and I jerked my hand away, barely holding back a scream. I scooted back a few inches and squinted into the shadows, wishing Bernice had left on a light so I could see what was on the deck with me.

I heard claws on the wood flooring and prayed that I wasn't alone in the dark with a possum. Those things scare me to death with their pointy noises and sharp teeth. The critter bumped my arm with its head and a tentative purr wiped away my nerves.

Laughing softly, I scratched the cat's head. It leapt onto the window ledge, its silhouette looming in the moonlight, then rejoined me on the deck, nudging my hand for more attention. I was so happy it wasn't a possum—or a ghost—I gave in to the petting. I wondered if I'd found Bernice's intruder. It wasn't a huge cat, but if you combined the element of surprise with the distortion of wind and shadow, the cat might have looked like a guy with a beard. "Well, friend," I said as I rubbed its fur, "who are you? Did you frighten the lady who lives here earlier? That wasn't polite, you know."

The cat didn't seem to care. It nudged up against me for a few more minutes before deciding it had had enough. With a twitch of its tail, it jumped onto the deck rail and strolled away. I laughed again and resumed the search for my flashlight. It was so late now, I decided to tell Bernice about the cat tomorrow. But I knew she'd be relieved at the very simple and logical explanation, and so would Miss Frankie.

A few minutes before eight on Saturday morning, I pulled into the parking lot at Zydeco. It had taken me another fifteen minutes the night before to find my flashlight, but I'd finally made it home and crawled into bed around one. I could have slept all day, but Evangeline Delahunt was giving up part of her weekend to meet with me. That's what had finally convinced me to get out of bed.

I didn't know what I'd find when I walked through the door this morning, but I hoped that everyone had thought about their behavior and had come to some grown-up conclusions. I hoped that Ox would keep his opinions to himself while Evangeline was in the building, and that Edie had seen the error of her ways. And I prayed that everyone else was in a forgiving mood. And for world peace and the end of human trafficking. I thought I might as well go for broke while I was asking for the impossible.

Zydeco is housed in a renovated antebellum house on the edge of the Garden District. It was built before the Civil War, but the only historical pictures I knew of were taken around the turn of the last century. At some point, someone had removed part of the extensive gardens to make an employee parking lot and build a loading dock onto the back of the house, but otherwise, it looks much like it did back when.

The day had dawned cool and sunny, and I'd have loved to do something fun outside in the glorious weather, but I needed to do what I could to prepare before my meeting with Evangeline Delahunt. Normally I'd have used the time to sketch out a few ideas for the cake, but this was an unusual situation. Edie hadn't set the appointment, so I didn't have the benefit of the extensive notes that usually accompanied my first meeting with a new client. I had no idea what kind of cake Mrs. Delahunt would want, what kind of menu she had in mind, how many people she needed to serve, or her personal likes and dislikes.

The lack of information made me a bit edgy. I don't like walking into a meeting at a disadvantage. On my way to work I'd decided the best use of my limited time would be to read up on the Crescent City Vintage Clothing Society. At least I'd know something about it and its history when Mrs. Delahunt arrived.

Trying not to anticipate the worst from my staff, I climbed the loading dock steps and let myself into the design room. Even on my worst days, this area can cheer me up. With its high ceiling and huge windows overlooking the remaining gardens, it's cheerful and sunny. Philippe had painted each of the walls in a different color using hues of gold, fuchsia, teal, and lime. That had been one of my ideas, by the way. What can I say? The use of bright, sunny colors is part of my Mexican heritage, and the color and creative chaos in this space fed my soul.

At least it usually did.

Today, the tension in the design room was so thick you'd have needed a butcher knife to cut it. I took one look at everyone's sullen faces and decided to talk to Edie first. If I could sort things out with her, maybe I could make headway with the rest of my very pissed-off staff.

I waved to Sparkle and Estelle, who were huddled together in Sparkle's corner—the one that never catches the sunlight—whispering about something. I hoped they were discussing work, but they both looked so guilty I suspected they were complaining about Edie and our ill-fated run to the hospital.

Dwight was pulling his beard guard over his whiskers

and hair to protect his work from fallout, and Ox sat alone at his workstation sketching something. That was unusual, since Ox and Isabeau usually arrived together and spent a few minutes running over the daily calendar while they had their first cups of coffee.

"Where's Isabeau?" I asked him. "Is she sick today?"

He shook his head without looking up. "She'll be in later. Said she had something to take care of." He flicked a glance at me, but didn't actually make eye contact. "That a problem?"

Well . . . kind of. If she'd had an appointment, she should have run it past me first, but after last night I wasn't going to say so. Sometimes you have to pick your battles. "It's fine with me as long as the work gets done. What's on the schedule for today?"

He shrugged and pushed the calendar across the table. "See for yourself. What time is your meeting?"

"Evangeline is supposed to be here at ten," I said. If we were talking about any other client, I would have asked him for ideas and invited him to sit in on the consult, but he'd made it clear how he felt about the job last night, and I wasn't in the mood to deal with his negative attitude or go down that road again. "I expect it should take an hour or so. After that, I'll work on the pumpkin cauldron for the Howard family reunion cake."

The Howards had commissioned a Halloween-themed cake for their annual get-together at the end of the month. We'd designed a three-tier tilted cake painted with spooky trees and a full moon, rimmed by a chocolate path that climbed up the tiers to the top of the cake. The path would be edged by fallen leaves, tiny pumpkins, and wooden signs made from fondant and gum paste. Each sign would bear the name of a family member from the oldest living generation. We planned to top the cake with a large jack-o'-lantern, its "lid" shifted to let a witch's brew of chocolate spill out to create the path. I was in charge of making all the fondant items. I'd already assembled two dozen tiny pumpkins and boxes full of colorful autumn leaves, so the large jack-o'-lantern was the only thing left on my list.

Ox nodded and reached for an eraser. "Sounds great."

Judging from the tone of his voice, that was a big, fat lie. It looked like bringing Ox around would require both finesse and persistence. I moved on and let myself into the front of the house, where Edie reigns over the reception area from behind a massive U-shaped desk.

It's a large room dominated by Edie's desk and an ornate staircase made of rich, dark wood. A couple of inviting seating areas take up space in front of the large front windows, and framed poster-sized photographs of extreme and elegant cakes adorn the crisp white walls.

Edie glanced up when I came through the door, but looked away quickly. "Morning."

I hoped that was contrition on her face, but I couldn't be sure.

I helped myself to a handful of M&M's—her snack of choice since she got pregnant—from a bowl on her desk. "Have you been back in the design room this morning?"

She shook her head. "Not yet. Why do you ask?"

"Because everybody back there is on edge. Would you like to guess why?"

Edie's glance landed on mine. "I suppose you're going to say it's my fault."

"Are you seriously going to suggest it's not?"

Her almond-shaped eyes narrowed and she turned her chair so that she was facing me head-on. "You ought to be thanking me. If I hadn't done what I did, you and Ox would have completely ruined the night for Dwight."

I couldn't believe my ears. "You're blaming *me*?"

"Not just you. Ox, too. Really, Rita, you should have heard the two of you. Half the people at the Duke were laughing. The other half were whispering. We've all worked too hard to build up Zydeco's reputation to ruin it in a barroom brawl."

I felt about two inches tall. "Okay. Maybe you have a point. Kind of. But that doesn't let you off the hook for your part in last night's disaster. We were all scared to death and we drove like maniacs to get you to the hospital, only to find out it was all a joke?"

"Not a joke." Edie flicked a lock of hair from her cheek. "I was going to have a trial run anyway. Last night just seemed like the right time to do it."

Unbelievable. "It was a very bad idea," I said. "You upset people who care about you, and I need you to apologize to them."

"Apologize for what?"

"For upsetting everybody. For lying to us. For making us think you were about to have the baby. Pick one."

Edie laughed, but she wasn't amused. "And what about you and Ox?"

I'd apologize when Ox did, but getting him to apologize wouldn't be easy. I'd deal with that later, though. First, I had to get him to look at me. "How about you just take care of your part? We have too much work to have bad feelings cutting into productivity."

Edie rolled her eyes. "I don't think I have anything to apologize for. Like I said, you should be thanking me."

Edie's always been one of the most hardheaded people I know. Pregnancy hasn't softened her any. "I appreciate you stepping in before our argument got out of hand," I said. It wasn't entirely true, but I wanted to show that I could be flexible. "But don't you think faking labor was overkill?"

"It worked, didn't it?"

"In a way," I admitted grudgingly. "But it just created a whole new set of problems."

"That's a matter of opinion." She looked away and I could tell it wasn't going to be easy to convince her. I could stay and argue (which would clearly be a waste of time), or I could give up for the time being and use the next hour or so to mentally prepare for my meeting.

The choice was obvious.

But that didn't stop me from trying to get the last word. I stood and gathered my things. "Just don't do it again."

Six

My conversation with Edie left me feeling edgy and dissatisfied, but I didn't have time to dwell on it. I grabbed a cup of coffee and holed up in my office—an elegant room with a bay of five floor-to-ceiling windows that look out over a broad street lined with graceful old trees. A couple of built-in shelves hold a combination of Philippe's extensive cookbook library and mine. I'd also inherited Philippe's beautiful cherry wood desk, as well as the office chair he and I used to good-naturedly bicker over when we were together.

I settled down, opened my browser, and Googled the Crescent City Vintage Clothing Society. Naturally I was curious to know why Philippe had refused to work with Evangeline Delahunt, but not so curious I'd let myself ask Ox for details. But since the cake and menu were for the society, not for Evangeline personally, I decided to focus on finding what I could about the society itself.

Within minutes I'd learned that "vintage" refers to clothing made between twenty and one hundred years ago. Anything older is antique. The society had been founded twenty years earlier, and Evangeline Delahunt was a founding member. She'd initially served as the society's president, a run of successive terms that had lasted five years. Afterward, she'd stepped into her current role as events coordinator, with her specialty being the Belle Lune Ball, held every year at the historic Monte Cristo Hotel.

I'd filled two pages with notes by the time Edie buzzed to let me know my appointment had arrived. I closed my computer, stashed my notes on one side of my desk, and took a couple of deep breaths before stepping out to meet my new client.

Evangeline Delahunt was an impressive woman. Tall, thin, and stylish. I guessed her to be about the same age as Miss Frankie. Her silver hair was cut short and she wore a tailored suit that seemed to float around her body as she walked. One look at her reminded me that I had not grown up in her world and would probably never fit into it.

I offered her a hand to shake, which she took after looking it over for a moment. Once she had her hand back, she ran her eyes slowly over every inch of me, starting at my head, going down to my flat and well-worn sandals, and then back up again. Her lip curved slightly as if she saw something distasteful.

Somehow, I resisted the urge to smooth my hair and tug at the neckline of my shirt as I led her into my office. "It's a pleasure to meet you, Mrs. Delahunt. Please, have a seat. I'm excited to hear your thoughts on the cake and menu you want us to put together for the ball."

She crossed the room slowly, giving everything in it the same curled lip inspection she'd given me. Finally, she arranged herself in one chair and put her purse on the other. "I'm here because Frankie insists that you people are capable of making a cake suitable for our event. You've heard of the Crescent City Vintage Clothing Society, I assume?"

I nodded. "Yes, of course."

"And you're aware that the Belle Lune Ball is one of the most prestigious society events of the year."

"Absolutely. We're thrilled to get this chance to work with you."

She relaxed her lips slightly, but still didn't smile. "As well you should. If I weren't desperate, I wouldn't take a chance on an unknown."

My shoulders stiffened, but I did my best to smile. "Zydeco is hardly an unknown."

"It is to me."

My nerves twitched but I managed to avoid showing my irritation. "Then I plan to make it worth the risk you're taking. Now, I'd love for you to tell me a bit more about the ball."

Evangeline ran a finger along the armrest of the chair, probably checking for dust. "What would you like to know?"

"The basics, to begin with. How many guests do you expect? What kind of menu do you have in mind? And how many do you need the cake to serve?"

"I thought you said you were familiar with our event."

"Well. Yes. Familiar." Familiar-*ish* anyway. I'd read about it online and planned to quiz Miss Frankie about it, but I hadn't had a lot of notice. What little time I'd been given had slipped through my fingers. "I've done my research," I said easily, "but I'd much rather hear about the society from you. I'd like to view the event through your perspective."

Evangeline tilted her head to one side, gave that some thought, and then began talking. "The Vintage Clothing Society's Belle Lune Ball is always a premiere event here in New Orleans, but this is a particularly important year for us. The society was founded twenty years ago in January, which makes next year a milestone for us." Everything about Evangeline's expression said she was taking full credit for the society's longevity.

"That's quite an achievement," I said, hoping I sounded sincere. "What's your theme this year?"

She gave me a *duh!* look. "It's our twentieth anniversary. That's our theme."

Well, that was helpful. I tried to remember what the tradition was for twenty years of marriage, but all I knew offhand was that it wasn't silver or gold. "Are the decorations already planned? Do you have a color scheme?"

Another annoyed look crossed her face. "We haven't revealed that yet and we won't until the night of the ball. That's a society tradition."

I was quickly becoming irritated with her. Did she not know the answers to my questions, or was she trying to be obnoxious? I refused to let her get the best of me. The more she stonewalled, the more determined I was to get this right.

I pointed out what should have been obvious: "If we're going to work on this event, my staff and I will need to know. I'll also need access to the other people working on the event. If I can meet with the person in charge of decorations, I'll be able to successfully tie in the cake design, the menu, and presentation of the dishes."

Evangeline lowered her head slightly in what could have been a nod. "I suppose I can put you in touch with the committee head—after you sign a confidentiality agreement, of course. I'll need one from anyone who will be working on the event."

Wow. Weird. But whatever. "Of course. We'll be happy to sign."

"Do you have a business card? I can have her call you."

I'd have preferred to make contact with the committee chair myself. I didn't know how long it would take Evangeline to pass on my phone number, but I'd take what I could get. I handed her a card and resumed my seat. "Terrific. The sooner the better. Are you thinking about a sculpted cake or something more traditional? We could do round tiers or square. Or if you want something more modern, maybe we could do a sculpted and decorate it to look like a vintage dress."

A little crease formed in her forehead. "I won't be able to say until I see what you have in mind."

"Yes. Of course. I'll run up some sketches and get them to you. Do you have a preference about the flavor or type of icing? We can do a lot with buttercream, but cream cheese is always popular. Or there's fondant . . ."

Evangeline didn't say anything for a moment. She just looked down her nose at me in silence. "So you're the girl Philippe married, are you?"

That was so unexpected, the pen slipped from my fingers. "Yes I am."

"It's strange that you're here now, running his bakery like this, don't you think? Tell me, why did we never see you around here when he was alive?"

Her audacity stunned me into silence, but only for a moment. I'd had my reasons and they'd seemed legitimate at the time. But legitimate or not, they were none of her business. I could have said so straight out, but I'd lose the contract for sure if I did, and I still had things to prove.

"Oh, you know," I said with a thin laugh. "Life gets in the way. Now, about the cake—"

"You two met in Chicago. Is that right?"

"Yes. At pastry school." I wanted to escape those cold, hard eyes so I grabbed the portfolio from the top of the filing cabinet. "Maybe you would like to look at some of the other cakes we've created. We have some extremely talented cake artists on staff. Looking at cakes we've made for other clients may give you some ideas."

After handing her the folder, I sat behind the desk again. "I'm sure you'll want the cake to tie into the idea of vintage clothing, so what if we did something like this?" I sketched a rough outline of a couple dancing, both in what I hoped was appropriate vintage clothing, and turned the sketch so she could see it. "It's off the cuff, of course, but it's a rough idea."

Evangeline glanced quickly down at the sketch and away. "It's *quite* rough, isn't it? It's also somewhat ordinary."

I was tempted to show her a whole bunch of ordinary, but I bit my tongue and swallowed my pride. "Meeting with your decorators will help." So would a few suggestions. If she was this unforthcoming about what she was looking for, no wonder the other bakery had failed to produce a design she could approve. "If you could help me narrow down what you're looking for—"

Just then there was a knock on the door and Edie poked her head inside. "I'm really sorry to disturb you, but you have a phone call, Rita."

The interruption surprised me. Edie knew better than to barge in on a client meeting. "Take a message, please. Tell whoever it is that I'm with a client and I'll call back when I'm finished."

"I tried that. It's Miss Frankie's neighbor, Bernice. She says it's an emergency."

She had to be joking. I should have called this morning to tell her about the cat. Quickly, I pondered my options. I could stay with Evangeline Delahunt and let her continue taking potshots at my self-esteem, or I could take a moment to reassure Bernice. Maybe the break would also help get Mrs. Delahunt back on track.

It took me roughly two seconds to make up my mind. "Would you excuse me, Mrs. Delahunt? I'll only be a minute. You can go through the portfolio to see if there's anything that sparks an idea for you."

Evangeline looked anything but pleased, but I hurried out to Edie's desk and picked up the call. "Bernice? What's wrong?"

"What's *wrong*?" she whispered. "There's a crazy woman sitting in my living room and she's got a voodoo whatever with her. You have to get over here right now and get rid of them."

Surely I'd heard her wrong. "I'm sorry, who did you say was there?"

"I just told you. You have to come now. I don't know what to do with them."

I wasn't sure why I was responsible for her visitors, but clearly she thought I was, so I tried to get a bit more information. "Are they friends of yours?"

"Of mine? No! The crazy girl says she's a friend of yours."

"But that's impossible."

"Are you saying you didn't send them over here? That you're not responsible for that frightening-looking woman I found on my porch? She was shaking something at me, Rita. I swear they're bones."

Bernice had to be imagining things. "I doubt that," I said gently. "Where are the women now?"

"In my living room," Bernice whispered. "I had to let them in so the neighbors wouldn't see them."

Seriously? "You let complete strangers into your house even though you thought they were carrying bones?"

"I had to," she insisted. "They said that they refused to

leave until I let the voodoo lady contact Uncle Cooch, and Polly Ebersol was out walking her dog. I didn't know what else to do. But don't worry. I'll be all right until you get here. I have my gun."

That did it. "Do not use your gun," I ordered. "I'm on my way." And then I bolted for my office to get rid of Evangeline Delahunt.

Seven

I finished up with Evangeline Delahunt as quickly as I could. She promised to have the decoration committee chair call me, and I said again that I'd draw up some sketches and make another appointment with her when I had them ready. I just hoped she would call her decorator pronto. We couldn't afford to lose a single day.

By daylight Miss Frankie's neighborhood looked festive and ready for Halloween. Corn husks and jack-o'-lanterns decorated sidewalks and porches. Fall wreaths hung on doors. A couple of neighbors had even created faux grave-yards on their lawns.

Bernice must have been watching for me because she opened the door and stepped out onto the porch before my car stopped moving. The moment I got close enough, she grabbed my arm and tugged me to the far side of the porch.

"I *told* you I didn't want anybody to know what happened last night," she scolded in a harsh stage whisper.

I pulled my arm away gently. "I didn't say a word," I assured her. "I have no idea what's going on, but I'll find out. Where are they?"

"In the living room," Bernice said with a nod toward the door. I hurried inside and she trailed behind me. As we passed the kitchen, I said, "Stay here. I'll come back when they're gone."

I was a little surprised that she obeyed me without arguing. I could hear soft voices as I walked down the hallway, but that still didn't prepare me for what I saw when I stepped into the room.

Isabeau sat on Bernice's giant leather sofa next to a tall black woman wearing a white turban, tiny oval-shaped sunglasses, and a black sundress sprinkled with yellow flowers. If it hadn't been for the small bones on a jute string she held in one hand, the woman would have looked perfectly normal.

Isabeau grinned when she saw me, and I flashed back to the night before at the Dizzy Duke. I hadn't meant to lie to Bernice a moment ago; I'd honestly forgotten that I'd told the group about Bernice's visitor. I'd also forgotten Isabeau's claim that she knew a way to help. Oops.

My stomach dropped and guilt settled on me like a pile of rocks, along with a sprinkle of outrage. "What in the hell are you doing here?" I demanded.

Isabeau popped up from the couch and bounced across the room to hug me. "I told you I knew someone who could help. Don't you remember?"

"I do now. Who is this?"

She turned back to her companion with a flourish. "This is Mambo Odessa, Ox's aunt."

You could have knocked me over with a feather. Ox had

an aunt who was a voodoo priestess? I offered Mambo Odessa a friendly sort of smile. After all, this wasn't her fault, and I didn't want to get on the bad side of someone who walked around town carrying bones.

"I didn't realize Ox even had an aunt," I said, "much less one who dabbles in voodoo."

Mambo Odessa's mouth curved down at the edges. "I do not 'dabble,' as you put it," she said. "And there's no need to worry. I only use my connection to the spirits for good."

Had she read my mind, or had she overheard what Bernice said to me? Either way, I hoped her definition of "good" and mine were the same. I assured her that I believed her and turned back to Isabeau. "Why didn't you tell me what you were planning to do?"

"Because you're busy. There's that big new contract and all. And you had the meeting with Evangeline Delahunt this morning. I didn't want to bother you when I could just do this myself."

"But you shouldn't have done *this* at all. You scared Bernice half to death, and now she thinks I've been blabbing about what happened last night to anyone who would listen."

Tears welled in Isabeau's usually bright blue eyes. "But you *did* tell me about it, and you didn't say that it was a secret."

"Because it never occurred to me that you'd do something like this." My conscience gave me a sharp prod, and this time I decided to listen. Isabeau wasn't to blame. I'm the one who broke my promise to Bernice. This was my fault alone.

I sighed and rubbed at the knots of tension that were forming in my neck. "You're right, Isabeau. I'm sorry. I apologize to you, too, Mambo Odessa. It's my fault you've wasted your time this morning." Keeping my voice down so that Odessa wouldn't overhear, I asked Isabeau, "Does Ox know you're here?"

Isabeau glanced at Odessa and smiled sheepishly. "No

way. I didn't want Ox to find out what we were doing. He doesn't like this kind of thing. So the two of us met for coffee this morning and rode over here together."

Mambo Odessa rose majestically and came to stand by me. "We'll leave now. But you should be careful, my girl. There's trouble in your future."

News flash: There was trouble in my present. I didn't want to offend her, especially since I already had trouble with Ox, but I couldn't pretend to believe in what she did either. "Thanks," I said, "but I could have told you that."

"Your friend here is headed for trouble, too. She got some old things coming back to haunt her."

I might have been impressed if Isabeau obviously hadn't already told Mambo about Bernice's Uncle Cooch sighting last night. "I'll make sure to warn her."

Mambo Odessa smiled. "You think I'm a fraud, but you'll find out I'm not. Somebody wants something from that lady and you have to help her. She doesn't have anybody else."

Another good guess, but anybody could have put those pieces together. Bernice thought she saw her dead uncle. When in trouble, she'd called me. A plus B equals C. As for me being all she had, that wasn't entirely accurate, but I saw no reason to mention Bernice's nephew Bernie and his family. Bernie was nice enough, but he wasn't the kind of guy who'd hold up well if confronted by the spirit of Uncle Cooch.

"Got it," I said. "I hate to seem rude, but I really have to ask both of you to leave."

Mambo Odessa took a step. "Be careful, child. You're going to uncover some secrets you may not want to know about. You're going to uncover some things others don't want you to know about. You watch your back, hear?" And then, pressing a business card into my hand, she smiled softly. "When you need me, call."

I mumbled something noncommittal and motioned for Isabeau to join us. "I know you're trying to help, Isabeau, but I'm really in hot water with Bernice. You guys need to go."

She looked disappointed, but she led Mambo Odessa out the front door and I breathed a sigh of relief. I didn't know what to make of Mambo Odessa's parting comments, but I didn't waste time thinking about them. I had to make sure Bernice was still speaking to me.

I found her at the kitchen table sipping sweet tea. She seemed all right, but I had a major apology to offer and some groveling to do.

"I'm so sorry," I said as I sat down beside her. "I did open my big mouth last night. I just had no idea Isabeau would do something like this."

Bernice ran a finger along the side of her glass, leaving a clear streak in the condensation. "You promised you wouldn't say anything."

"I know. I just—" *No excuses*, my conscience whispered. It sounded a whole lot like Aunt Yolanda, and I knew it was right. "I screwed up. Big-time. Can you forgive me?"

Bernice looked at me for a long time. "I suppose there was no real harm done. I just hope Polly Ebersol didn't see them. She's as sweet as she can be, but she can't keep a thing to herself. I know it's not her fault really. She's been lonely since her husband died. When she finds someone to talk to, she just can't stop herself."

I bit back a smile. "Well, I'm sure that even if Polly saw them, it will be okay. Everybody knows you don't believe in voodoo, and if it helps, Mambo Odessa says she only uses her spirit connections for good."

Bernice wiped her wet finger on a napkin. "Well, of course she'd say that. It's what you wanted to hear."

"She said a few things I didn't want to hear," I said. I

hadn't really believed Mambo Odessa, but the fact that she was Ox's aunt stirred up some weird kind of protectiveness in me. My own version of the six degrees of separation game, I guess. "Anyway, they're gone and they won't be back."

"Well, good. Thank you."

"How are you feeling?" I asked. "Are you okay?"

Bernice shrugged one shoulder. "Oh, I'm fine. Or I will be. Having that woman in my house stirred up some old memories—ones I'd rather leave behind."

Uh-oh. "Anything you want to talk about?"

"No. Not really." Bernice stared at her glass for a heartbeat or two and then let out a big sigh. "It's funny how things from your childhood never really leave you, you know?"

I nodded but I don't think she saw me. Her eyes had taken on a faraway look.

"Maybe it's just because I saw Uncle Cooch last night—or thought I did. He was a lot of fun when he was alive, but there were times when he scared me a bit. He believed in all those old swamp superstitions, especially those about fishing and hunting. He absolutely believed in the rougarou, and sometimes he'd tell us bedtime stories about it."

She'd lost me. "The what?"

"The rougarou." Bernice shuddered and linked her hands together. "It's a creature of the swamp that's a cross between . . . oh, probably Big Foot and a werewolf. Uncle Cooch used the rougarou to keep us kids in line. He didn't like for us to break the rules."

So he'd used some hideous creature to frighten them into obedience. I took an instant dislike to Uncle Cooch. "Good thing Aunt Yolanda didn't know about the rougarou when I was a girl," I said with a grin. "I was so angry about my parents' accident, I made sure to break as many rules as I could get away with for a while."

Bernice smiled, but her eyes still seemed far away. I tried another tack. "Does that mean you grew up in the swamp, too?"

"I sure did. Little bitty town out in Terrebonne Parish called Baie Rebelle."

"Rebel Bay?"

Bernice nodded. "I could hunt and fish with the best of them when I was a girl. Even beat my cousin Eskil one year in the catfish contest." She smiled at the memory. "But that was a long time ago. I haven't touched a pole in years."

"What brought you to New Orleans?"

She laughed. "I got married. What else?" She looked around her kitchen and let out a yelp. "Gracious! Where are my manners? Would you like some sweet tea? I brewed some fresh this morning. Or I can stir up some lemonade in a blink."

I said that tea would be fine and she poured me a glass.

"I suppose you think I've lost my mind, don't you?" she said as she put the glass on the table.

"No! Not at all. I'm sure you saw something last night. As a matter of fact, I came back to look around and found a cat on your deck. It seemed pretty comfortable. Maybe it jumped up on the window—"

"That was no cat," Bernice said with a scowl. "It was my uncle Cooch, plain as day. But please don't repeat that to Frances Mae. She's already convinced I'm seeing things."

After betraying her confidence last night, I was determined to avoid a repeat performance. "I won't say a word," I promised. "To anyone."

"So you came back last night," she said after a moment. "Does that mean you believe me?"

"I believe you saw something," I said. "I thought that if I could find footprints or some other physical evidence of neighborhood kids pulling Halloween pranks, it would set your mind at ease."

"And did you?"

"Well, no. But that doesn't mean there wasn't someone here."

She sighed again and took a drink. "I appreciate you checking, baby. Really, I do. I know how crazy it all sounds. What I saw simply couldn't have been Uncle Cooch, but I don't have any other explanation for it." She winked at me as she put her glass on the bar. "I'll just have to pray extra hard tonight, won't I?"

"Would you feel better if you weren't alone? I'm sure Miss Frankie would let you stay with her again if you want to." I didn't doubt my mother-in-law's hospitality for a moment, and besides, it was my turn to volunteer her for something without asking. She owed me at least a dozen times over.

Bernice shook her head. "Oh no, honey. I'll be just fine. But if I do get nervous, I'll give Frances Mae a call."

She seemed calmer and her nostalgia had faded, so I stood to leave. As I did, the phone shrilled. The harsh ring in the quiet house startled us both.

Bernice let out a chirp and one hand flew to her throat. Her eyes flashed to the phone uncertainly. "Excuse me for a minute, won't you, dear? Let me see who that is."

Okay, so maybe she was still a bit nervous. Besides, it seemed rude to slip out while she was on the phone, so I wandered into the dining room to give Bernice some privacy and sent Ox a text letting him know I'd be back soon. Just as I pressed Send, Bernice let out a cry of alarm and the phone dropped with a clatter onto something hard.

Maybe I'd sent that text too soon.

Eight

In response to Bernice's cry, I rushed back to the kitchen. I hoped she hadn't hurt herself or, worse, had had a heart attack or something. Last night had been troubling for her, and this morning's visit from Isabeau and Mambo Odessa hadn't helped. Had the phone call been the last straw?

We ran into each other at the kitchen door. I was relieved to see her walking around on her own, but just like the night before, her face was pale and her expression alarmed.

"What is it?" I asked. "Bernice? What's happened?"

She weaved a little on her feet and I worried she might faint. "Oh, Rita! It's my cousin Eskil. He's gone." Her voice was thin and reedy, but I was relieved to know she wasn't seriously ill.

"Gone? You mean he . . . died?"

Her eyes flew wide and she gaped at me in horror. "You think he's dead?"

"No. I mean I don't know. What did you mean when you said that he's gone?"

"Oh. I meant that he's missing. He went fishing yesterday morning and he hasn't come back. They're afraid he's lost out in the swamp."

I put an arm around her and helped her into the living room with its comfortable chairs. I made soothing noises the whole way along the lines of, "I'm sure they'll find him. He's probably just fine. Maybe he stayed out too late and slept somewhere else."

Bernice clutched my arm gratefully. "Oh, I do hope you're right." She sank into an overstuffed armchair and pulled a handkerchief from her pocket. "It's just so distressing. It's like Uncle Cooch all over again! This is exactly what happened when he disappeared."

Coincidence? I had trouble believing that, but I didn't want to upset Bernice any more than she already was. I sat in a nearby chair and kept an eye on her. "Try not to jump to conclusions," I said. "It's probably not the same at all."

She wiped a few tears away and tried to smile. "Do you really think so?"

"Of course," I assured her, which wasn't entirely true, but it seemed like the right thing to say. "Who called you just now? How much information do they have at this point?"

Bernice sniffed and dabbed and made an effort to pull herself together. "It was Eskil's sister, my cousin Bitty. She lives with Aunt Margaret now. In fact, all the children do. Eskil never left. He's been there taking care of Aunt Margaret ever since Uncle Cooch disappeared. Tallulah came back after her husband left her for another woman, and Bitty . . . well, the poor thing. She was left at the altar when she was just a young woman. We don't talk about it, though. It makes her too sad."

All very interesting, but not what I asked. "So Bitty called you. What exactly did she say?"

Bernice gave me a cross look. "Just what I told you. Eskil went fishing yesterday and he never came home. Bitty says Aunt Margaret is fit to be tied, but of course she would be, wouldn't she? After what happened to Uncle Cooch. I hope this doesn't set her back. She's a bit frail, you know."

I nodded as if I knew all about Aunt Margaret and asked, "So the missing cousin . . . Eskil? He's Cooch's son?"

Bernice nodded and patted her forehead with a handkerchief, then reached for my hand. "That must be why Uncle Cooch came to me last night. He was trying to tell me about Eskil, wasn't he?"

I didn't want her to go there. I shook my head. "I don't think—"

But Bernice wasn't listening. Her eyes grew as round as quarters and she shot to her feet. "I think I know what he wanted to tell me. He wants me to go to them. They need my help!"

Mambo Odessa's warning that Bernice was heading for trouble echoed in my head, but I stuffed it into a corner of my mind and ignored it. I needed all my powers of concentration just to follow the conversation. "Do they have people out looking for Eskil?" I asked.

"Bitty says the whole town is out there. She and Tallulah are doing their best to keep up, but what a job. It's too much for the two of them." She skipped from one subject to another like water in a hot pan, which made it tough to keep up.

"What job is that?"

Bernice *tsk*ed her tongue against the roof of her mouth. "Feeding the volunteers, of course. You don't think they're going to let people go hungry?"

"Well, no, but—"

She flapped a hand at me and took a few steps toward her chair, stopping on her way to pluck some dead leaves from a plant. She moved nervously, as if she was having trouble remaining in one place. "I can't just sit here while they're going through such a thing. Honestly, Rita, imagine how you'd feel if we were talking about your family."

The argument I'd been about to deliver withered on my tongue. I'd been thinking about Bernice and her health. After all, she wasn't exactly a spring chicken. But she wasn't ancient either. Clearly, she cared about her aunt and cousins. I could relate to that. Losing my parents in that car accident had been horrific. I couldn't imagine how it must feel for a family member to go missing in a swamp filled with man-eating creatures.

Maybe it would do Bernice good to see her family. Maybe it would do them good to see her. "What can I do to help?"

Bernice wiped away a few more tears and sat down again. "I knew you'd understand. Thank you, dear. You'll drive me, won't you? I can't see as well as I once could, and I don't like to drive at night."

Wait. Me? In the swamp? At *night*? Was she out of her mind? This wasn't what I'd had in mind when I'd asked if she needed my help. Pros and cons ping-ponged around in my head. I knew I should say yes, but I desperately wanted to say no. I had work to do. Lots and lots of important, time-sensitive work. I was a busy, busy woman. And most important, I don't do swamps.

When I didn't respond immediately, Bernice released my hand and waved the handkerchief in front of her face. "Oh, it's too much to ask. Forget I said anything. It's just that with Uncle Cooch gone, Eskil is the only man in the family. He takes care of all the women, you know." She let out a distressed cry and fluttered her hands some more. "But I'm sure they'll be all right. I certainly don't want to put you out. I know how busy you are."

Guilt gave both my heart and my stomach a big old squeeze. I could have handled a straight-out assault. If she'd told me I had to take her as penance for opening my big mouth last night, I could have argued with her. But plucking at my heartstrings like that? It was too much. I couldn't take the thought of poor Aunt Margaret out there all alone with nothing but her two daughters and a swamp full of alligators for company.

"Well, of course you need to go, and I'll be happy to drive you. Do you want to leave right now?" I said.

Just like that, Bernice's tears dried right up. It was a miracle. "I need to make a few phone calls first," she said matter-of-factly. "And I'd like to pack a few things to take Aunt Margaret in her time of need. Could we leave around four? That way we can get there before supper and help the girls get food on the table. Those people will have been searching all day. They'll need to be fed."

Right. Four o'clock. Subtracting time for travel, that would give me roughly two whole hours to work on ideas for the Belle Lune Ball. Whatever would I do with all my spare time?

"You wanted to see me?"

The unexpected sound of Ox's voice startled me. I'd been so engrossed in the blog I'd been reading, I hadn't heard him come to my door.

I didn't want to give him the upper hand, so I tried not to let him see that he'd surprised me. "Yeah, come on in."

He moved into my office and took a chair. Usually, I talked things over with Ox in the design room while we worked, but I didn't have enough time to do that today. Plus, I figured it didn't hurt to remind him occasionally that the butt in the boss's chair was mine.

"Everything okay?" he asked.

"Sure," I said. "In a manner of speaking. You know how it is."

He didn't even crack a smile. "What's up?"

I didn't know if Isabeau had told him about the way she and Mambo Odessa had ambushed Bernice that morning, but I wasn't going to tell him. He and I might be on rocky turf, but I knew better than to stir up trouble in someone else's relationship.

"I'm going to have to leave early this afternoon. It's important."

"Oh?" In that one word I heard the whole list of accusations: I'd been gone most of the morning and now I needed to leave again? Maybe Ox *should* be the one running this place. Then again, it might just have been my own guilty conscience speaking.

"You remember Miss Frankie's neighbor Bernice? Her cousin has gone missing in the swamp. Bernice needs to get to her family and she can't drive at night. She needs me to take her to some place called Baie Rebelle."

"Okay. You coming back?"

I laughed, hoping to lighten the mood. "Of course . . . assuming I don't get eaten by an alligator."

"You're going today?"

"Later this afternoon. I'll be in tomorrow to take care of a few things. I just need to leave a little early today."

He regarded me through narrowed eyes. "Let me guess: You want me to take over while you're gone?"

Okay. So he still wasn't over last night. I was determined to take the high road. "It's just for a couple of hours, and everybody seems to be on task and working well. Or is there a problem I don't know about?"

Ox shook his head and drummed his fingers on the armrest. "Nope. Unless you count the fact that I'll have to get someone else to finish the Howard reunion cake."

"I'm almost finished with it," I said. "It won't take long to make the jack-o'-lantern for the top. I can finish that before I leave." He didn't say anything so I waited a moment and then said, "Okay. Good. I'll have my cell phone on me, so if you run into any problems, just call."

He snorted softly. "Right. If there's something I can't handle, I'll make sure I find you. But you really think you'll have cell reception in the middle of the swamp? Good luck with that."

He really was in a mood. I sucked in a calming breath and reminded myself that no good would come from prolonging the argument, even if he was being a jerk. "Have you ever been to Baie Rebelle?"

Ox shook his head. "Never even heard of it."

"Well, then, maybe it's an exception to the no cell service rule. We can only hope."

I thought he'd leave, but he settled more comfortably in his chair. "How did your appointment with Evangeline Delahunt go?"

The question sounded innocent enough, but the challenge in his eyes was unmistakable. I like to think that I'm an honest person, but there are times when it's necessary to be careful with the truth. This was one of them. No way was I going to give Ox the satisfaction of saying he told me so. "It went fine," I said with a sugary smile. "She seems like a lovely woman."

Okay, so that was an outright lie and I'd probably be struck by lightning for telling it. But I just couldn't—or wouldn't—admit that he'd been right.

He grinned but there was nothing friendly about the smile on his face. "Lovely? Are you sure you met the real Evangeline?"

"Of course I did. Somewhere in her sixties? Tall. Thin. Short silver hair? She was delightful." And this is why I try not to lie. Once I get started, it's hard to stop.

"Delightful. Really."

I lifted my chin and met his gaze. "Yes. Really."

"So what was the decision? What are we making?"

"We haven't made the final decision yet," I admitted reluctantly. "I'll be meeting with the decorator. We'll make a decision after that."

"Sounds interesting. When is the meeting?"

"Tomorrow." The word slipped out before I could stop it.

One of Ox's eyebrows arched. "You're meeting on Sunday?"

The lies just kept on coming. "Yes. They're very eager to work with us."

"Really. Maybe I should join you. If that's okay, that is. Isabeau and I don't have any plans."

Again, it wasn't what he said; it was the way he said it. Almost as if he knew I didn't actually have an appointment. As if he was trying to catch me out. I nodded and tried to look pleased with his suggestion. "Great idea. I don't remember the time off the top of my head, but I'll let you know." Which was a ridiculous thing to say with my phone, my computer, and my calendar all sitting right in front of me.

Ox smirked. "Why don't you just check now?"

His attitude was really starting to rankle. I was ready to be finished with the conversation, but I couldn't see a way out . . . except to change the subject. It was a low blow, but I felt backed into a corner. "You have family around here, don't you?"

Ox nodded uncertainly, probably confused about where I was going with my question. "My folks are from Georgia, but I have an aunt and some cousins here. Why do you ask?"

I felt a little fizz of pleasure at throwing him off balance. Plus, he looked genuinely baffled, which convinced me he didn't know about Isabeau and Mambo Odessa's morning house call. I backed up a bit. "Bernice mentioned that her family is superstitious, but I don't know much about the local folklore. I'm curious to know what I'll be running into. How much do you know about all that woo-woo stuff people around here believe?"

Ox almost smiled, but he caught himself before he could. "I know a little. Are you asking about something in particular?"

"I don't know enough to ask about anything in particular," I admitted. "But here's what I do know: Bernice's uncle disappeared about fifteen years ago and nobody has seen any sign of him since. Now her cousin—his son—is missing and the circumstances are the same. She mentioned something about the rougarou and said her uncle used to tell them bedtime stories about it to keep them in line. Are there any other swamp legends I should know about?"

Ox nodded slowly. "Lots of them. Too many to list in one sitting. I've heard that some people believe the *feu follet* are hanging out in the swamp. Some people say that they're the souls of children who were never baptized, but don't worry. It's actually just swamp gas." He eyed me for a moment and asked, "You don't believe in any of that, do you?"

I shook my head. "Not at all. I'm just curious." I was relieved that some of his hostility had faded, and I gave myself a mental pat on the back for not rising to his bait. I'd been working on my people skills, and I liked thinking that my efforts were paying off.

"What about Bernice? Is she a believer?"

I wagged my hand in a "maybe, maybe not" gesture. "I don't think she wants to be, but the legends are part of her childhood. That can be hard to shake."

"Sure can."

"She told me that her uncle had a moonshine still out there in the swamp," I said. "Nobody knew where it was. Do you think that's why he fed them stories about a swamp monster?"

"To keep them from exploring and finding it?" Ox shrugged. "Could be. I'm sure some of those legends seemed bloodcurdling to a bunch of impressionable kids." He stood and stared down at me for a moment. "Good luck. Try not to run into the rougarou while you're out there."

"Funny." I got out of my chair, too, so he wouldn't have the advantage of standing over me. "Guess I'll see you in the morning then."

"Okay."

I thought he might say something else, but he turned and left without another word. We hadn't patched up our differences entirely, but I had hope that we might eventually.

I just hoped "eventually" wasn't too far away.

Nine

Miss Frankie was waiting with Bernice when I arrived to pick her up, which didn't surprise me. The three of us loaded into the Mercedes with Bernice in the front so she could give me directions, and Miss Frankie in the back.

We traveled a few miles on the freeway, but the rest of our trip was on a narrow two-lane road that wound back and forth over water and swampland. If there had ever been lane markings, they'd long ago disappeared. We were deep inside Terrebonne Parish surrounded by forest of pine, live oak dripping Spanish moss, and a few other trees I couldn't identify. Thick undergrowth and squatty palmetto trees carpeted the forest floor.

Every once in a while we passed a cypress swamp dotted with those otherworldly trees and nubby stumps, apparently called cypress knees, sticking up out of the water. Spots of civilization showed up now and then, but the people who lived out here seemed to like their privacy. Homes were usually solitary and far apart.

Bernice and Miss Frankie kept themselves busy debating about almost everything under the sun. Bernice told us about her grandmother's favorite remedy for a headache—cow dung and molasses rubbed on the temples—and Miss Frankie declared a deep and abiding gratitude for the man who invented aspirin. Then Bernice explained how her daddy had always been careful not to let his shadow fall on the water when he was fishing because it would bring bad luck, and Miss Frankie declared it wasn't luck but common sense, so that the fish wouldn't see a shadow on the water and swim away. They had gone on that way for a while, so I'd tuned them out and daydreamed about different designs for the Belle Lune cake.

After nearly two hours, Bernice lunged up in her seat, straining against her seat belt. "We're getting close now! Slow down. The speed limit is only twenty-five here in town and they'll get you if you go over."

I put on the brakes and slowed to a near crawl, and a few seconds later the trees parted to reveal a small clapboard building. The sun had sunk low in the western horizon, but it was still light enough to see the uneven lettering on the sign: T-REX'S GENERAL STORE.

If this was the "town," it was little more than a wide spot on a very narrow road. Besides the general store, I saw a ramshackle gas station with two old-fashioned pumps, a bar called The Gator Pit with a faded sign I could barely read, and a single-wide trailer, home of the Baie Rebelle Church. The church parking lot was empty and the gas station was deserted, but a handful of cars were nosed up to the bar.

A man wearing raggedy overalls, white rubber boots, and a dirty ball cap caught my eye. He was bent to look through the window of a white Ford Ranger and he waved his arm in sharp, angry gestures. My natural curiosity stirred, making me wonder who was in the truck and what had made Overall Man so angry. By the time we passed the bar, I'd come up with three different scenarios, all of which were probably way off the mark.

"Aunt Margaret's house is probably ten minutes away," Bernice said. "Just turn left here and follow this road until I tell you to stop."

She'd been giving me those same instructions for over an hour, but I really didn't mind. The joy on her face as we drove through her home turf warmed my heart. If it weren't for the worry shadowing her eyes, I would have said Bernice looked twenty years younger.

Maybe it was a good thing Miss Frankie was with us. Seeing how happy Bernice was to visit home, even under difficult circumstances, she might understand why I wanted to go home for Christmas. She might even agree to ask Pearl Lee for help with the holiday festivities instead of me.

"I must confess, Bernice, I had you pegged as coming from an entirely different background," I said as I made the turn onto a red dirt road.

Bernice sighed softly. "I married when I was just a girl. Sixteen years old. It wasn't so unusual back then. I took one look at my husband and fell hard. He'd been off fighting in Vietnam, and when he came back, he just swept me off my feet. I thought we'd settle down here and live the kind of life we were both used to, but going off to the other side of the world had changed him. We left the swamp and he never looked back." She smiled at me and a twinkle danced in her eye, momentarily replacing the worry. "I may've peeked back over my shoulder a time or two, but I loved that man hard enough to put the past behind me."

Miss Frankie stirred in the backseat, but she didn't say a word. It didn't matter. I knew what she was thinking. In the beginning, I'd loved Philippe as much as I knew how to love anyone, but I'd never felt comfortable around his wealthy relatives. After spilling red wine on Miss Frankie's white sofa and carpet on my first visit, I'd avoided coming back with him when he visited New Orleans. Maybe I hadn't loved him enough. Maybe I'd been too selfish to make sacrifices. Maybe if he'd understood my emotional baggage better, I would have found my way through it.

We'd never know, and I didn't want to start dwelling on past mistakes, so I concentrated on Bernice instead. "So your husband grew up around here, too?"

Bernice nodded. "David's people live about thirty miles east. Close enough that we used to run into each other from time to time. You know how it is."

Not really, but I pretended I did. "If he'd been off serving in the military, he must have been a little older than you."

"Seven years," Bernice said. "These days you'd worry about a man that age setting his sights on a girl as young as I was, and you'd probably be right to. But like I said, it was a different world when I came up. It was no big deal for a girl to leave school and get married. A boy either, for that matter. People around here didn't worry much about education in those days."

From the looks of the ramshackle houses we were passing, I guessed that not much had changed. We rounded a few more turns in the road and Bernice pointed to the roof of a large house visible behind a grove of leafy green trees. "That's it. That's Aunt Margaret's place there. Slow down now. The driveway's coming up just after this bump in the road."

The undergrowth was so thick I would have missed the

turnoff if she hadn't warned me. I turned onto a wide dirt driveway that led to a clearing and a large and surprisingly modern home. A broad porch stretched along two sides of the house and at least a dozen trucks and cars were scattered in the clearing, but I couldn't see anyone moving around. Either the search party was still out looking for Eskil, or they were back and dinner was already being served.

There was no room left in the clearing, so I parked on the edge of the driveway next to a deep ditch filled with weeds and a few inches of brackish water. We took a few minutes to get out of the car and stretch, and then Bernice led us to the front door.

She gave a courtesy knock and let herself in. Miss Frankie and I followed. Just as the screen door banged shut behind me, I saw a broad woman wearing a plaid shirt and jeans squeal with delight and throw her arms around Bernice. Two other women came to see what all the commotion was, and Bernice was swallowed up in a round of hugs and excited chatter.

Eventually the dust settled and the excitement died away, and Bernice introduced Miss Frankie and me to her family. Aunt Margaret was a tiny woman with hair the same snowy white as Bernice's. She had a narrow face covered with a network of wrinkles and kind eyes.

The squealer turned out to be Cousin Bitty, a friendly woman with a wide smile and arms like bands of steel. Her sister Tallulah was a bit more reserved. She was as short as her mother, but three times as wide, and her brown hair was cut short in no particular style. Tallulah watched us with wary eyes, sparing only the slight curve of her full lips before returning to what she was doing.

I couldn't tell how old any of them were. Life on the swamp had given them all a weathered appearance. Aunt

Margaret might have been anywhere from sixty to ninety, and I thought Bitty and Tallulah were probably in their fifties, but I could have been off by ten years in either direction.

I'd expected to walk into a house hushed with worry, but nobody seemed terribly concerned about Eskil's fate. Aunt Margaret certainly didn't look as frail and fragile as Bernice had led me to believe.

After a few minutes Bitty herded us into the kitchen and passed out aprons while she explained the menu and assigned chores. Miss Frankie and I were put in charge of a tossed salad and stationed at one end of a massive pine table so scarred it had to be a family heirloom. Bernice started stirring together a batch of cornbread large enough to feed everyone in Terrebonne Parish, and the other three went back to what they'd been doing when we arrived.

Once we were all working, I broached the subject uppermost in my mind. "Is there any news about Eskil? Have they found him yet?"

Bitty shook her head. "Nothing yet, but the swamp is a big place. There are a thousand and one places to look for him. They'll find him yet."

Tallulah gave her sister an irritated look. "He went out fishing like he always does. He would have gone to the places he always goes. If they were going to find him, they'd have done it already."

I glanced at her mother to see how she'd react to such a negative prediction, but Margaret just kept rolling out a piecrust and barely glanced at Tallulah. "This isn't like when your daddy disappeared," she said. "Eskil's careful."

Tallulah *tsk*ed her tongue and chopped a large sausage link into bite-sized pieces. Some wonderful aromas were coming from the pot she had on the range, and suddenly I was glad Bernice had invited us to share their dinner.

"Mama, I don't know where your head is. Eskil's been butting heads with Silas Laroche over that hunting lease for months. And you know Silas. He'd as soon shoot you in the back as look at you. What if Eskil got up in his business?"

"Your brother isn't stupid," Aunt Margaret said patiently. "Now stop fretting and get that gumbo ready. Eskil is fine. If he was gone, I'd know it."

I wanted her to be right, but I thought the potential for something bad to have happened out there in that wild and rugged land was huge.

"Are there many people searching?" Miss Frankie asked.

Bitty bobbed her head up and down. "Most everybody in town, except probably Silas. I didn't see him leave with the others, but he's not as social as most. He likes to keep to himself."

"He keeps to himself all right," Tallulah said. "Except when he's setting lines over somebody else's. He doesn't believe in rules and regulations," she explained for our benefit. "He doesn't think people can own land or lease rights. He doesn't care one bit what the law says. If he wants to hunt or fish somewhere, he's going to do it, and he expects everyone else to get out of his way."

"He's not easy to get along with," Aunt Margaret agreed. "But you know he wouldn't hurt Eskil. They've known each other since they were in diapers."

Tallulah cut up another sausage and pulled a plastic bag full of shrimp from the refrigerator. "Like that ever stopped anybody." She paused and tilted her head for a moment. "We'd best hurry y'all. I hear 'em coming back."

Conversation ceased and everyone went to work to finish the meal. After a few minutes even I picked up the sounds of people approaching. At first it was the low murmur of voices. Then a soft laugh and the steady sound of footsteps.

The voices fell silent not far from the house and a moment later something heavy hit the wooden porch.

The screen door flew open with a bang and a large man with shaggy gray hair and a long gray beard loomed in the doorway. A small football-shaped birthmark bounced around on his cheek, and a powerfully rank smell wafted off him. I guessed it was a mix of swamp water, rotting vegetation, and spoiled meat. "I heard y'all were worried about me," he boomed in a voice that shook the boards under my feet.

So this was Eskil? I glanced at Bernice, and from the stunned look on her face, I guess she'd reached the same conclusion I had. Uncle Cooch hadn't come to see her last night, but I was almost certain Cousin Eskil had.

Ten

When Eskil Percifield walked through the kitchen door, I expected a few tears of relief from the womenfolk. Maybe even a hug or two. But both his sisters and his mother looked at him with bored expressions.

"I might have known you were all right," Tallulah said, sounding almost disappointed. "What happened?"

Eskil plucked a stray piece of sausage from the cutting board and tossed it into his mouth. "The damn boat ran out of gas on me. I coulda sworn the tank was full when I left."

"You need to be more careful," Bitty cautioned as she slapped his hand away. "Now go wash up. You stink." She leaned over to look out the door at the assembled crowd and called out, "That goes for the rest of y'all. Supper's on the table but none of y'all are sitting down until you wash yourselves."

A lot of good-natured tussling over water from the hose

and the bathroom sink took place over the next few minutes.
Bitty and Bernice did their best to tell Miss Frankie and me
who they all were, but with two dozen cousins, uncles, and
neighbors roaming through the house, I got lost in a hurry.
There were even a couple of women in the search party, both
of whom seemed more comfortable with the men in the yard
than the women in the kitchen. I checked a few other faces
for that birthmark, but Eskil seemed to be the only one
present who had it.

While glancing out the window, I noticed one of the
women talking to a young man with shaggy dark hair. He
cut her off with an angry wave of his hand and stalked away.
She called after him, but her voice got lost in the dozen
conversations floating around me so I didn't hear what she
said. She was old enough to be his mother and I wondered
if she was.

The look on her face and the angry set of his shoulders
tripped my imagination and sent it racing forward twenty
years. Would that be Edie and her baby in the future? Or
the baby and *me*? I felt a little light-headed at the thought,
but there was nothing I could do about it now so I stuffed
my concerns into the back of my mind and focused on putting together the meal for the search party.

Eventually everyone was clean—in a manner of speaking—
and everyone found a place to sit, or lean. A dozen people
crowded around the huge table and the rest spilled into the
living room and out onto the porch. Cousin Somebody-or-other
said grace, then everybody dug in with enthusiasm.

The food was delicious and hearty. A rich gumbo with just
the right amount of spice, fried okra, melt-in-your-mouth
cornbread dripping with honey, a crisp salad of fresh-from-
the-garden greens and tomatoes, and a roast that could have
been anything from beef to raccoon for all I knew. It was

seasoned with peppers and onion, and enough cayenne pepper to make a hole in the ozone layer. Dessert, a rhubarb-orange pie, was to die for. The crust was flaky and buttery, the filling perfectly tart and sweet. I knew plenty of professional pastry chefs, myself included, who couldn't make a better crust or match the flavors Aunt Margaret had coaxed out of the fruit.

Conversation was lively, if a bit confusing, but I found myself enjoying the company more than I'd expected to. After a while, the meal wound down and people began to drift away. That's when the real work began. Miss Frankie and Bernice cleared the table while Tallulah and Bitty gathered dishes from the living room and porch. I scraped food into the trash and stacked dishes beside the sink, and Aunt Margaret put away the leftovers. Now that I'd seen Eskil and formulated a theory about him being Bernice's late-night visitor, I was dying for a chance to talk to her. I'd seen the shock of recognition on her face, and I assumed she had some idea why he'd showed up on her back deck last night. She was having such a good time with her family, though, I didn't want to interrupt.

We'd almost finished cleaning up when Bernice gasped and put a hand on her chest. I was at her side in a flash, alert for any sign of trouble. It had been a long, troubling day for her, and I didn't want the stress of it to get to her.

"What's wrong?" I asked. "Are you feeling okay?"

"Oh. Yes." She looked a little embarrassed by my reaction. "I just remembered my pills. I'm supposed to take them with dinner and I plum forgot."

I wondered how serious it would be for her to skip a dose. "You left them home?"

Bernice laughed and shook her head. "No, baby, they're in my purse. I left it in your car. I'll have to run out there and get it."

Oh. Well, shoot. I hadn't been raised to let a nice older lady go wandering around in the dark, so even though I was spooked by the dark swamp outside, there was no way around it. I told Bernice to stay where she was, grabbed my keys, and turned on the tiny LED light on my keychain. After giving myself a mental pep talk for courage, I stepped out into the night.

A thousand stars lit the sky, and the moon looked gigantic without city lights to dull it. Something rustled in the nearby bushes, and something else let out a loud warning buzz. I was nervous, but I could also hear voices floating on the air so I knew I wasn't alone.

Even with odd sounds coming from the shadows, being outside wasn't as frightening as I'd imagined it would be. Still, this part of the world was completely foreign to me. I'd spent my entire life in cities, as had generations of family before me. There'd been no childhood visits to an *abuelo*'s farm. No summers at camp. I was completely out of my element in nature.

When I was a few feet in front of the car, I used my keyless entry to unlock the doors. The headlights flashed, momentarily blinding me with the bright light. I moved cautiously to the passenger's side door and found Bernice's purse.

So far, so good.

I pressed the remote to lock the car, and this time I saw something long and dark in the ditch illuminated by the headlights. My heart stopped beating and my mind screamed *alligator!* but the rest of my body froze in fear.

Car. I needed to get inside the car.

Scrambling like a madwoman, I tore at the door and threw myself inside. I had no idea if an alligator could get through a locked car door, but I sure hoped it couldn't.

Unable to stop myself, I leaned up to look at the beast. And in that moment, I realized it wasn't an alligator at all—unless alligators in Baie Rebelle wore hunters' orange vests and white rubber boots.

I started the car and turned on the lights, and I sat there for a long time just staring at the body and willing it to move. It didn't, so I made myself get out of the car for a closer look. He was facedown in the brackish water, but I didn't think he'd been part of the search party who'd stayed for supper.

I checked my cell phone, but just as Ox had predicted, I had no service. I walked back to the house and went straight to the kitchen, where I'd seen a telephone earlier. Aunt Margaret was there chatting quietly with Miss Frankie and Bernice. Tallulah and Bitty had disappeared somewhere.

Miss Frankie smiled at me when I came through the door. "Margaret has kindly invited us to stay overnight, sugar. Do you think we should, or do you need to get back?"

"I don't think we're going anywhere for a while," I said. "I just found a dead man in the ditch."

Things move a lot slower in the country than they do in the city. It took a local sheriff's deputy nearly an hour to show up at Aunt Margaret's. During that time curious onlookers— those who were still hanging around after dinner—trampled all over the driveway and the banks of the ditch. I didn't know how the poor man had died, but I thought it would be easier for the sheriff to determine what happened if the evidence wasn't disturbed. Every effort I made to keep people away fell on deaf ears, however. I had a hard time believing that the citizens of Baie Rebelle were that naïve—it seemed far more likely that they didn't mind destroying whatever evidence there might be, which made me think the man in the ditch probably hadn't keeled over from a heart attack.

While we waited for the authorities to show up, rumors began circulating. Nobody had touched the body, but everyone seemed to know that it was Silas Laroche, the neighbor Eskil had been having trouble with. I didn't like the sound of that, his body being in Eskil's ditch and all, but nobody else seemed all that upset that Silas was dead. The women just kept the sweet tea and coffee flowing, as any self-respecting Southern woman would if a dead body showed up in her front yard.

After a long wait, a police cruiser pulled up the driveway and a small woman in a blue uniform got out. She looked to be in her midthirties, about my age, with a slight build and brown hair pulled into a ponytail. She took a look around and then approached the porch, where we were all sitting, hands on hips. "What's goin' on here, Miss Margaret?"

"Well, hello there, Georgie. Come on up and set. I'll get you a glass of tea."

Georgie shook her head. "Thanks, but I can't. Got a call about some trouble out this way." She pulled a paper from her uniform shirt pocket and glanced down at it. "Is there a Rita Lucero here?"

I waved my hand over my head and stood to make it easier for her to spot me.

She motioned for me to sit. "I need you to stay there, ma'am. You're the one who called dispatch?"

"I am."

"What seems to be the problem?"

I'd already explained the problem to the dispatcher, but I'd had enough experience with the police to know this was how they worked. Besides, Deputy Georgie had a look in her eye that convinced me I'd be smart not to argue. "I went to my car to get something and noticed a body lying in the ditch. It's just down there if you want to take a look."

"It's Silas Laroche," Tallulah interjected. "Looks like he finally did what we always knew he'd do: got himself drunk and fell in a ditch."

Georgie looked surprised. "You positive it's Silas?"

"It sure looks like him," Bitty said. She put on a virtuous expression and stood a fraction of an inch taller. "Of course, I could be wrong. We didn't touch the body."

Georgie nodded curtly. "Y'all stay right here. I'll go have a look."

She took a brisk walk toward the ditch, scrambled down the bank to check the body, and made a call using the radio on her shoulder as she walked back toward us. "It's Silas all right," she said when she finished her call. "Only it doesn't look like he drowned in the ditch. I'd say somebody hit him over the head with something hard enough to crush his skull." She zeroed in on me. "You're the one who found the body, then?"

I said again that I was, and after warning everyone else to stay put, Georgie led me inside. I swallowed my questions and tried to give off a cooperative vibe. The kitchen smelled of fresh coffee, underscored by Tallulah's gumbo.

We settled at the table and sized each other up. Now that we were closer, I could see that Georgie had clear gray eyes and a smattering of freckles on her nose and cheeks. "I've never seen you around here before," she said. "You aren't from around these parts, are you?"

I said that I wasn't, and rattled off my address and cell number before she could ask.

She introduced herself as Georgie Tucker and put both elbows on the table. "You're all the way down here from New Orleans, huh? Funny, you don't look like the kind to hire a hunting guide."

"I'm not," I said with a smile. "I drove my mother-in-law and her neighbor down here this afternoon. Bernice got a call this morning that her cousin Eskil was missing out on the swamp. Naturally she was worried about him."

"Bernice is your mother-in-law?"

I shook my head. "My mother-in-law is Frances Mae Renier. Bernice Dudley is her neighbor."

Georgie made a few notes. "You ever meet Silas Laroche?"

"Never." My mind flashed back to the man I'd seen outside the bar when we pulled into town, but I told myself it couldn't have been the same guy. Plenty of men wore ball caps and white rubber boots. "I'd never even heard of him until tonight."

"So you had no reason to want him dead?"

"No."

"You know of anybody who did?"

I shook my head. "I never even met any of these people until tonight. This is my first time in Baie Rebelle."

I wasn't sure Georgie would believe me, but to my surprise, she nodded. "That's what I thought. So tell me, what did they do between the time you called in and when I got here?"

The question surprised me. Not including my friend Liam Sullivan, the last dealings I'd had with a cop had left a bitter taste in my mouth. Georgie's easygoing manner and apparent lack of suspicion helped me relax.

"I think just about everybody had a look around. I tried to stop them, but they weren't in the mood to listen. For what it's worth, I'm pretty sure Bitty was telling the truth. They trampled all over, but I don't think anyone touched the body."

"Did you see anybody arrive? Or leave?"

"Lots of people," I said. "Like I said, Eskil was stranded out on the water somewhere and people were out looking for him. They used this place as command central. The clearing was full of trucks and cars when we arrived. People left at various times. Some left after they found Eskil and some after we finished eating. I wish I could tell you who left when, but I met so many people, I don't remember more than a handful of names."

"That's okay," she said. "I can get a list from the family and maybe you can look it over at some point to see if you notice anyone they left off."

"I'd be happy to, though I'm not sure how much help I'll be."

Georgie smiled and stood. "Whatever help you can give me will be just fine. Folks out here aren't real obliging in cases like this. They like to protect their friends and neighbors."

I got out of my chair and nudged it up to the table. "Even if one of them is a killer?"

"That depends on who did the killing and who they took out," Georgie said. "If there's anybody more hated in these parts than Silas Laroche, I couldn't tell you who it is. But he's also a native of the area, and I expect the locals will circle the wagons. So be careful, okay? This little town didn't get its name by accident. People around here are friendly enough, but they're not known for welcoming strangers or following the rules."

"Thanks. I'll keep that in mind. But I don't plan to stick around any longer than I have to. As soon as you say it's okay for us to leave, we'll be out of here."

Georgie gave me a weary smile. "You can go whenever you want. I've got your contact info so I can find you again if I need to."

Even though the interview had gone well, hearing that made my knees weak with relief. I followed her back to the porch and sat down in the cane rocking chair next to Miss Frankie's.

She ran her eyes over me and spoke softly. "How did it go, sugar?"

"Fine. We're free to leave so once Bernice is ready, let's get out of here."

Frowning lightly, Miss Frankie glanced at her watch. "It's nearly ten now. We won't get home until almost midnight."

"That's not so late," I said. "You and Bernice can sleep in the car if you want."

"Of course." She glanced at Bernice, who sat between Bitty and Aunt Margaret. "This looks bad for her family, doesn't it?"

"How so? The family was here with us all evening."

"Except for Eskil."

Okay, so there might be something to worry about there, but I had a free pass to get out of Baie Rebelle and I wanted to use it before Deputy Georgie changed her mind. "I wouldn't worry about Eskil. He was lost out on the water, remember?"

Miss Frankie glanced toward the family. "Yes, but Tallulah told us that he's had trouble with that Silas person. I'm sure you remember that."

I sighed. "I do."

Miss Frankie leaned her head back against the rocking chair. "So this Silas is dead and Eskil has several hours he can't account for. And I'm sure you've noticed his resemblance to Bernice's ghost."

"Yes, but if he was in New Orleans, wouldn't that give him an alibi?"

"Maybe. But he had plenty of time to get back here before Silas died. I expect Bernice will want to stay until this whole mess is cleared up. Margaret already gave us a blanket invitation, and I think we should accept it."

"But I can't stay here, Miss Frankie," I said. "I've got work to do."

"Tomorrow's Sunday," she reminded me. "Zydeco is closed."

"That's true, but I have a lot to do for the Belle Lune Ball," I countered. I didn't mention the current hostility among staff members. Hopefully, it would blow over before Miss Frankie had to hear about it. "I need access to the Internet and my cell phone, and I doubt very much Baie Rebelle has reliable Internet service."

To my surprise, Miss Frankie didn't argue with me. In fact, she patted my knee and smiled. "Well, whatever you think is best. I do think I'll stay here with Bernice, though. Maybe, if it's not too much trouble, you could stop by after work tomorrow and pack a bag for each of us. Just enough for a few days. Or would that be asking too much?"

She knew I couldn't say no when she put it that way, even though another trip to Baie Rebelle and back would eat half a day. But I didn't care. I'd actually won an argument with her. It wouldn't hurt me to compromise a little. I collected both of their house keys and set off for home. I wasn't all that worried about them being safe at Aunt Margaret's. Everybody in that house was probably carrying at least one gun. And if that was what Miss Frankie wanted, who was I to argue?

Really, I should've known better by now.

Eleven

By some miracle I got myself out of bed on Sunday morning after hitting the snooze button only three times. I drove to work, arriving just before eight, and headed straight for the break room, where I made a pot of coffee, laced a cup of it with sugar and creamer, and then stifling a yawn, carried it to my office.

Morning sun bathed the front of the building, and I opened the blinds to enjoy it while I worked. Like the rest of the city, this neighborhood was all decked out for Halloween, some shops opting for a festive look and others trying for a more ghoulish atmosphere. At Zydeco we'd gone the festive route, tying bundles of hay with wide orange and black ribbons and arranging pots of mums and colorful gourds around them. I filled a dish on my desk with an assortment of Halloween candy—a guilty pleasure from childhood—and settled in to check my voice mail.

I had a couple of hang-ups, several inconsequential business calls, and a message from Uncle Nestor. Actually the last one wasn't really a message for me. It had probably been a pocket dial, and I could only understand about one-quarter of what my uncle was yelling at someone in his kitchen since most of it was in Spanish, which I'd never learned as well as I should've. My parents hadn't spoken Spanish at home so I didn't learn the language when I was young. When I moved in with my aunt and uncle, I'd been hurt and angry with the world, and for a while I'd viewed the differences between my dad and his older brother as some kind of betrayal. I'd stubbornly refused to respond to anything but English, and to my continued amazement, Uncle Nestor had given in to placate me. I hadn't recognized it at the time, but now I saw it as a measure of how much he loved me.

I'd picked up a few words along the way, of course. Uncle Nestor hadn't given up Spanish entirely. But most of the words I'd learned were the ones Aunt Yolanda would have washed out my mouth with soap for repeating.

Uncle Nestor seemed oblivious to the fact that he was being recorded. Not that he would have behaved all that differently if he'd been aware. He's fiery and hot-tempered, but under that rough façade he has a heart as big as the Grand Canyon. I always find his tirades more amusing when they're directed at someone else. Hearing him now made me homesick. Grinning, I hung up and made a mental note to call him later. And by later, I mean that I would call after I'd locked down the Vintage Clothing Society contract and told Miss Frankie about my Christmas plans.

The last message was from a woman who identified herself as Simone O'Neil, a member of the Belle Lune planning committee. She left two phone numbers and said she was eager to hear back from me. I had no idea what her office hours were, but I thought eight thirty on a Sunday morning might be a bad time to return her call.

I added another mental reminder to call her later as well then spent a few minutes sorting the mail that had piled up on my desk when I wasn't looking. After that, I wandered into the design room to check on the cakes in progress.

When I opened the door, I found Isabeau at her workstation rolling out some pale blue fondant. She was wearing pale pink sweats and a white T-shirt, and her summer blond hair was piled on her head in a messy bun.

I glanced around for Ox, figuring he must be around somewhere. He and Isabeau had been pretty much joined at the hip since they started seeing each other last year. It's not unusual for staff members to work on Sunday, especially when we have a large contract or we're running behind. As far as I knew, we were right on schedule, so I was surprised to find anyone other than me working that morning. Seeing Isabeau made me wonder if something had gone wrong after I left yesterday.

"Hey there," I said to Isabeau. "Is there something on the schedule I don't know about?"

She gave me a low-wattage smile and shook her head. "No. I'm just playing around. I had some nervous energy and needed to burn it off."

I tried to imagine a world in which I had energy to spare, but it wore me out just thinking about it. "I just made coffee. If I'd known you and Ox would be here, I'd have stopped for doughnuts."

Isabeau picked up her knife, and then immediately put it down again. "You didn't say anything to Ox about what happened yesterday, did you?"

Uh-oh. I glanced around again to make sure he wasn't lurking somewhere. "No, I didn't."

She sighed with relief. "Thank you! And don't worry, he's not here."

I didn't know if that made me more confused or curious. "Is everything okay between the two of you?"

Isabeau nodded. "Sure. It's just that he gets so mad when I consult Mambo Odessa, and I don't know why. She's wonderful! A few months ago he told me not to go to her anymore, but I can't just stop consulting her, so now I have to sneak around behind his back."

I'd known Ox for a while, and I knew that sneaking around on him, for any reason, was a bad idea. Isabeau hadn't asked for my advice, but I felt compelled to say something. "Do you think that's wise? If he finds out—"

Isabeau sat on her stool. "He's not going to find out. I'm way too careful."

Famous last words of sneaks the world over.

"Anyway," she went on, "he was acting weird last night and I thought maybe you'd said something."

"I take it he's not a believer."

"No, he's not. But that's what confuses me. Mambo Odessa is great at what she does. She's one of the best around, and she's perfectly normal."

"If you don't count the bones she carries around on that string."

"Sure, but she doesn't do a lot of weird, hinky things," Isabeau protested. "You saw that for yourself."

"She seemed pretty normal," I agreed, privately thinking, *Except for the bones. On a string. Followed by predictions of trouble for both Bernice and me.* Which were completely bogus as long as you didn't count Cousin Eskil getting lost on the swamp and the dead body I'd found in the ditch.

"And she's his aunt. His own aunt!"

I laughed and moved a little closer to her table. "I'm sure

he loves her. You can love somebody and not agree with all their choices, you know. Sometimes you have to love people in *spite* of the things they do."

Isabeau cut a straight line down a long piece of pale blue fondant. "Yeah. I guess."

"Well, your secret is safe with me as long as there's no repeat performance of yesterday's house call. You said Ox was acting weird last night. How did things go after I left? Did you finish the Howard reunion cake or did you run into a problem?"

"No problems," she said with a shrug. "We finished the cake last night and delivered it with time to spare. But since you asked, could you talk to Edie? She's being a real pain in the neck."

I didn't tell her that I'd already tried talking to Edie. I didn't want to make things worse. "She's eight months pregnant," I said, channeling my inner Captain Obvious. Isabeau didn't even blink so I caved in and asked, "What has she done now?"

"It's not what she does, it's the way she does it." Isabeau blew her bangs out of her eyes and shifted her weight from one foot to the other. "She's just being . . . Edie, only worse."

On another day I might have laughed at that description, but Edie had been a walking time bomb for months now. The closer we got to her due date, the more emotional and irrational she seemed to get. "Hey, we were all upset by what happened the other night," I said, "but the only real damage was that Dwight's birthday party ended too soon. Give it a day or two. Let's see if things blow over."

Isabeau rolled her eyes dramatically. "I wouldn't hold my breath. Yesterday Edie told River she doesn't even want him around when the baby is born."

I groaned inwardly. "I'm sorry to hear that, but their relationship is none of our business."

"It was our business on Friday when she had us all race to

the hospital. It was our business when she gave us 'helpful hints' about how we could improve our performance. Sparkle and I were standing right by her desk when she told River that he's not reliable enough and she doesn't want him floating in and out of the baby's life. You can just imagine how Sparkle reacted."

My least favorite part of supervising a staff is handling the personality conflicts and personal problems. Even though the staff at Zydeco is relatively small, they're all creative and sensitive and emotional. For the most part, I try not to get involved when they have problems with one another. I prefer to let them work out their issues on their own. Was I being cowardly or smart? I wasn't sure.

Isabeau seemed to read my mind. "You *have* to talk to her, Rita. You're her best friend and everybody is fed up with her. Sparkle's so afraid that her brother won't get to know his baby, she can hardly function. Plus, you're the baby's godmother. It's kind of your duty, isn't it?"

In all the excitement of the past two days, I'd almost forgotten that I'd made a lifetime commitment while under duress. I wasn't convinced that talking with Edie about her family issues fell under my jurisdiction as the baby's godmother, nor was I sure that I qualified as her best friend. Then again, maybe I did—but even that didn't make the prospect of having a chat with Edie about her personal life any more attractive.

To get involved, or not to get involved. That was the question. I promised Isabeau that I'd see what I could do and escaped to my office. I told myself not to even think about dead bodies, family feuds, or baby daddies. Channeling all my energy into staying focused on work, I checked e-mail and updated Zydeco's Facebook status. I wrote a couple of blog posts and scheduled them to automatically publish during the upcoming week.

But despite my best efforts, Silas Laroche's body kept flashing through my mind. I tried to remember how everyone had reacted to the news that he was dead, and struggled to recall where everyone had been throughout the evening. Unfortunately, the details escaped me. There had been too many people milling about, and too many faces with no names attached.

I was just shutting down my laptop when my cell phone began playing Inner Circle's "Bad Boys," which meant it was Liam Sullivan calling. He'd been tied up with a case for the past few days so we hadn't spoken in a while. Hearing the theme from *Cops* chiming made my heart jump around in anticipation. Still, I tried not to sound like I was getting all jiggy inside when I answered.

My "hello" came out on a squeak, which killed the semi-sultry tone I'd been trying for.

"Hey there," Sullivan said. "What are you up to?" He's got a great voice. I'm just saying.

"I'm at Zydeco catching up on some work. What about you?"

"Wondering if you're free for dinner tonight. Sorry about the short notice, but we just wrapped up a case and I'm suddenly at loose ends."

Aunt Yolanda had always warned me not to appear too eager when it came to men. That's not always easy, especially when the man in question is as great as this one. And Sullivan with free time was one of my favorite things. "I'd love to," I said, trying to sound nonchalant. "Do you have someplace in mind?"

"I haven't even thought about it," he admitted. "I just picked up the phone and dialed as soon as I knew I was free. What are you in the mood for? Chinese? Italian? Or would you prefer something homegrown? I know a great Cajun place in Houma. It's a bit of a drive, but the food is worth it."

I'd been so glad to hear from him, I'd forgotten all about my promise to take Miss Frankie and Bernice their bags later on. I felt the drag of disappointment, but then I remembered how close Houma was to Baie Rebelle, and realized that I could kill two birds with one stone.

"I vote for the place in Houma. And while we're out that way, how would you like to take a drive to a little town called Baie Rebelle?"

He hesitated, but only for the space of a heartbeat. "Okay. Sure. What's in Baie Rebelle?"

"Miss Frankie and Bernice. They're staying with Bernice's aunt for a few days, and I promised to take them some clothes and things after work today."

Sullivan chuckled. "I'm not even going to ask what they're doing there. You can fill me in on the way. It'll be good to see the two of them again."

It was tempting to take him up on that offer not to tell him until later, but with Sullivan, honesty is always the best policy. Especially when I had nothing to hide. I told him about finding Silas Laroche in the ditch and filled him in on what little I knew about the man—which was almost nothing.

"He seems to have been universally disliked," I said as I wrapped up the story. "Even the sheriff's deputy who responded to the call said as much. Miss Frankie is worried that they'll try to pin the murder on Bernice's cousin, but he was out on the water for most of the day. His boat ran out of gas and most of the town was searching for him. The thing is, I've been thinking about it all day and I'm sure the body wasn't in the ditch when we got there. Plenty of people would have seen it earlier. That means somebody put it there while we were inside having supper."

"Maybe you just didn't notice."

"No, it wasn't there when we arrived, Liam. I'd swear to it."

"Okay. I believe you. You said that you called the local sheriff?"

"Right."

"And they seemed competent?"

"I only met one deputy, but she seemed to be on the ball. Don't worry, though. I'm not trying to get involved. I don't have time to get involved. I just don't want you to find out about this when we get there and think I was trying to hide it from you. Call this a preemptive strike."

He laughed. It's a good, honest sound that always puts a smile on my face. "Okay. So what time should I pick you up, and where will you be?"

"How about three, at my place? I'll leave here in a few minutes and head over to Miss Frankie's. Packing their bags shouldn't take long. I should still have plenty of time to get ready."

"I like the sound of that." Sullivan's voice grew low and suggestive, but I also detected a teasing note. "What are you going to wear?"

"Oh, I don't know . . . Something that looks like I just threw it on without giving it much thought. I should be able to accomplish that in a couple of hours."

"Well, don't hurt yourself," he said with another laugh. "I'm not all that interested in what you're wearing anyway. I'd just like to spend some time with you. And for what it's worth, I'll probably spend about two minutes brushing my teeth. I may even put on fresh deodorant. I'm going to go all out, so try not to show me up too badly."

There wasn't a chance of that happening. Sullivan's a tough act to top.

Twelve

Sullivan showed up at my place a few minutes before three wearing tight-fitting jeans and a white T-shirt under a light-weight blazer. As always, he looked great. And he smelled like soap and aftershave. And toothpaste. His light brown hair was cropped close to his head, and his killer blue eyes were hidden behind a pair of sunglasses.

I smiled, and ran my eyes all over his six feet something of finely toned muscle, which he maintains thanks to a personal fitness regime and probably some police department regulations. I admire him for being so committed to staying physically fit. I consider it a public service.

He gave me a hug and a quick kiss, and made all the right noises about how nice I looked. I'd settled on a comfortable pair of jeans and a white cotton blouse over a yellow tank top, pulled up my hair in a vain attempt to reduce the frizz that is the bane of my existence, and added a pair of dangly earrings that had been an impulse buy a couple of weeks earlier. I was pleased with the effect, and the look in Sullivan's eye when he leaned in for that kiss told me I'd done well.

After loading the bags into the trunk of his Impala, we were on our way. It was a good thing he didn't work undercover. That car's red paint and chrome thingamajigs would never let him go anywhere under the radar.

As he drove, we made small talk about everything and anything except his work, my work, or Silas Laroche's murder. The most pressing question on our agenda was the best order of events for the evening. After a brief debate, we decided that, since it was still early, we'd drive to Baie Rebelle first then stop for dinner in Houma on the way back.

You'd think that since both of us were adults with some experience under our belts, we'd've known what happens to good intentions, and opted to eat first.

By the time we pulled into Baie Rebelle and turned toward Aunt Margaret's house, long shadows stretched across the road. We caught glimpses of the sun on the western horizon, a deep yellow ball sitting on the water and reflecting brilliant oranges and blues onto the clouds overhead. After surviving my first visit to this remote location, with Sullivan now at the wheel, I could relax enough to appreciate its raw beauty.

It wasn't until Sullivan had parked in the clearing and opened my door that he brought up the subject we'd so carefully avoided for the past couple of hours. He jerked his chin toward the sagging crime scene tape on the driveway behind us and said, "Let me guess. That's where you found the body?"

"There's a reason you're on the fast track in the Homicide Department," I said with a grin. "You're quick. What gave it away?"

"Sorry. I can't give away my professional secrets." Sullivan put his hand on the small of my back, and we set off toward the crime scene tape. I'd anticipated his interest in looking at the scene, so I'd opted to pair running shoes rather than heels with my outfit. His smile faded slowly and he fell silent as he studied the ditch and the ground around it. "Well, you're right about one thing. The folks around here did a good job of messing up the crime scene."

"I did my best to keep them away, but it was impossible."

Sullivan nodded slowly. "One of you against all of them? You were smart not to try taking them all on."

"Hey!" someone shouted from somewhere behind us.

We both turned and saw Tallulah standing on the porch aiming a shotgun at us. I gave her my friendliest wave and shouted, "It's me, Tallulah. Rita. Bernice's friend? I brought some clothes for her and Miss Frankie."

Tallulah slowly lowered the shotgun and brushed at her short brown hair. "Well, okay then. I didn't recognize you. Who's that with you?"

I didn't dare move yet, so I shouted back, "This is Liam Sullivan. He's a friend of mine from New Orleans."

Seemingly satisfied, Tallulah rested the shotgun across her arm and jerked her chin at us. "Well, what y'all doing out there? Come on up to the house."

I wasn't going to argue with her, and apparently neither was Sullivan. We crossed the clearing and came to a stop in front of the porch, where I finished the introductions.

Tallulah looked Sullivan over carefully, then asked, "Y'all hungry? Bitty's working on supper now. There's plenty to go around."

"I'm afraid we can't stay," I said. "I'll just drop off these bags for Bernice and Miss Frankie and we'll be on our way. Are they inside? We should say hello."

"I'll grab the suitcases," Sullivan offered. "Where would you like me to put them?"

Tallulah answered his question first. "Just bring 'em up to the porch. I'll take 'em on down to their room later." She scratched lazily at a spot on her arm and turned to me. "They ain't here. Been gone about half an hour, I guess. You might as well stay until they come back."

Sullivan carried the suitcases to the porch and Tallulah ushered us inside. She propped the shotgun by the door and invited us to sit. Sullivan and I took the couch. Tallulah claimed a recliner and then we all looked at one another for a while. When I couldn't stand it any longer, I broke the awkward silence.

"So Miss Frankie and Bernice have gone out? Do you know if they'll be back soon?" I love the two of them, but I didn't trust them to stay out of trouble, especially when they were together. It wasn't as if Baie Rebelle was full of places to eat and shop.

"I don't have any idea where they went," Tallulah said. "They borrowed my car is all I know."

"They didn't tell you where they were going?"

Tallulah spent a moment adjusting her shirt over her ample bosom. "Why are you asking me? They're grown women. I'm not in charge of their schedule."

She wouldn't have said that if she knew my mother-in-law. "Maybe they said something to Bitty or your mother," I said as sweetly as I could. "It's a long drive back to New Orleans. If they'll be a while, maybe we shouldn't wait."

"Bitty took Mama to the Walmart, so they're gone, too," Tallulah said. "That's why Bernice took my car."

"Maybe Bernice is showing Miss Frankie around," Sullivan suggested. "She grew up here, didn't she?"

"She sure did, but I don't think that's it," Tallulah said.

"Come to think of it, they did say something about paying their respects to Junior Laroche. But that's really all I know. And I don't even know for sure they went there."

Sullivan's eyes locked on mine. "Junior Laroche? Is he related to the guy who died?"

Tallulah nodded and gave her shirt another twitch. "He's Silas's older brother."

A red flag popped up and started waving around in my head. "I'm sorry, but I'm confused. Is Junior a friend of Bernice's? I was under the impression she didn't know the Laroches well."

"He's not a friend to speak of," Tallulah said. "I think they're just curious to find out what Junior knows about Silas's last days. Not that he'll know anything, or tell them if he does. I don't think those two brothers spoke more than a handful of words to each other the past twenty years."

Sullivan leaned forward, resting his elbows on his knees. "You don't think Junior would know who wanted his brother dead?"

Tallulah actually smiled at him. I'm not sure, but I thought she even batted her eyelashes. "Sure he could. If you want to know what *I* think, I'd put Junior's name at the top of that list."

I almost popped off my end of the couch. "Why do you think that?"

The smile slid right off Tallulah's round face when she looked at me. "Because Junior hated Silas and everybody knew it."

"And you let Miss Frankie and Bernice go over there?" I didn't mean to sound panicked—or angry—but I'm pretty sure the shrillness of my voice made me sound both. No wonder Miss Frankie had been so quick to let me go home last night.

"They went to offer their condolences," Tallulah said. "What's wrong with that?"

"That's not why they went," I reminded her. "You just said they went to ask him questions." I looked to Sullivan for backup and saw concern darkening his eyes.

"Where does Junior Laroche live?" he asked. "Is it far from here?"

"It's a bit down the road," Tallulah said. "Go on down this road another . . . ten miles? Maybe twelve. Junior's got some waterfront property, and there's a big sign out front for JL Charters. Do you want me to show you?"

Sullivan shook his head. "That won't be necessary, but if you could draw us a map, that would help. What kind of car are they driving?"

"It's an oh-six Nissan Sentra. Orange." She drew a rough map and handed it to him, and we rushed out the door.

"Do you think they're in trouble?" I asked as we trotted across the clearing to his car.

Even though we were in a hurry, Sullivan did the Southern gentleman thing and opened my door for me. "I hope not," he said as I got inside. "I'm actually more worried that Miss Frankie is about to start some."

We followed Tallulah's map and found her rusty orange Nissan parked in front of a small house with peeling blue paint. On the edge of the road, a huge weathered board sign told us we'd reached JL Charters. I might have worried about Junior's cash flow situation, but the new Dodge Ram beside the house told me he was probably doing all right.

Miss Frankie and Bernice were sitting on mismatched chairs arranged on a rickety front porch. With them was a man I assumed to be Junior Laroche. Miss Frankie and Bernice each had a glass of ice water on a plastic table between them. The man clutched a beer can.

He was tall and thin, about fifty years old, with a receding hairline and a well-trimmed beard. I watched him carefully as we approached, half expecting a wary reception like the one Tallulah had given us. To my relief, the man put the beer on the porch and came toward us with a used car salesman smile.

He pumped Sullivan's hand enthusiastically. "Welcome to JL Charters. If you're looking for a hunting or fishing guide, I'm your man. The name's Junior Laroche."

"Thanks but that's not why we're here," Sullivan said. He jerked his chin toward the porch, where Thelma and Louise suddenly got real busy pretending they couldn't see us. "We're looking for Miss Frankie and Bernice. We were told we could find them here."

Junior looked back at his guests. "Well, then, you might as well come and set." He dragged a couple of extra chairs from the far side of the porch. "Can I get you a beer? Water? I don't have much else right now."

I wasn't sure those sagging boards could hold all of us, but I climbed the questionable-looking steps and eased my weight onto a scratched wooden chair, leaving the rusty metal one for Sullivan. We both said that water would be fine and Junior disappeared inside.

I waited just until I couldn't hear his footsteps any longer then turned to Miss Frankie and Bernice. "So . . . what are you two doing here?"

Miss Frankie tried to look surprised. "Isn't it obvious? We're paying a condolence call on the bereaved."

"You don't even know him," I pointed out. "And neither do you, Bernice. I'm no expert, but I'm willing to bet there's no rule of etiquette demanding that you call on a complete stranger after a loved one dies."

Miss Frankie leaned forward and whispered, "Oh, but, sugar, that's just the point. I don't think Silas actually was a loved one. Junior doesn't seem to care much about his brother's untimely demise."

Sullivan groaned and rubbed his face with one hand. "With all due respect, Miss Frankie, I sure hope you're not thinking you can investigate the murder."

She lifted her chin and gave him a stern look. "No, but I don't see why I shouldn't. Poor Eskil did not kill that man, even if everybody seems to think he did."

"Define *everybody*," I said.

Bernice leaned up and spoke in a stage whisper. "Half a dozen people stopped by Aunt Margaret's this morning. Every one of them thanked Eskil for getting rid of Silas. Eskil told them all that he didn't do it, but he can't prove it and nobody believes him."

We heard Junior coming back and we all pretended to be enjoying the view from the porch. It wasn't easy. Junior's waterfront property backed up on a narrow inlet of brownish water rimmed with vines, weeds, and low-hanging trees. His front yard looked out over a poorly maintained road and a stand of half-dead trees. In the middle of it all stood a shack missing half of its weathered boards.

Junior handed glasses to Sullivan and me and took his seat again after removing a couple of unopened beer cans from his pockets. He settled those at his feet and reached for the open can, gulping greedily. "Is one of you gonna tell me what I've done to deserve all this attention, or do I have to guess?"

I didn't want to encourage Miss Frankie, so I answered before she could. "I wanted to offer my condolences," I said. "We've never met, but I'm the one who found your brother's body last night."

Junior cocked an eyebrow. "You?"

"Yes."

"And now you feel responsible or something?"

"Not responsible," I said. "But I do feel terrible about what happened. I just wanted to tell you how sorry I am."

Junior belched under his breath. "You don't have to be sorry. Silas was my brother by birth, but we lost him a long time ago."

"I hate to see a family fall apart," Miss Frankie commiserated. "It's the saddest thing in the world."

"I'd say that depends on the family," Junior said with a cool smile. "Wouldn't you? Now you've said what you came to say, so if you don't mind—"

Sullivan sipped some water, which made me think he wasn't ready to leave. "Are you saying you and your brother weren't close?" he asked.

"That's exactly what I'm saying. We hadn't been close for a long time. Now suppose you tell me why that's any of your business."

"It's not," Sullivan said. "But you can understand why Bernice here is upset. Silas was found on her family's property, and some folks think her cousin was responsible for putting him there."

"That's probably because he was," Junior said. "It's no secret that Eskil and Silas had bad feelings between 'em. Everybody around knows that."

"It would help us understand if we knew why," I said.

Junior cut a glance at me. "Why don't you ask Eskil? I'm sure he'd tell you."

"Eskil isn't talking," Miss Frankie said. "Not to us. Not to the sheriff's office."

"That's right," Bernice said with a bob of her curly white head. "So we thought we'd come to the person most likely to know the story."

Junior's mouth curved into a slow, sly smile. "Well, you came to the wrong place, folks. Because I don't know a thing about my brother."

"Do you know if he had any other enemies?" Sullivan asked. "Was there anyone who might benefit from his death?"

Junior gave him a long look. "Just what are you asking?"

Sullivan shrugged. "Exactly what I said. Is there anyone who might benefit from your brother's death? Did he own land or have money?"

Junior laughed. "You wouldn't ask that if you'd known Silas. He didn't care about money and he didn't believe people could own land. That's why he ran off in the first place. Our old daddy wanted to build a legacy. Something big to leave his family when he died. Silas didn't want any part of it. He ran off and the old man cut him out of the will. And that was that. Other than that, I don't know anything about him or what he did."

I thought about the man I'd seen yelling at someone through a car window on our way to Aunt Margaret's house yesterday. I knew it was a long shot, but I asked anyway. "Do you know anyone around here who drives a white Ford Ranger?"

Junior narrowed his eyes, but he kept that cheesy grin on his face. "How long you got? I could tell you at least a dozen names."

Somehow I doubted that. I wondered if he was lying or just annoyed by the question. "You and your brother lived in the same small town," I said. "You said that everybody knew that he and Eskil had issues. How could you know that but not know what those issues were?"

Junior polished off one can of beer and popped the top on another. "Because folks around here mind their own business. If you're smart, you'll do the same. You go around sticking your nose into other people's business, you could make some enemies. Now unless you want to book a hunting trip or something, I'm through talking."

Thirteen

Junior's abrupt dismissal left us with no choice but to leave. Sullivan stood and shook Junior's hand again. "We'll get out of your hair then. Sorry for the intrusion."

I wasn't ready to go but I bit my tongue and followed Sullivan back to the street. Bernice and Miss Frankie brought up the rear. I heard the screen door slam shut behind us with a *bang!* and I let out a regretful sigh. Junior knew a whole lot more than he let on. I'd have bet on it.

"Well, you were right," I said when we gathered beside Sullivan's car. "He certainly doesn't seem upset by his brother's death."

"Clearly not," Miss Frankie agreed. "But I'm not convinced that he doesn't know why Eskil and Silas were at odds."

Sullivan folded his arms across his chest and leaned against the car. "Neither am I. What was that about the white Ford Ranger?"

I squinted into the setting sun and shook my head. "Nothing really. I saw a guy wearing boots like the ones Silas Laroche had on talking with somebody in a truck like that when we pulled into town yesterday. Then again, it could have been anyone. The guy seemed angry, though, and I thought I'd toss it in and see what we got. And you saw what happened. We got a big fat nothing."

"Yeah," Sullivan said, but he seemed thoughtful. He shook it off and smiled at Miss Frankie and Bernice. "Listen, ladies, I don't like the two of you getting involved in all of this. Somebody around here killed Silas Laroche, and whoever it was might not hesitate to lash out again. My advice is to stay out of it. Let the sheriff and his deputies do their jobs."

Miss Frankie gave Sullivan a wide-eyed stare. "Why? Because you think we're too old?"

He laughed and shook his head. "Don't you go putting words in my mouth, Miss Frankie. My mama would skin me alive if I suggested such a thing. It's because I think this could be dangerous. I've got a gut feeling about this and I don't want to see either of you get hurt."

Bernice's cheeks burned deep pink. "My cousin is the one who'll get hurt if somebody doesn't help him. And I'm as sure as I can be that he's innocent."

Miss Frankie gently touched Bernice's shoulder. "We're not going to let that happen. There are plenty of people around here who can tell us why Eskil and Silas were at odds. Let's go talk to someone else."

"Whoa!" Sullivan said, stepping in front of them. "I have a better idea. Let's go back to your aunt Margaret's and have something to eat."

I knew why he'd made the suggestion, but I didn't want our dinner date to evaporate. Sitting at the table with Tallulah glaring at me and making eyes at Sullivan just wouldn't be the same as the private dinner I'd been anticipating.

Miss Frankie stepped around him. "And leave Eskil to fend for himself? What's wrong with you?"

Sullivan took her arm and fell into step with her. "I admire you for caring so much, Miss Frankie, and I know how much Bernice means to you. But you aren't thinking about how much Rita cares about you. I can't let you do something dangerous while I'm around. She'd never forgive me."

It was a bold stroke, but genius. Miss Frankie's shoulders almost sagged. "You're right, Liam. Let's go back."

I didn't know whether to feel relieved or aggravated. She never gave in that easily for me. I opted for relief. The only thing that really mattered was getting the two of them back to Aunt Margaret's. If Sullivan could do that, more power to him.

Just when I thought it was settled, Bernice chirped in dismay. "Oh my Lord! I completely forgot. I promised Tallulah I'd pick up some Old Bay Seasoning while we were out."

Sullivan didn't even miss a beat. "Give Rita the keys to Tallulah's car. She'll pick it up. You ladies can ride with me."

Miss Frankie handed over the keys without argument, and Sullivan got the two women settled in his Impala. After tossing a smile and a promise to see me back at the house, he made a U-turn and sped off down the road.

I don't think I've ever liked him more.

It took me three tries to get Tallulah's car started. When I finally did, the Sentra bucked a couple of times and jumped forward, raring to go. Three of the car's seats were split open, revealing dusty puffs of stuffing. A pile of mail—mostly junk, I think—was crammed into the space between the front seats, and a couple of empty soda cans rolled around on the floor in back every time I accelerated. I sure hoped

T-Rex stocked Old Bay Seasoning in his general store because I wasn't sure the Sentra would live long enough to go any farther.

A couple of muddy pickup trucks and a sheriff's car were parked in front of T-Rex's when I pulled up. After the dust settled, I spotted Georgie Tucker eating at a picnic table a few feet away.

She smiled when she saw me and wiped her mouth with a napkin. "Hey there. I thought you'd gone back to the big city."

"I did," I said. "I had to come back to bring a few things for Miss Frankie and Bernice. Any news about how Silas died?"

"Not a whole lot. Eskil's refusing to talk to me at all. His mama and sisters have clammed up except to offer me something to drink." She laughed and shook her head. "There sure are some eccentric folks around here."

That seemed like an odd thing to say. Not that it wasn't true, but . . . "I thought you were one of them."

"Not yet, but I'm working on it. I moved down here from Tennessee about five years ago so I'm still an outsider."

I grinned and sat on the bench across from her. A cool breeze fluttered the treetops and raised goose bumps on my arms. A few monarch butterflies drifted past, the first of the annual autumn migration to the southern end of Mexico. "If the family's not talking, does that mean you don't have any leads?"

"Nothing concrete so far. I talked with Silas's brother Junior earlier. I'm on my way to talk to his widow as soon as I finish my dinner break."

His widow? "I didn't realize Silas was married."

Georgie opened a small bag of chips and munched on a couple. "You sound surprised."

"I guess I am. Nobody mentioned anything about him having a wife. Did he have kids, too?"

"Just one. A son. Kale's twenty-two and lives with his mom. Probably nobody thought to mention it because Silas and Nettie haven't lived together in twenty years." Georgie shrugged and ate another chip. "Way I heard it, Silas got tired of city living one day and just moved off into the swamp."

Yeah. I could see how the big city of Baie Rebelle might be too crowded for some people. "How did his wife feel about that? Do you think she had a motive for killing him?"

"Not that I know of after all this time. But she and Kale have had their struggles. If it weren't for Junior, I don't know where they'd be."

Interesting. "Junior takes care of his brother's family?"

Georgie nodded. "He's been more of a daddy to Kale than Silas ever was. Kale's a good kid. He's had a little trouble, but nothing serious. Anyway, Silas mostly kept to himself after he left town." She munched for a minute and said, "We were out to his place looking around this morning. I think we've found the murder weapon."

She dropped that piece of news like an afterthought. *Oh . . . I almost forgot . . .* I wondered if she'd done that on purpose to get my reaction. "Can you tell me what the weapon was, or is that classified?"

Georgie washed down her lunch with Coke. "I guess it won't do any harm. We found blood and hair on a toilet tank lid on Silas's property. Looks like that's what did him in."

I gaped at her in disbelief. "A toilet tank lid? Are you serious? Who would think of using *that* as a weapon?"

"Somebody looking for a weapon in the moment, I suppose. That probably makes this a crime of passion."

"I *knew* he wasn't at Aunt Margaret's when we arrived.

It's almost as if the killer wanted to throw suspicion on Eskil. Was Silas killed at his house?"

"Outside, down by the creek. We'll have to wait for the tests to come back to prove our theories, and that might take a while, but I'm pretty sure that's what did it."

I turned that over in my mind for a moment. "Did you find any fingerprints?"

"Sure. A whole lot of 'em, in fact. Don't know yet if any of them belong to the killer."

"It would take some serious muscle to swing a tank lid with enough force to kill a man. Are you thinking the killer was male?"

Georgie did a so-so thing with her head. "Not necessarily. There's women in these parts who could handle that heavy piece of porcelain as well as any man." She nodded toward the Sentra and changed the subject. "I see you're using Tallulah's car. Something wrong with yours?"

I wasn't ready to abandon the subject of Silas Laroche and his toilet lid–wielding killer, but I didn't want to press my luck. I shook my head. "I came with a friend today, and got put in charge of picking up some Old Bay Seasoning. Do you know if they carry it here?"

"I reckon so. You can get just about anything you need here at T-Rex's. If he doesn't have it, he knows where to get it. And they're open twenty-four/seven. You need something at two in the morning, just ring the bell. T-Rex'll get out of bed and sell you whatever you want."

"All the conveniences," I said with a laugh. "The only thing missing is a drive-through window."

The sound of a truck pulling into the gravel parking lot caught our attention. Georgie waved and I glanced over my shoulder in time to see a tall, heavy-boned woman wearing a baseball cap getting out of a maroon pickup. I started to look away again but realized that she looked familiar and kept an eye on her. I could count on one hand the number of people I actually knew in Baie Rebelle, so the fact that she looked familiar had to mean that I'd seen her at Aunt Margaret's the previous night.

Georgie had polished off her dinner and got up to toss the trash. "How you doin', Adele?"

Adele slowed her step but she didn't stop walking. Even from a distance, I could see that she looked awful. Her eyes were red and puffy, her complexion mottled. "I'm all right," she said. She opened the door and added, "See ya later," and shut the door behind her firmly.

"Call me crazy," I said, "but I don't think she's all right at all. Was she a friend of Silas's?"

Georgie laughed and shook her head. "Hell no. Probably just allergies or something."

She seemed certain so I didn't argue, but I wasn't convinced. I said a quick good-bye to Georgie and followed Adele into the store, hoping I could figure out a way to strike up a conversation.

T-Rex's was a tiny building filled with a few built-in wooden shelves, portable metal shelves squeezed into every available space, and a couple of old-fashioned chest-style coolers. I could have picked up anything from canned vegetables to live bait, a true one-stop-shopper's delight.

The aisles (if you could call them that) were too narrow for more than one person; depending on the person, they might even have been too narrow for one. Behind a high counter holding a cash register, miscellaneous fishing stuff, and a telephone, two middle-aged women laughed over something in a magazine. I guessed neither of them was T-Rex.

I noticed Adele near one of the coolers, so I made a

beeline for her. "Sorry to bother you," I said, "but didn't we meet last night?"

She shook her head and tugged the brim of her cap lower over her eyes. "I don't think so."

"You weren't one of the search party who met at Margaret Percifield's house last night?"

I could feel the two clerks watching us, and I knew they could hear every word in that tiny space. Adele must have realized the same thing because she gave me a grudging nod. "Oh. Yeah. I guess I was."

"I'm Rita Lucero," I said, still trying to come across as the friendly type. "I just wanted to say thank you for your help."

Adele flicked her gaze over me. She wasn't a pretty woman, but she had beautiful eyes—green with flecks of brown—and lashes some women would have given their firstborn to have. "Yeah. It was no big deal. It's what we do out here." She returned her attention to a yellow bottle in her hand, and something about the way she moved made me remember the woman in the backyard with the angry young man. I had a gut feeling Adele had been that woman. So maybe what had her so upset today was trouble with her son, and not Silas's death.

I didn't want to take advantage of her when she was down, but I had doubts about Eskil's story and I might not get another chance to talk to one of the search party. Hoping she'd respond to a friendly face, I turned on my inner Chatty Cathy. "I'm just glad someone found Eskil when they did. It's amazing that he got through the night alone on the swamp."

"Not really," Adele said without looking at me. "He knows what he's doin'." She returned the bottle to the shelf and tilted her head in my direction. "Strange thing, though. I could've sworn I checked that arm of the swamp earlier and he wasn't there. Then a few hours later, there he was big as day."

"Maybe you just thought you'd checked that spot," I suggested. "I'm sure it gets confusing out there. Or maybe he got to the shore and made camp."

Adele shook her head. "Now *that* would have been dangerous. He was a lot safer in the boat."

Unless he was somewhere else entirely. "Was anyone with you when you checked that part of the swamp the first time? Your son maybe?"

"I was alone. I don't have kids." She folded her arms over her chest. "Why? You think I'm lying about where I looked?"

I was more concerned about how many people knew that Eskil hadn't been in the swamp overnight and what it might mean for him if the truth got out. Bernice had obviously seen Eskil in New Orleans on Friday night, but even if the sheriff believed her, that still gave Eskil plenty of time to get back to Baie Rebelle and dispatch Silas Laroche.

"I'm not saying you're lying," I assured Adele. "I'm just trying to figure out what really happened. I thought I saw you talking to a kid at Aunt Margaret's last night. He was around twenty. Maybe a few years older. Shaggy dark hair? I thought it was you anyway."

"No."

"That's too bad. My friend Bernice is worried about Eskil. He's her cousin, you know."

"So I heard."

"And I was hoping one of you might be able to convince the sheriff's department that Eskil couldn't have killed Silas."

"Why would I do that?"

"Because he's innocent. I mean, it's a shame about Silas, of course. Did you know him?"

Adele rolled her eyes slowly in my direction. I could read fear in her expression, but also a deep sadness. The look in her eyes hit me like a fist. "Everybody knows everybody around here," she said. "So yeah. I knew him."

"I'm sorry," I said. "I don't mean to pry but you just seem upset and I thought . . ." I trailed off, trying to figure out exactly what I thought. That she might like someone to talk to? That she might want to bare her soul to a complete stranger? I backed a step away and repeated myself. "Sorry. I really didn't mean to pry."

Feeling like an idiot, I looked around until I found the Old Bay Seasoning, paid for my purchase, and hightailed it out the door. But I had a feeling that Georgie was wrong about Adele. I was almost positive that Silas's murder had upset her deeply.

Fourteen

❖

I rattled my way back to Aunt Margaret's in the Sentra and breathed a sigh of relief when I saw Sullivan's car in the clearing. If he was there, I could trust that Miss Frankie and Bernice were also there and, hopefully, behaving themselves. The instant I got out of the car, the smell of wood smoke hit me along with the mouthwatering aroma of something cooking on a grill. I also caught a whiff of cake baking and my stomach growled, reminding me that Sullivan and I still hadn't eaten.

I left the Old Bay Seasoning in the kitchen with Bitty and Tallulah and went in search of the others. I found them in the backyard. Sullivan was reclining in a cushioned patio chair. His eyes were closed and a cold drink sat on a table beside him. Miss Frankie and Bernice were chatting with Aunt Margaret beneath the spreading shade of a huge old tree. Across the yard, Eskil manned the grill.

Trees and undergrowth surrounded the property, so wild and thick I thought it must take constant work to keep it under control. Somewhere out there, Bernice's Uncle Cooch had kept his still hidden, and seeing how dense the forest was gave me a better understanding of how generations of Percifield men could've managed to keep the still's location secret.

Sullivan didn't look like he planned to go anywhere for a while, so I seized the opportunity to have a chat with Cousin Eskil. He didn't notice me walking toward him until I was almost upon him, which was a good thing because when he did see me, he glanced around like an animal wanting to escape a hungry predator.

My friend-making skills had fallen flat with Adele, but I wasn't ready to give up on them. I smiled all friendly-like and sniffed appreciatively. "Whatever you're grilling smells amazing. What is it?"

He looked me in the eye and took his time answering. "Gator steaks." His voice was so low, I wasn't sure I'd heard him correctly.

"Really? Alligator? I've never heard of cutting steaks from a gator. Which part of the animal do you use?"

Eskil stroked his beard thoughtfully. "Guess I shouldn't lie, should I? I'm pulling your leg. It's pork. I *wanted* to fix up a mess of gator, but Ma told me not to. She thought y'all might turn up your noses."

So the man had a sense of humor. Grinning, I leaned forward to see what he was doing with the pork. At least eight huge chops were sizzling on the grill and a heavenly smelling barbecue sauce had created a glaze that made me think twice about driving back to Houma for dinner. "I'm a professional chef," I said. "I don't turn up my nose at much of anything."

"Good to know. Next time we'll do the gator. Ma's got some boudin cooking. You'll like that."

I knew a little about boudin, a spicy Acadian sausage that was originally made as a way for a family to stretch its protein and feed more hungry mouths. Traditionally made from pork and rice and flavored with green onion, parsley, garlic, and cayenne, it's still a staple among Louisiana Cajuns. I'd had boudin a couple of times, but I couldn't wait to try the homemade variety.

We fell into a companionable silence. I hated to destroy it, but after talking with Junior and Georgie and then meeting up with Adele, curiosity was eating me alive. "Do you mind if I ask you a question?"

Eskil slid a look at me from somewhere between his eyebrows and his beard. "Depends on what it's about."

"Listen, I know I'm an outsider and this is all none of my business. But please understand that Bernice is a friend and I care about her. She's worried sick about you."

"About me? Why?"

"Because some people around here seem to think you may have killed Silas Laroche. Bernice is convinced you didn't do it, and she wants me to help clear your name."

Eskil's eyes grew serious. They were the only part of his face I could actually see. "That's real nice of her, but I don't need help. I didn't kill Silas."

I hoped he was telling the truth. "Do you have any idea who did?"

Eskil shook his head and closed the lid on the grill. "Nope. But if I did, I'd shake the man's hand and buy him a drink. Whoever took Silas out did the world a favor."

I hoped he wouldn't talk like that around anyone else. Somebody might get the wrong idea. "You think it was a man then?"

"Figure of speech. Coulda been anybody."

"I have another question if you don't mind. Friday night, Bernice saw someone looking in her window. From the description she gave me, it was either you or her uncle Cooch, which we both know is impossible. Would you mind telling me what you were doing there? And why didn't you just knock on her door?"

"That's two questions, not one."

"Well, then, take your pick. I'll be happy with the answer to either."

"Why would I go all the way to New Orleans to see Bernice?"

"I don't know. That's why I'm asking. You scared her half to death, and you're lucky you didn't get shot."

Eskil chuckled softly. "Bernice still owns a gun? Well, good for her. I was afraid that husband of hers made her go soft. That wouldn't have taken much. She always was afeared of her own shadow."

"I think you're underestimating her," I said. "She's tougher than you think. But you still haven't answered my question. Why did you go to see her?"

"I never said I did."

"Well, someone did. Someone who looks a whole lot like you. Or are you suggesting your father came back from the dead to pay her a visit?"

The skin around his eyes crinkled. "Coulda been the rougarou."

"But it wasn't."

"You never know. There have been sightings around here for years."

"You're seriously asking me to believe that the rougarou drove up to New Orleans to frighten Bernice?"

"I'm not asking you believe anything." Eskil wiped his

hands on his pant legs, leaving streaks of red barbeque sauce on the denim. "Who says my daddy's dead anyhow? They never found his body. He could be alive for all we know."

"Do you really believe that?"

His eyes grew serious. "I know you're trying to make Bernice happy, little girl, but what I believe is none of your business."

"Look," I said, ignoring the "little girl" thing, "I'm just worried about Bernice and about the timing of everything that's happened. You can understand that, can't you? Friday night someone who looked like you was outside Bernice's house. You say it wasn't you, which is too bad because Saturday morning someone reported you missing. The whole town rallied to search for you and they found you that night on the swamp. You said that you ran out of gas, but it turns out that someone had already checked that particular part of the swamp earlier and you weren't there. If that information gets out, I have a feeling the sheriff is going to be interested in hearing where you really were."

Eskil stared at me for a long, uncomfortable moment. "You threatening me, girl?"

"No. I'm just saying that it's pretty clear you have a few secrets. You might have some trouble keeping them now that Silas Laroche is dead."

"You think *I* killed him?"

"I didn't say that," I assured him. "But his body was found on your mother's property, so I think somebody wants it to look like you did. Georgie says that you're not talking to the sheriff's department. Don't you realize that refusing to cooperate is making you look guilty?"

Eskil raked his cool blue eyes across my face. "What I realize, young lady, is that you're too nosy for your own good." And with that he strode off, leaving me to wonder if

I'd been wrong about him. *Had* he killed Silas? He looked strong enough to do whatever he wanted with a toilet tank lid. Nobody had seen him for almost twenty-four hours, during which time somebody had sent Silas to his great reward.

Maybe Bernice was right to be worried.

Sullivan was awake and surrounded by the womenfolk by the time Eskil left me standing alone by the grill. Aunt Margaret fussed over Sullivan like he was her favorite grandson. Bitty fluttered to and fro, refreshing the tea in his glass anytime he shifted his weight and blushing every time he spoke. Her behavior gave me glimpses of the young woman who had been left at the altar. After learning just how small Baie Rebelle was, I wondered if the man who'd jilted her lived nearby. That could have made for some awkward situations.

Bitty wasn't the only one who seemed fascinated by Sullivan either. Miss Frankie and Bernice flanked him, urging him to tell stories about some of the cases he'd worked, which seemed to pull even Tallulah under his spell.

I was ready to get back into the Impala and make a clean getaway, but Sullivan couldn't seem to resist the urging of five females who had their hearts set on keeping him around for a few more hours. I'm not going to say his decision made me happy, but I wasn't going to get all bent out of shape about it. After all, if I'd been able to resist Miss Frankie and Bernice, we wouldn't be in Baie Rebelle in the first place.

With Sullivan's attention divided among the members of his new fan club and Eskil glowering at me between bites, dinner was an awkward experience. At least the food was good. The barbecued pork chops were perfectly cooked, moist and tender on the inside with a nice crust on the outside. His homemade barbecue sauce was both sweet and tangy. The boudin was heavenly, hearty and rich with a pleasant spice that made my lips tingle. Bitty's coleslaw was both creamy and crunchy, and Tallulah's green beans cooked with bacon were amazing. But the highlight of the evening was Aunt Margaret's pea-pickin' cake, also known as pig-pickin' cake, cotton-pickin' cake, and even Mandarin orange cake, depending on where you find the recipe.

There are as many stories about how the cake came by its name as there are names for the cake itself. It might have been named by country singer Tennessee Ernie Ford, known for his signature line, "Bless your pea pickin' heart," or because it was the perfect cake to serve after a hot day in the sun picking peas. Or it might have been given its pig-pickin' moniker because it was traditionally served at Southern barbecues, where the pig was cooked low and slow until the meat was falling off the bones, allowing the guests to pick off the meat at the table. We'll probably never know the true story, but the cake was so good I didn't care. The cake was light and moist and slightly citrusy thanks to the mandarin oranges. Between layers, whipped cream laced with pineapple gave the cake a bright, summery flavor.

We finished the meal and Eskil led Sullivan off to do something manly while the women stepped back in time again to clean up. I don't mind doing dishes, and I didn't begrudge doing my part to help my hostesses, but watching the two men swagger off across the lawn while assuming the kitchen was the women's domain grated on my nerves.

Okay, so maybe I was a bit more irritated about having to share my romantic evening alone with Sullivan than I'd first thought. I did my best to sweeten my mood—or at least not let my face show what I was really feeling.

We all fell back into the jobs we'd filled last night with Miss Frankie and Bernice clearing the table, Aunt Margaret putting away, me scraping dishes and stacking, and Bitty and Tallulah washing and drying. It didn't take long to exhaust the basic topics of conversation not covered during dinner. We generally agreed that the weather had been delightful and the food delicious. Aunt Margaret caught Bernice up on a few items of family gossip—who had what health issues, who was getting married, and who had been divorced.

After a while Tallulah told everyone that T-Rex was talking about selling fresh boiled peanuts, which made all of them a bit giddy with excitement. Personally, I didn't understand what the fuss was all about. I'm told that boiled peanuts are an acquired taste. It's one I had not yet managed to develop.

I'd been listening politely, offering comments or agreeable noises when appropriate, but the subject of T-Rex and his general store gave me an opening I couldn't resist.

"Speaking of T-Rex's store," I said as I scraped bones into a paper bag, "I ran into that sheriff's deputy when I stopped there to get the Old Bay Seasoning. She seems nice."

Aunt Margaret and Bitty agreed wholeheartedly, but Tallulah's endorsement lacked enthusiasm. I didn't know if she had some reason for withholding her stamp of approval, or if that was just her personality. I suspected the latter.

"I also saw one of the women who was out searching for Eskil last night. Adele something?"

"That would be Adele Pattiere," Aunt Margaret said. "She's a sweet thing, isn't she?"

That wouldn't have been the word I'd have used to describe her, but I agreed that she was and fell silent while I scraped another plate so I wouldn't seem unduly nosy. "I thanked her for taking part in the search. Maybe I'm wrong, but she seemed upset about something."

"Adele was?" Concern formed shadows on Bitty's face. "Did she say why?"

"Not to me," I said, and rinsed the plate under the tap. "I could've sworn I saw her talking to a young man last night who seemed angry with her. I thought maybe it was a family issue, but she said I must've been mistaken. So then I thought maybe she was upset about Silas Laroche. Was she a friend of his?"

Tallulah snorted. "Adele and Silas? Friends? She's not that stupid."

Aunt Margaret sent her daughter a warning look. "It's not right to speak ill of the dead." For my benefit, she explained, "Silas wasn't very popular around here, I'm afraid. He rubbed a lot of people the wrong way."

"I've been getting that impression," I said. "I have to admit I'm curious about why nobody liked him."

Miss Frankie stopped working and sidled closer.

Bernice looked almost breathless with anticipation. "Why *does* everyone think Eskil killed him? What was going on with the two of them?"

That was a little more direct than I'd intended to get, but Bernice was family, so she could get away with more than I could.

Tallulah looked at me pointedly, but she answered Bernice. "Eskil didn't kill him. I don't know why everybody thinks he did."

"But there was bad blood between them," Miss Frankie pointed out.

"There was bad blood between Silas and everybody else," Bitty said. "Not just Eskil."

"So people think Eskil did it because Silas's body was found here?" I asked. "Is that the only reason?"

Tallulah turned away sharply. "I'm not going to air my family's dirty laundry in front of the whole world."

"Rita and Miss Frankie aren't the whole world," Bernice said. "They're friends of mine and they're only trying to help."

Tallulah sent Bernice a withering glance. "You had no right to bring all these strangers here. This is a family matter."

Bernice shoved the salt and pepper shakers into a cupboard, closed the door with a bang, and rounded on her cousin. "It's a police matter, Tallulah, and it could easily become a court matter. I know you don't want your privacy invaded, but you'd be smart to convince Eskil to start talking. Because this is mild compared to what will happen if he's arrested."

Whoa! Bernice!

Tallulah opened the cupboard and made a show of moving the salt and pepper to their proper places. "Fine. Then if you ask me, it was that boy of his that killed Silas. How do you suppose Kale feels knowing his daddy lived just a few miles away but didn't care to see him? Or maybe it was Nettie. What kind of woman stays married to a man like Silas for twenty years after he deserts her?"

Bitty let out a dreamy sigh. "Did it ever occur to you that maybe she loved him?"

"Love? Silas?" Tallulah laughed. "Nettie's got a better head on her shoulders than to get all dewy-eyed over a man. There's something in it for her, you mark my words."

Bitty looked astonished. "I think you've lost your mind. Nettie's . . . well, she's . . ." She took a deep breath and sighed heavily. "Nettie's a regular member of the Thursday night ladies' Bible study group, which you'd know if you ever bothered to go."

Tallulah pushed air between her teeth. "You're too trusting, Bitty. You always have been. You think just because somebody shows up at church twice a week, they can do no wrong."

Bitty looked so wounded, I decided to step in, but Miss Frankie beat me to it. Just as well. I consider myself a nice person, but Miss Frankie has Southern comfort down to a science.

Bitty sniffled and Miss Frankie patted and made soothing noises. Bernice and Tallulah shared a weary look. And I still had no idea how Adele Pattiere felt about Silas Laroche's death.

"We shouldn't be talking about any of this," Tallulah muttered. "Eskil wouldn't like it."

Aunt Margaret slapped her hand on the table with a *whack!* that stunned everybody in the room into silence. "I appreciate how you feel, girls. I truly do. But your brother's in trouble and we've got to help him." She sank down at the table and looked straight into my eyes. "Frances Mae tells me you're good at solving puzzles like this one. Is that true?"

I wiped my hands on a towel and joined her. "I don't know if I'm good at it, but I've had a little luck in the past. Do you know something that might help clear Eskil of suspicion?"

"I know he didn't run out of gas in the swamp last night," she grumbled. "That boat of his started right up this morning. And I know he and Silas have been at each other's throats for years. If you promise you'll try to help him, I'll tell you what I think."

Tallulah gaped at her mother in shock. Bitty wrung her hands and skittered from the room. Miss Frankie and

Bernice raced to the table with a speed and agility I didn't know either of them possessed.

"It's all about his daddy's still," Aunt Margaret said when we were settled.

Bernice clasped her hands together. "Lord have mercy. I told you about that still, didn't I, Rita?"

Aunt Margaret smiled sadly. "You remember hearing the stories, Bernice. Running that still was a family business. My husband got it from his daddy. His daddy got it from Cooch's granddaddy, and so on back four or five generations. By rights, it all should've gone to Bernice's daddy, but he was in Korea when their daddy got sick, so Cooch got it. He made a good living at it for a while. And then one day he up and disappeared. He was still a young man. Didn't anybody think he was going to go so soon, least of all Cooch himself. Trouble is, he took the location of that still and the family recipe with him. After that, the girls had it rough, but Eskil . . . well, he got hit the hardest. And he blamed it all on Silas Laroche."

Fifteen

"Let me see if I have this straight," Sullivan said as we drove home later that night. Fog had rolled in from the water, creating an eerie backdrop for the Impala's headlights. I couldn't see more than a few feet in front of us. "Coolidge Percifield, otherwise known as Uncle Cooch, ran a still somewhere out there in the swamp. He made good money off it—hence the big house for Aunt Margaret."

I leaned forward as far as my seat belt would let me, looking out for other cars and wildlife. "Exactly. But could that possibly be true? I thought stills went out with the repeal of prohibition."

Sullivan shook his head. "Nope. Making moonshine is still a thriving business. A multimillion-dollar industry. It's legal in a couple of places, but there's mostly a big underground network."

"I guess you learn something every day."

Sullivan chuckled. "True enough. You said that nobody but Cooch knew the still's location or the family recipe, right?"

"That's what Aunt Margaret said. Apparently, both things were part of the family legacy. The location was passed down once a generation from father to son. That went on for a hundred years or so until Cooch disappeared without having a chance to pass the information down to Eskil. He took the location of the still and the recipe with him."

"And Eskil thinks Silas Laroche had something to do with his father's disappearance," Sullivan finished for me.

"Yes. According to Aunt Margaret, Eskil has always suspected Silas of doing something to Cooch. It may be true that a gator got him, but Eskil believes that Silas set up the meeting." I shuddered at the thought.

"Even if that were true, it happened fifteen years ago," Sullivan mused. "Why would Eskil suddenly go off the deep end and whack Silas over the head with a toilet tank lid after all this time?"

That image made me shudder again. "That's the sixty-four-thousand-dollar question. The other thing that's bothering me is why would someone kill Silas at his own house but then carry his body all the way to Aunt Margaret's house to dump it? I mean, look at the country out here. Why not just throw his body behind some trees? Nobody would ever find it."

"I'd say that the killer wanted everybody to know that Silas was dead. He or she probably also wanted to make Eskil look guilty."

"Well, they accomplished that," I said. We drove out of the dense patch of fog and I relaxed back in my seat. "You don't think he is guilty, do you?"

"He'd have to be pretty stupid to kill the guy and dump

him in his mother's ditch. Eskil might be a character, but he's not stupid."

"I wonder who else wanted Silas out of the way," I mused.

"Junior wasn't exactly torn up over his brother's death," Sullivan reminded me.

"No, but Adele Pattiere sure was."

"That's speculation on your part. She could have been upset over something else, like her argument with the mystery kid."

"It's not speculation, it's woman's intuition," I corrected. "Totally different. You didn't see her face when I mentioned Silas."

Sullivan grinned and accelerated slightly. "Just so you know, neither intuition nor speculation is admissible in court. Eskil told me that nobody had much to do with Silas. He poached other people's lines, fished property where other people had paid to lease the rights, and pretty much pissed everybody off. If Adele had been friendly with him, nobody would've had anything to do with her again."

We rounded a curve and drove into another heavy patch of fog. Sullivan didn't seem worried about his inability to see, which made me worry even more. Tensing, I leaned up to help him watch the road. "The sheriff's deputy, Georgie, told me that Silas was still married. He's been living off on his own for twenty years, but his wife and son apparently live right there in Baie Rebelle."

"Is that right? Strange that Junior never mentioned that. And I thought we were getting along so well."

"I don't think Junior was a fan, but cheer up. You won the hearts of all the women in Bernice's family. Even Eskil warmed up to you. But Junior? Not so much. Try not to let it hurt your feelings."

"I'm devastated."

"I can see that," I said with a grin. "Apparently Junior has been taking care of his brother's family all this time. He didn't tell us about that either. I wonder why."

"*I* wonder why the wife never filed for divorce."

"Nettie," I said. "That's her name. Tallulah thinks she stayed because there was something in it for her. But maybe it's as simple as not being able to afford to go to court."

Sullivan flicked his gaze at me. "Maybe. And maybe Tallulah's right. Maybe she had a reason for staying married to him."

"Well, if she did, it wasn't because of *his* money. Remember, Junior told us their father cut Silas out of his will."

"Are you sure Junior was telling us the truth?"

Interesting question. "You're not?"

"I don't know. It's an intriguing situation for sure."

He didn't know the half of it. I hadn't even told him about Eskil's visit to New Orleans or Mambo Odessa's warnings. I didn't like keeping secrets from him, but I'd broken my promise to Bernice once—technically twice if you counted the conversation I'd had with Eskil by the grill—and I was reluctant to do it again. Unless I knew that Eskil's ghostly visit had a bearing on Silas's murder or he desperately needed the alibi, her secret was safe with me. Besides, Sullivan would want to know why I hadn't told him about Bernice's scare before, and that wasn't a conversation I wanted to have just then. As for Mambo Odessa, I didn't see any reason to mention her at all for the same reason.

I was suddenly tired of talking about Silas Laroche and his messed-up life. We'd missed out on our quiet dinner together and I wanted to make up for lost time. "We didn't get the evening we had planned," I said. "I'm sorry I dragged you into that."

Sullivan grinned. "It wasn't so bad."

"You only say that because you had all the women making eyes at you," I teased. "Even Tallulah has a little crush on you."

"Little? I got her to smile. Twice. And you call that little?"

"I could have gotten her to smile," I protested. "If I'd broken a leg or something."

Sullivan laughed and took his eyes off the road just long enough to turn my insides to mush. I defy any woman to remain unaffected by those eyes. "We're going to do this again real soon," he said. "And by *this*, I don't mean hanging out with my new girlfriend. I mean dinner, alone with you, someplace nice."

Poor Tallulah. She never really had a chance.

Monday morning, I carried coffee upstairs to Zydeco's conference room so I could get ready for our weekly staff meeting. Driving to Baie Rebelle with Sullivan the night before hadn't exactly been the romantic evening I'd been hoping for, but it had been eventful and I was looking forward to that rain check.

I had high hopes that having a day off had given the staff a chance to cool down. I didn't want to confront Edie again, wasn't in the mood to argue with Ox about Evangeline Delahunt and the contract for the Belle Lune Ball, or for that matter with anybody about anything. I just wanted the day to go smoothly. I didn't think that was too much to ask.

The staff gathered, and while things weren't exactly cheerful, we got through the meeting with a minimum of snarky comments and dirty looks. Ox asked about my pretend meeting the day before, and I pretended that it had been rescheduled. I could tell he didn't believe me, but he didn't push the issue, for which I was grateful. The staff and I went over the designs for a couple of wedding cakes and came up with a game plan for making sixteen dozen cupcakes for a private school Halloween party the following week. Everyone walked away with their work assignments and nobody tried to kill anyone else, which I counted as a win.

I carried my notes downstairs, pausing when I reached the first-floor landing. Edie wasn't back at her desk yet, which wasn't that unusual, but the strange sounds coming from the end of the hall were. Leaving my notepad on Edie's desk, I followed the noise to the employee break room, where I found Edie mopping her tear-streaked face with a napkin.

I tried not to stare. I was always uncomfortable when Edie cried. Or when anyone else did, for that matter. Even after eight months of Edie's pregnancy, I never knew quite what to say when she fell apart.

She hiccupped softly and wadded the napkin in her hand. And then she looked at me as if she expected me to do something.

I gave a little finger wave. "Hey."

Sniff.

"Is everything okay?" I know it was a ridiculous question. The answer was painfully obvious.

She gave me the requisite answer for a woman in emotional distress: "Yeah. I'm fine."

I didn't want her to think I'd come looking for her, so I went to the fridge and pulled out a can of Diet Pepsi. Leaning against the counter, I popped it open and took a drink. "I think the staff meeting went well, don't you?"

"Yeah. It was great."

"Oh, good." I sat down at the table with her. "Because I thought maybe the tears meant that something was wrong."

She blew her nose loudly and a sob shook her body. "They hate me, don't they?"

I recognized the signs of a pity party. I've thrown a few for myself over the years. I wasn't clear on the details of Edie's, since I thought the staff had been remarkably civil that morning, but letting her get bogged down in negative emotion wouldn't help any of us.

"No," I said firmly. "They're still a little upset about that surprise trial run to the hospital on Friday, but they don't hate you. An apology would go a long way to making things better, you know."

She tossed one tissue and pulled a fresh one from her pocket. "You still don't get it, do you? If Isabeau had done what I did, they would have thought it was cute. Because it was me, they're all pissed off."

I didn't completely agree with her, but I didn't disagree either. Isabeau had people skills that Edie hadn't yet mastered. Not that Edie was working on them. But I didn't know how to say that without making her feel worse.

I bought some time by slugging down another few swallows of delicious ice-cold beverage. "You and Isabeau are different people with different personalities," I said when I came up for air. I was channeling Aunt Yolanda. She's way smarter about stuff like this than I am. "Comparing yourself to her is like comparing apples and oranges. They're both great, they're just different."

She gave me an annoyed look. "People don't like me. I know that."

"That's not true," I told her. "We *all* like you. A lot."

Edie put the new tissue to work and hiccupped again. "How can you say that? You saw the way they acted during the staff meeting. They'll be glad when I'm off on maternity leave."

"Only because it means the pregnancy will be over. For

you. Not for us. We'll be glad for you. And excited to meet the baby."

There. That was mainly true. We *would* all be glad for Edie, and excited to meet the baby . . . and we'd also be pretty glad for ourselves that Edie's emotional roller coaster of a pregnancy would be over.

Edie still looked doubtful, but just then the phone rang. We both looked at it. Answering incoming calls was Edie's job, but she was in no condition to talk to clients, so I answered it myself with a chipper, "Zydeco Cakes. This is Rita. How may I help you?"

"Rita Lucero?" It was a woman's voice, one I didn't recognize.

"Yes."

"Simone O'Neil here. I'm with the Crescent City Vintage Clothing Society. I left a message for you yesterday, but I thought I'd follow up and call you again. I hope I'm not being too pushy."

"Not at all," I assured her. "I was about to call you myself. I'm hoping to meet with you to discuss the decorations and theme for the Belle Lune Ball."

Edie pulled herself together, tossed her tissues, and waved as she left the room. I wouldn't say she looked happy, but at least she wasn't crying any longer. That would have to do for now. I hadn't given up hope that I could convince her to apologize, but that would have to wait. I hoped not too long, though.

While Simone O'Neil checked her calendar, I covered the receiver and called, "Edie? Are you busy for lunch?"

She reappeared in the doorway and shook her head. "Not really. Why?"

"Do you want to grab a bite with me?"

"You don't have to do that," she said with a frown. "I'll be fine."

"It's not a pity invitation," I said. "So don't get the wrong idea. Say twelve thirty?"

She nodded uncertainly. "Sure. Okay. I guess."

Her response was underwhelming, but I was determined to get the staff back to normal. I flashed a BFF-worthy smile and Edie disappeared again. A moment later, Simone came back on the line. We agreed to meet the following afternoon at her office, and I hung up feeling pretty good about my day so far. I don't get that feeling very often, so I enjoyed it while I could.

Sixteen

⚜

Edie and I spent our lunch break talking about the baby and Edie's plans for decorating the baby's nursery. She'd even offered me the chance to change my mind about being the baby's godmother. Since she'd more or less tricked me into saying yes, I could have backed out with a clear conscience, but I didn't. The idea of taking on a lifetime of responsibility made me a little dizzy, but I kept hearing Aunt Yolanda telling the teenage me that sometimes things weren't all about me, and I knew this was one of those times.

I still thought Edie could have made a better choice, but she'd been caught off guard by the pregnancy and she was scared to death by the looming reality of becoming someone's mother. I guess we'd just have to muddle through together.

She didn't bring up the argument she'd had with River after our trip to the hospital, and I didn't ask. I didn't want her to think I'd invited her to lunch to lecture her about her choices. She got far too much of that as it was.

On the way back to work, I paused in front of a gift shop to admire a Halloween tea setting in a store window. A delicate black lacquer teapot had been paired with black-and-white plates and crisp white napkins tied with orange satin ribbon. I'm not a tea drinker, but the setting appealed to me.

"You didn't have to do this, you know."

I glanced away from the window. I must have looked confused because Edie said, "I mean, I enjoyed having lunch together but, well, you didn't have to."

"I didn't do it because I had to," I assured her. "I asked you to have lunch with me because I get tired of eating alone."

"You asked me because I had a meltdown at work," Edie said, but she was smiling—and she was right—so I didn't argue.

I craned to see the price tag on the teapot and made a mental note to come back and look at it more closely when I had some free time. "I have an appointment with a woman named Simone O'Neil tomorrow afternoon," I said when we started walking again. "She's in charge of the decorations for the Belle Lune Ball. Have you ever heard of her?"

Edie nodded. "I've seen her name around, usually connected with charity work, but I've never met her."

"What about Evangeline Delahunt? Why does everybody freak out when they hear her name?"

"You met her," Edie said. "What do you think?"

"I thought she was thoroughly unpleasant. Is she always like that?"

Edie hitched her purse higher on her shoulder. "She and I don't exactly hang out," she said, "but I hear she's a real pain in the neck."

"Who do you hear that from?" I was pretty sure I knew the answer, but I asked anyway in case she'd picked up talk from someone other than Ox.

"Ox knows her," Edie said. "Philippe knew her."

Back in pastry school, Edie had nursed a crush on Philippe. He'd never returned her interest, but it always stung a little when I realized she knew something about him that I didn't. This one was the emotional equivalent of a mosquito bite, so I brushed it off. "Is it true that Philippe refused to work with her?"

Edie nodded. "Yeah. Miss Frankie sure tried to get him to do it, though."

"That's the part that confuses me. Why was it so important to her?"

"I don't know. People don't confide in me, you know. I meant what I said earlier. I don't really have any friends around here."

That wasn't exactly true; when she wasn't pregnant and emotional, people confided in Edie all the time. She was a font of information, and not just because she ran the front of the house at Zydeco. She was also adept at accidentally overhearing other people's conversations. Commending her on that talent didn't seem like the most effective way to make her feel appreciated, though, so I swallowed that comment as well.

I didn't say anything until we'd put another block behind us. That's how long it took for me to grow uncomfortable with the silence. "How are things with River?"

Edie turned her face toward a storefront window filled with silk leaves in fall colors. "Don't start, okay?"

"I'm asking about your life," I said. "I'm interested in knowing what's going on. Isn't that what friends do?"

She stopped walking and shrugged. "Yeah. I guess so."

"So? How *are* things with River?"

"They're not."

I didn't want to throw Isabeau under the bus by admitting that she'd told me about their argument, so I pretended ignorance. "Why? Did he leave again?"

"No. But he will. You know he will."

"No, I don't. And neither do you."

"He was raised by hippies," she argued. "In a commune. He's not even sure who his own father is. He's spent his entire adult life traveling all over the globe doing God knows what. How can I trust a man like that?"

I shrugged. "I don't know. I thought I could trust Philippe, but it turned out I couldn't. Sometimes you get hurt. Sometimes you don't. But the fact is, River is the baby's father. Doesn't he deserve a chance? If not with you, at least with the baby?"

"I've given him a chance," she said. "He blew it."

"Oh, come on! He arrived a few minutes late to your pretend labor. That's hardly a hanging offense."

Edie's good mood evaporated. "So you expect me to let him be part of our lives forever just because I made one stupid mistake?"

Ouch! I hoped she wouldn't say things like that in front of the baby. If you asked me, letting your kid know it was a "stupid mistake" could easily fall into the "Scar Your Kid for Life" category.

"I don't know," I said cautiously. "Maybe sleeping with River was a mistake. Maybe it wasn't. You won't know for sure unless you stop looking for reasons to push him away and see how it plays out."

She huffed impatiently, a sure clue that she didn't appreciate my opinion.

"Look, Edie, I can't tell you what to do and I'm really

not trying to. But you're the one who decided to sleep with him. You're the one who picked him to be the baby's daddy, even if you didn't really mean to. The baby had no choice in the matter, but *your* choice is going to affect him or her forever. Just because you don't want River around doesn't mean the baby won't. That's all I'm saying."

She glared at me.

I glared right back. "Hey, you asked me to be the baby's godmother. I'm just doing my job."

"Your job is to be there for the baby, not to start dictating to me."

"Who's dictating? I'm just offering a suggestion."

"Well, don't!"

I might have come up with a great reply to that, and I might not have. Before I could, my cell phone chimed Uncle Nestor's ring tone and Edie took advantage of the distraction to walk away. She said something as she left, but I couldn't hear what it was.

Maybe that was for the best.

I seriously considered ignoring Uncle Nestor's call, but my uncle is a persistent man. The longer I avoided talking to him, the more he'd call. I knew this from experience.

Swallowing my frustration with Edie, I answered with a chipper, "Hey, *tío*! What's up?"

"I have great news, *mija*," Uncle Nestor boomed. He sounded happy. That was good. "Ramon's been looking for flights to get you home for Christmas. He found a great deal this morning."

That was my family for you. To them I'd always be a little girl, incapable of looking out for myself. I went for a cautiously optimistic tone. Not so excited that Uncle Nestor thought he could continue doing this. Not so off-putting that he'd take offense. It's a fine line.

"Oh. Well. That's great. I hope it will work with my schedule." Maybe I should have mentioned that my schedule was up in the air, but until I locked in the Vintage Clothing Society contract, nothing was certain. Why waste energy arguing over something that might not happen?

Uncle Nestor rattled off a few details, but I didn't even try to retain them. Once I knew whether or not I'd be up to my eyeballs in work during December, I'd know whether or not I could get away for Christmas. Either way, I wouldn't be able to help Miss Frankie with her Christmas plans, but I saw no reason to drag out the unpleasantness. I'd just handle it all at once, like ripping off a Band-Aid. Besides, Miss Frankie was in Baie Rebelle for the foreseeable future, and I didn't know when I'd get a chance to talk to her privately. This wasn't the kind of news I wanted to give her over the phone.

"Have Ramon e-mail the details to me," I suggested. "I'll check out the flight as soon as I can."

"No need for that," Uncle Nestor said. "I've looked at it myself and it's perfect. You'll fly out of New Orleans the Monday before Christmas and go back a week later. There were only three seats left this morning. You can't wait when you find such a deal."

A car missing its muffler drove past, making it impossible to hear or be heard. I waited until the noise died away and said, "I understand the ticket is a good deal, but I can't do anything about it right now. I'm not at my desk and I don't have my calendar in front of me. I'll need to look at the staff's vacation schedule so I can make sure there's someone available to cover while I'm gone. I promise I'll check it out as soon as I have a few minutes to spare."

Uncle Nestor put his hand over the phone and shouted at

someone in Spanish. When he came back, his voice was much softer. That's not necessarily a good sign. "You're not trying to get out of coming home, are you?"

"No! I can't wait to see all of you."

"Because I warn you, *mija*, if you don't make it home this year, your aunt will be very disappointed."

"She's not the only one," I assured him. I came up behind a mother with two toddlers in a stroller, both holding black cat balloons. I had to slow down until I could get around them.

"She's planning to make all your favorite dishes," Uncle Nestor bargained. "There will be chilies *Rellenos* and the *queso blanco* you like so much. And flan. She's already working on the menu."

I finally got around the stroller and balloons, only to get stopped at a corner by a traffic light. My mouth watered just thinking about my aunt's cooking. And let's not even get started on the dishes Uncle Nestor made every year. "That's not fair," I protested. "You know Aunt Yolanda always starts working on Christmas early. It's her thing."

"Maybe, but she's very excited this year. It's all she can talk about."

Gee thanks, Uncle Nestor. No pressure there. The light changed and I trotted to the other side of the road. "Okay. Okay. I promise to look at the information before the end of the day. Will that make you happy? Just tell Ramon to send it to me. He has my e-mail address. Now stop trying to make me feel guilty. I thought we were on the same side."

Uncle Nestor laughed and switched subjects. "Have you talked to Manuel lately?"

Manny was the third of my four cousins, all of whom were as close to me as brothers. Over the years, each of us has disappointed my aunt and uncle in some way. Manny's claim to infamy had been his decision to leave Uncle Nestor's restaurant and devote his life to music instead.

Uncle Nestor had been livid about Manny's choice for a long time. Aunt Yolanda spent the first five years assuring him that Manny would eventually come to his senses, but it had been ten years, and they were still waiting. Manny had been making the rounds of bars, and women, ever since.

"I haven't talked to him," I admitted. "Should I?"

"He's seeing someone," Uncle Nestor said.

"Is he okay?" I asked tentatively, uncertain about why we'd suddenly bounced from Christmas to Manny's female companion of the week.

"He's fine," Uncle Nestor assured me. "They've been together awhile."

Still confused. "Define *awhile*."

"Six months. She's special, this one."

My gasp of surprise was completely genuine. This was huge! "Who's the woman? Where did he meet her? Have you and *tía* met her?"

"Yes, we have, and we approve."

Oh. My. Gosh! Uncle Nestor approving of something Manny did? Had the world come to an end?

"Manny told us last week that he wants to propose at Christmas."

"No! Are you serious? How did this girl ever pin him down?"

"I can't say more. I'm sworn to secrecy. But I can tell you that he wants you to be there when he pops the question."

Ah! Everything clicked into place. So that's what this was about. "You mean the others don't know? Santos? Aaron? Julio?"

Uncle Nestor laughed softly. I was hooked and he knew it. "They don't know a thing. Yolanda and I are the only two he's told. And now you know. You cannot breathe a word, *mija*."

"No. I won't. But—"

"Not a single word. But now you understand why Christmas is so important to your *tía*."

"I get it, but—"

"She wants to make a good impression on the young lady's family."

"She doesn't need to worry about that," I said. "Aunt Yolanda is amazing."

"Of course she is, but this is important to her. You understand."

"I do." Oh boy, did I! I knew how worried Aunt Yolanda'd been about Manny. I could only imagine how thrilled she was that he'd decided to settle down. "I really want to be there," I said. "I'll make reservations, I promise. Just as soon as I have my schedule nailed down."

"Well, I've saved the best for last, *mija*. I already booked the flight for you. It's my gift. Ramon will send the ticket in your e-mail."

"You booked the flight?" My voice came out louder than I'd intended, and several people turned to look at me. I gave a little *oops* grimace and lowered it again. "Uncle Nestor—"

"It was a great deal. I couldn't pass it up. And you *said* you were coming home for the holidays."

"Yes, I did," I said with a sigh. "But I don't know exactly when I can get away and how long I can stay." Or if I could get away at all. "You should have checked with me before you spent all that money."

"Aren't you the boss at that place? Make it happen, Rita. Put your foot down." This from the man who'd taken maybe two vacations my entire life—and one of them had been ordered by his doctor.

I knew this was partially my fault. I should have told him about the Belle Lune Ball and the possibility that I might not make it home at all, but that would have just opened another can of worms. "Yeah. I'm the boss. But please, *tío*, get your money back. I'll book my own flight."

"Don't be so stubborn. I'm trying to do something nice for you. And I can't get the money back. The ticket is non-refundable."

Of course it was. Uncle Nestor has always been frugal. In the past he'd had to be. There had never been enough money to go around. He made a more comfortable living now, but old habits die hard.

I looked around for a wall I could bang my head against. "We're going to have to talk about this later," I said. "I've got to go."

"Rita?"

"Yes?"

"Remember, not a word about Manuel."

I disconnected and stuffed the phone into my pocket and I channeled my inner Scarlett O'Hara. I'd think about Christmas in Albuquerque tomorrow. After all, tomorrow was another day.

Seventeen

❧

I stayed busy the rest of the day preparing for my meeting with Simone O'Neil. I printed off our flavor choices for cake, fillings, and buttercream and made notes about combinations that worked well together. I updated our portfolio, adding photos of the most impressive cakes we'd made in recent months. Even though Simone wouldn't be the one to make a final decision about hiring Zydeco, I hoped that if she saw the options we offered, she could help steer Evangeline Delahunt toward a mutually beneficial decision.

It was well after ten that night when I left the building and nearly midnight when I finally fell into bed. The next morning I took extra care with my appearance, choosing a pair of classic black pants and a white silk top with silver earrings and a matching bangle bracelet. I thought about adding heels but decided I might make a better impression if I could actually walk across the room without falling over.

I slipped on a pair of ankle strap ballet flats and called it good.

I worked all morning on paperwork and left for my appointment in plenty of time to allow for traffic and getting lost in unfamiliar parts of the city. I found the Crescent City Vintage Clothing Society in a beautiful old building on Royal Street. After driving around the block several times— not an easy feat on those narrow French Quarter streets—I snagged a parking space within easy walking distance and gave myself a mental high-five for having incredible luck.

Suddenly nervous, I gave myself a quick check in the rearview mirror. My hair was behaving itself, and my makeup hadn't run. No stray black marks from mascara or eyeliner and nothing in my teeth. Even my lip gloss still appeared fresh. I was good to go.

I presented myself to the receptionist a full five minutes early. She directed me to a seating area filled with cane-back chairs and lush tropical greenery. While I waited, I gave myself a pep talk along the lines of Stuart Smalley from the old *Saturday Night Live* sketches. I told myself that I was smart enough and talented enough to hold my own, and that the insecure little Hispanic girl I once was had grown into a confident, competent woman.

After roughly a hundred repetitions, I saw an elegant woman about my age walking across the lobby. She had short dark hair and a friendly smile, and I liked her immediately. "Rita? Thank you for coming. I'm Simone."

We shook hands and I thanked her for making time for me in what I knew was a busy schedule. You know, the usual. After the pleasantries were behind us, she led me down a long hallway and out into a magnificent courtyard garden. I was learning that these hidden surprises were some of the best things about New Orleans. Incredible beauty was often hidden in the most unexpected places.

We sat at a table near a small fountain, and while I got settled, Simone gave me a brief rundown on the building's history. The property itself had originally been occupied by barracks for French troops, though they were eventually torn down and the present-day building erected in 1845 by a French merchant, who lived there until tragedy and bankruptcy left him broke and broken.

It was a fascinating story, but it left me feeling guilty that I didn't know much about the history of Zydeco's building. Just one more thing to put on my to-do list—the one I'd eventually get to in my spare time. Maybe if I'd had a few interesting facts at my disposal when Evangeline Delahunt came to Zydeco, she'd have been more impressed by our first meeting.

Simone motioned to someone I couldn't see, and a young woman in white appeared out of nowhere with a tray holding a pitcher of lemonade and two glasses. She put the tray on the table and Simone poured for both of us. "I understand you're new to New Orleans."

I nodded. "That's right. I only moved here last summer."

"How do you like it so far?"

"I like it very much," I said. "It's a fascinating city full of history and diversity, and there's always something to do." I thought I sounded like a poorly made travel video, but Simone didn't seem to notice.

"We do like to party," she said with a laugh. "Are you sure you're up for the challenge the Belle Lune Ball represents? It's a grueling schedule for everyone involved and expectations are high."

Was that an innocent question or was she trying to deter

me? "We're up for it," I assured her. "I have the best staff in town, and the most talented."

"I hear good things," she said. "Tell me, did you keep the staff after Philippe died?"

"Most of them."

"Is Ox still with you?"

I nodded slowly. "He is. You know Ox?"

Simone smiled and crossed her legs. "Very well. We're old friends. He didn't tell you?"

I felt as if I'd been slapped but I think I kept a smile on my face. "He didn't mention it, but we've been busy."

"Of course you have," she said. "Silly of me to think otherwise. I'm looking forward to seeing him again. Please tell him hello for me."

"I'll be sure to," I said and tried to steer the conversation in a direction I thought would be more comfortable for me. "When I met with Evangeline, she was vague about the colors, the theme, and the decorations for the Belle Lune Ball. I'm hoping to get more details today so we can start working on a design for the cake. Do you have a color scheme in mind?"

Simone looked disappointed by the change of subject, but she shifted gears quickly. "Glass and candlelight. The ball takes place in January, so we want ice and warmth together. On the tables, tall glass vases filled with water and cymbidium orchids. Frosted white candleholders." She pulled pictures from a file folder as she talked and spread them on the table in front of me. "White tablecloths, of course. Or maybe a pale gray. I haven't made the final decision on that, but we still have some time."

"It's beautiful," I told her. And it was. Understated. Elegant. Classy. Ideas began to flow and I felt a buzz of excitement. "Do you have any idea what kind of cake Evangeline wants for the event? She really didn't give me much to go on."

"No, she wouldn't. She likes to challenge people."

"Consider me challenged. I don't know if she's looking for a sculpted cake or something more traditional. After seeing what you have planned here, I'm leaning toward the traditional. Maybe a stacked cake with four or five tiers and a fall of orchids." I began to sketch out my idea. "If the cake itself is pale silver-gray, we could put fondant ribbons here and here, or maybe a light stencil pattern in white. And we could surround the cake with candles to match the centerpieces."

"I love it," Simone said when I'd finished roughing out my idea. "I'd tell you to go ahead with that idea right now, but you know it's not up to me."

"Yes, I know." But I wished it was her decision to make. She would be so much easier to work with than Evangeline. In fact, Simone seemed to be Evangeline Delahunt's complete opposite: warm, friendly, accepting, and enthusiastic. I decided to be honest with her. "Do you think Evangeline would like it, or should I focus on something else entirely? I don't want her to fire us before we even have a chance to please her."

A tiny crease appeared in Simone's forehead. "I don't want that either. Would it be possible for you to work up a couple of different sketches for your next meeting with her? You know, hedge your bets?"

I laughed. "And I'm right back where I started. Don't get me wrong, I'm not complaining. I'll see what I can do, but I'm a little nervous since I'm aware Gâteaux couldn't produce a design Evangeline liked and they had months to come up with an idea. It would mean a lot to me if I could hit a home run my first time at bat."

Simone put a hand over mine. "I'm sure you will. I've heard great things about you. And I do hope the two of us can work closely together. We'll have so many things to coordinate, we should meet often, don't you think?"

The suggestion both surprised and pleased me. "I'd like that."

"Good." Simone uncrossed her legs and began to gather her pictures. "I'll tell Mama."

Everything inside me turned to ice. "Mama?"

"Why, yes. You didn't know? Evangeline Delahunt is my mother. We've been working together for the society since I got married. It's been more years than I like to admit to."

I'm sure she meant for me to smile, but I was feeling a little sick. I tried to remember everything I'd said about Evangeline that might have been construed as insulting, but my memory was sketchy. I remembered every thought I'd had, but I wasn't sure how many of those thoughts had made it out of my mouth.

"No. I—I didn't realize."

"Ox didn't tell you that either?" Simone's laugh tinkled like water splashing in the fountain. "I can't believe he did that. When you speak with him, tell him he's just as bad as he can be. He shouldn't keep you in the dark like that. Not if we're going to be spending time together."

I couldn't agree more. Moving on autopilot, I pulled myself together, stuffed my notebook and pencil back into my bag, and stood. I followed Simone back through the building, vaguely aware that she was talking but too angry with Ox to pick up much of what she said.

I *really* hate being blindsided. Simone had just hit me hard and my mind was reeling.

After saying good-bye to Simone and promising to call in a few days to make another appointment with Evangeline, I walked out onto Royal Street and hurried away from the building as quickly as I could. It had been cool in the shade of the courtyard, but in the sun the temperature was uncomfortably warm. Or maybe it was the anger boiling inside me.

Blinking back tears of frustration, I strode to the

Mercedes and tossed my bag into the backseat. I was about to get into the car myself when I heard a voice right behind.

"Rita?"

It was so unexpected my heart jumped into my throat. I spun around, assuming that Simone had followed me for some reason, but I was even more surprised to see it was Mambo Odessa, who stood only a few feet away.

How had she gotten there?

Okay, sure, I'd been upset after my meeting with Simone but I would have sworn the street was empty. Maybe I hadn't been paying attention to my surroundings, but why hadn't I heard her footsteps on the pavement? Or the jingle of her jewelry—and bones?

If I hadn't known better, I'd have sworn that Mambo Odessa had appeared out of nowhere.

Just like the other day at Bernice's, Mambo Odessa looked elegant, not creepy. Today she wore a black-and-white turban with a geometric pattern and a flowing white dress. Again, her sunglasses made it difficult to see her eyes.

"You look alarmed, child. Are you all right?"

"I'm fine," I said. "I didn't see you so you startled me. That's all."

She dipped her head slightly. "Well, then, I apologize. I was on my way to see someone and noticed you walking down the street. I thought I should say hello."

That sounded like a perfectly logical explanation—at least one that didn't involve magic spells or voodoo chants. I knew I should say something, but I just didn't have the skills to make small talk at the moment.

Mambo Odessa didn't seem to notice. Or maybe she could read my mind and knew that I was struggling. "If you have time, you should stop by my shop. You may find what you're looking for."

A solution to my multiple-family Christmas problem? A way to make Evangeline Delahunt fall in love with my menu and cake designs? Proof that Eskil hadn't conked his arch-enemy over the head? If Mambo Odessa had any of those things for sale, she really was remarkable.

I had to say something, so I said the first thing that came to mind. "I didn't realize you had a shop."

"Oh, yes. It's on Dauphine Street. Not far from here."

I nodded as if I knew my way around the French Quarter.

And she smiled as if she saw right through me. "One can walk through the entire Quarter in a fairly short time. The next time you're here, come by and see me."

"I'll do that," I said, but it was an empty promise. Aunt Yolanda had always been vehement about avoiding anything that smacked of magic or witchcraft. I wasn't quite as adamant as she was, but if something gave me a hinky feeling, I steered clear. Voodoo definitely fell into the "hinky" category.

"Until then," she said and held out a hand to reveal a small bracelet consisting of five or six purple beads on braided hemp string. "I have something for you."

For me? Okay, now that was weird. I stared at her hand without moving. "You just happen to be here as I leave an appointment and you have something for me? Did Isabeau tell you where I'd be?"

"I haven't spoken with Isabeau since the day you and I first met." She urged the bracelet toward me. "It is to help you overcome obstacles."

"Thanks but . . ." I wasn't ready to just take those beads and go on my way. "If Isabeau didn't tell you where I'd be this afternoon, how did you know where to find me? Did Ox tell you?"

"I haven't spoken with Ox either. Please. Take it. It will help you."

I didn't want to insult Mambo Odessa, but I didn't want to take the beads either. "It's kind of you, but I don't think the bracelet will help unless I believe it will. I'm sorry, but I don't."

Mambo Odessa looked cool and unruffled in her white dress. "It won't hurt you, child. It's simply a Brazilian wish bracelet."

I was growing warmer by the minute standing out there in the sun. "It's not that—" I began.

"You don't trust me. I know that. I understand. But I sense many obstacles in your path. I know they will present a challenge so I made this for you. You must wear it until it falls off."

I still didn't believe the beads held any special power, but maybe her intentions were good. I hoped that counted for something. I took the bracelet and smiled. Besides, I didn't want her putting some kind of spell on me for being rude. "Then thank you."

"I know that you are important to many people."

I laughed before I could stop myself. I knew people cared about me, but I'd never considered myself *important* to anyone except, at first, Philippe. I didn't think anyone's world would spin out of orbit if I disappeared tomorrow.

"Isabeau speaks very highly of you," Mambo Odessa said earnestly.

"That's nice to know. She speaks well of you, too." I noticed that she didn't say Ox was a fan of mine, but in light of the way he'd been acting, I wasn't surprised. I was raised to keep my nose out of other people's business, but I also struggle with a healthy, active curiosity. Curiosity won over manners. "Isabeau mentioned that Ox isn't a believer in what you do. She said she has to sneak around to see you."

Mambo Odessa smiled. "Ox is a stubborn boy, but he has a good heart."

"And a little trouble with the truth," I mumbled. She looked at me oddly and I realized that I'd spoken aloud. I should never let my frustrations get the best of me. "Maybe it's none of my business, but they both work for me so I'm concerned that you're encouraging Isabeau to go behind Ox's back."

"You worry that he'll be angry with her."

"Yes. And if he's angry with her, she'll get all wigged out. If he's angry and she's wigged out, that will affect their work. And then the rest of the staff will think they have to take sides and everybody will get involved, and before you know it, nobody will be getting anything done. It would be better for everyone if you encouraged Isabeau to tell Ox the truth."

Mambo Odessa smiled softly. "They are going to be just fine. Their relationship won't make the others stop working."

Her certainty annoyed me. "I hope you're right. Maybe I'm the only one who has a problem with trusting someone who keeps secrets." I didn't have anything else to say so I dangled the bracelet from a finger and said, "Thanks for this. I really should get going."

"You'll wear it?"

"Um . . . sure." I slipped it on my wrist and fumbled to secure it with one hand.

Mambo Odessa leaned in to help. The strong scent of incense rose up from her hair and clothes, and my eyes watered. "Don't remove the bracelet," she said softly. "Let it fall off when its work is done. And don't be too hasty to judge. We don't always know what another person is thinking." She squeezed my hand tightly and looked me in the eye. I think. It was hard to tell with those sunglasses. "Look for the blue shutters."

I blinked. "What?"

"When you come to the shop. Look for the blue shutters. That's how you'll find me."

"Oh. Yeah. Sure. I'll remember that."

She walked away, as if we'd just had a perfectly normal encounter. At least I wasn't worried about how she'd known where I'd be. All that stuff about Ox and Isabeau could mean only one thing: Ox had known what I'd learn during my meeting with Simone O'Neil and he'd sent his aunt to do damage control.

After Mambo Odessa disappeared (through a doorway, not in a puff of smoke or anything), I got into my car and pulled out onto the street. I had no idea why Ox had kept his friendship with Simone a secret, or why he thought it was so important to keep it from me, but I was getting tired of all the secrets. I thought it was time for a little honesty.

Eighteen

✤

By the time I left the French Quarter, it was nearly six. Knowing that Zydeco would be closing soon and Ox would be leaving the bakery any minute, I decided to head him off at the Dizzy Duke. The good angel on my shoulder warned me to wait until I'd cooled down. I told her to shut up and mind her own damn business.

Traffic was so thick it took nearly an hour to get back to the Garden District, which did nothing to improve my mood. To make matters worse, I had to park around the corner and two blocks down from the bar in a seedy part of the neighborhood that always made me nervous after dark. After I locked my doors, I threaded the keys through my fingers and vowed that if anything happened to me, I'd make sure Ox knew it was his fault.

Muted music and laughter drifted out of the bar as I got closer. I wished I could just go inside and relax. Why couldn't

Ox just man up and be honest? Part of me knew I should let my irritation with him go, but I'd had an hour in traffic to get worked up over that poorly disguised visit from Mambo Odessa. The whole way across town I'd tried to pull off that cheap bracelet but jute—or whatever it was—is surprisingly strong.

Inside the Duke, I immediately looked behind the bar. Seeing Gabriel Broussard working cheered me up a little. Gabriel and I have gone out from time to time. He's one reason Sullivan and I aren't more serious. That and the fact that I'm still gun-shy after my almost-divorce. Plus, I honestly care for both men. Besides, Sullivan is solid and dependable and hot, while Gabriel is charming and mysterious and . . . well, hot. How's a girl to choose?

Gabriel gave me one of his sexy Cajun smiles—the ones that always turn my blood to warm honey.

I made a beeline for him and thrust out my wrist. "Scissors, please."

A lazy lock of dark brown hair fell across his forehead, and his eyes roamed over me with stark appreciation. "Why do you need scissors?"

I shook my wrist in front of him. "Just cut this off, okay? Scissors, a butcher knife, a chainsaw, whatever. I don't care what you use."

He didn't move. "You know what that is?"

"Yeah. A cheap bracelet."

He cocked an eyebrow.

"Okay. It's a Brazilian something or other. Wish beads, I think."

"Exactly. You've been shopping?"

"If I'd paid for it, I wouldn't be asking you to cut it off," I pointed out reasonably. "It was a gift, but I don't want it. So just cut it off already, okay?"

Gabriel found a knife by the sink and came back. "You're sure that's what you want?"

His reluctant reaction stunned me. "What is wrong with you? Are you afraid of it or something?"

"Afraid? No. Do you know what it's for?"

"Something about obstacles, blah, blah, blah."

"Overcoming obstacles," Gabriel said. He looked completely serious.

So serious, that all I could do was laugh. "Don't tell me you believe in this voodoo stuff."

Gabriel gave me half a smile. "I respect it. I've seen what it can do. Who gave it to you?"

"A woman named Mambo Odessa. She's some kind of voodoo priestess."

"And she felt that you needed this?"

I jerked my hand away. "Oh, for Pete's sake. I'll ask somebody else."

Gabriel laughed. "Virgin margarita?"

"A regular one," I said. "With salt."

Gabriel tossed a coaster onto the counter in front of me and gave me another long, slow look. "You look great, *chérie.* What's the occasion?"

I'd almost forgotten that I'd dressed up for my meeting with Simone O'Neil. I glanced down at my outfit and back up into Gabriel's dark brown eyes. "I just came from a business meeting. A very important business meeting." Which, of course, made me remember why I'd stopped by in the first place. "Has Ox been in yet?"

"I haven't seen him. You seem upset. What's going on?"

"Secrets," I snarled. "More secrets. I'm getting really, *really* tired of them." I followed this up with a pointed look, which Gabriel understood immediately. We'd pretty much worked through our issues over his own failures to be honest with me, but I was pissed at Ox and he wasn't here, so unfortunately for him, that left Gabriel as target practice.

"Who got on your bad side today?" Gabriel said, grinning as if he found my righteous anger amusing. "I know it wasn't me this time."

I took a sip of my margarita and moaned a little when heaven hit my tongue. Among his many other talents, Gabriel is a master of his craft behind the bar. His margaritas are a perfect blend of tart and sweet. "Pick one of the following," I said when I'd recovered. "Uncle Nestor. Bernice. Ox. Isabeau. Cousin Eskil. I'm sure there are more but those are the top five."

Gabriel leaned on the bar and gave me a sympathetic look, which might have made me feel better if his eyes hadn't been dancing with mirth. "What has your uncle done this time?"

I explained briefly about Miss Frankie and her family party, the bid for the Belle Lune Ball contract, about Uncle Nestor and the airline ticket and the bribe he'd used to make sure I kept my word. "If I'm like a daughter to him, why doesn't he trust me? I *said* I'd be there for Christmas."

Gabriel shrugged. "He probably knows you well enough to pick up on *your* secrets."

I almost choked on my drink. "What secrets?"

"You just said that you haven't told Miss Frankie about your plans. That counts, right? And you haven't told your uncle that you may not be able to get back to Albuquerque for Christmas. That makes two."

"Those aren't the same thing at all. They're not secrets, I've just been waiting for the right time to tell them." I rested my chin in my hand and sighed. "And if I'm working the Belle Lune Ball for the Vintage Clothing Society, I still won't have time to handle a week with Miss Frankie's family. So they'll both be upset with me anyway. On the other hand,

Miss Frankie may not be a problem if Cousin Eskil doesn't start talking to the police."

Gabriel's brows furrowed. "I almost hate to ask, but who is Cousin Eskil, and what does he need to talk to the police about?"

"He's Miss Frankie's neighbor Bernice's cousin, and it's a long story." I told him about finding Silas Laroche in the ditch and my two trips in as many days to Baie Rebelle. Out of respect for the promises I'd made, I left out the part about Eskil's visit to New Orleans on Friday night and Isabeau's unannounced visit with Mambo Odessa. Out of respect for Gabriel, I didn't mention my ruined date with Sullivan. The omissions robbed Gabriel of the full impact of my week, but what else could I do?

His smile faded quickly as I talked. No big surprise there. It was quite a story, but it wasn't sympathy that put the frown on his face. "I suppose you've convinced yourself that you just have to get involved," he said when I finished.

"Ha! I thought you'd say that, but you suppose wrong." I'd finished my margarita while I talked, so I nudged my glass toward him, a signal that I needed another. "I have no intention of getting involved in that murder. It's Miss Frankie and Bernice you should be worried about."

"Those sweet old ladies? Why? What are they doing?"

"Miss Frankie thinks she's some kind of amateur sleuth now. We managed to rein them in a bit, but I have no idea what they've been doing since I came back. They could be in jail by now. Or worse."

"And Ox? Whatever it is, you should just fire the man. He's more trouble than he's worth."

I knew he didn't mean it. He and Ox got along well. But I liked being able to blow off steam so I went with it. "You have no idea. I have a chance for this great contract—an amazing opportunity for Zydeco. Actually Miss Frankie's the one who made the contact, but that's not the point. The point is, it's going to be great for us. I told everybody about it the other night when we were in here for Dwight's birthday. Did they get excited? No! In fact, Ox got all bent out of shape and said I was making a big mistake but he wouldn't tell me why. Like I'm supposed to do whatever he tells me just because he says to. And then he sent me off to a meeting today with Simone O'Neil without bothering to tell me that she's a friend of his. Oh! *And* she's Evangeline Delahunt's daughter. I don't think I said anything to Simone I shouldn't have, but Ox should have told me."

Gabriel listened to the whole spiel without interrupting. "Ah. I see. He didn't give you the whole history, eh? Well. He probably should have. Fire him. Be done with it."

I gave him a look. "You know I don't want to fire him. I just want him to stop doing stuff like this."

"Stuff like what?"

"Like I just told you. Were you even listening?"

Gabriel brushed my cheek with the backs of his fingers, and a slow burn started deep inside me. "Yes. I was listening."

Sexy Cajun and tequila are a lethal combination. I might have forgotten all about being angry if Ox and Isabeau hadn't walked through the door right then. Such rotten timing!

Ox acted as if he didn't see me—which only inflamed me more. Especially since Isabeau gave me a little wave as they headed toward our usual table. Anger and Sexy Cajun had a little tug-of-war but anger won out.

I hopped off my stool and grabbed my drink. "Don't you dare serve him until I get a few answers," I warned Gabriel and set off across the bar.

Ox looked annoyed when I dropped into the seat beside

his. I didn't care. Right then I could have taught him a few things about annoyed. The music on the PA system blared, making it almost impossible to carry on a conversation. I didn't care about that either. "Why didn't you tell me that Simone O'Neil is Evangeline Delahunt's daughter?"

Ox stared at me for a long moment. "You didn't ask."

"Are you kidding me? I had to ask? That's nuts! You also didn't tell me that you know Simone well. She said to tell you hello and she's looking forward to working with you again. So what's the deal? How do you know her, and why did Philippe refuse to work for her mother?"

"This isn't the place," Ox said.

"That's a lame excuse. Just where is the place, Ox? This place was good enough when you decided to tell me how I was signing Zydeco's death warrant. What's so special about your story that you can't tell it here?"

Slowly, he turned his head until our eyes met. "You don't know what you're asking."

I was *so* tired of the power struggle between us. "That's kind of the point, isn't it? Why don't you put yourself in my place for five minutes? Think about how you'd feel if I knew something important about a job but didn't tell you. Or how you'd feel if every time you made a decision, I challenged you."

Isabeau said something conciliatory. I tuned her out. This was between Ox and me.

Ox's nostrils flared and his eyes flashed. "What do you want me to say, Rita? That you're right? Okay. You're right. You feel better now?"

"No! I don't feel better at all. I thought we were friends. I thought we were working together. I thought we'd put all of this"—I waved my hands around as if I could pluck the right word out of the air—"this stupid . . . *this* behind us.

What do you want from me? What will it take to get you on my side for once?"

"You think I'm not your friend, Rita? Really? Has it ever occurred to you that maybe I don't tell you things because I *am* your friend? There are some things it's best not to know."

I was vaguely aware of Isabeau wandering away. Maybe that should have warned me that something big was coming, but it didn't.

"How could not knowing that Evangeline Delahunt is Simone O'Neil's mother be best for me? You let me walk into that meeting without all the facts. I could have said something completely inappropriate. I could have ruined everything for all of us because you withheld information from me. So who's signing Zydeco's death warrant now?"

Ox's breathing had become labored, and his eyes had narrowed to tiny slits. "You want the truth? Fine. I didn't tell you about Simone and Evangeline because I thought if you knew, you might find out the rest of the story."

"The rest of what story? Why would I care?"

"You really want to know?" he said. "Okay, here it is. Before Philippe left here for pastry school, Evangeline set her sights on him. She thought he'd make a perfect husband for Simone and the perfect son-in-law for her. He had the right credentials, the right breeding, and the right social standing. She did everything she could to push them together."

I blinked a couple of times. It explained why Philippe had resisted working with them, but I wasn't sure why Ox thought it would upset me. Learning about an old girlfriend from before he even met me wasn't going to send me into a tailspin. "So?"

"It wasn't just Evangeline who was trying to push them together, Rita." Ox turned in his seat to face me, and gave me a look full of meaning, like he expected me to put two and two together so he wouldn't have to keep talking.

I tried, but came up blank.

Ox closed his eyes and let out a deep breath. "Miss Frankie wanted the match, too. She wanted Simone Delahunt— O'Neil now—to be her daughter-in-law. She was already planning the wedding, the reception, the whole shebang, when Philippe left for Chicago."

My stomach lurched and my head began to swim. I'd worked through most of my issues with Philippe, but knowing that Miss Frankie had handpicked someone else to be his wife brought up all the issues I'd struggled with since I was a kid.

"You want the rest?" Ox asked.

"There's more?"

"You know Miss Frankie. She didn't give up hope for a while."

The margaritas churned again. "How long is 'a while'?"

"A while," Ox said. Then his expression softened. Oh God, was that pity I saw? "She did give up eventually and got completely on board with you and Philippe."

I couldn't make myself ask when that transformation had taken place. Was it before we got married or after? I realized that Ox had been right in the first place. There are some things I didn't want to know.

Miss Frankie told me often that she loved me. That I was like a daughter to her. But I wondered now if she was telling the truth when she said those things. Or was that just her way of manipulating me to stay in New Orleans so she wouldn't be alone?

My stomach flopped hard. I lurched to my feet and clapped both hands over my mouth as I tried to get out of my chair and away from the table. I raced to the ladies' room. Or maybe *raced* is the wrong word. I stumbled over feet and purses and chairs and table legs, but I finally made it through the crowds of happy, laughing people and threw myself through the door. I bounced off a woman who staggered out as I burst in and lunged into a stall just in time.

If I could give one piece of advice, it would be this: Never, ever, *ever* get sick in the ladies' room at a bar.

Nineteen

❦

I spent most of Wednesday swallowing ibuprofen and trying to calm my upset stomach. I also spent it trying to avoid Ox. I wasn't ready to talk to him yet. Actually, I wasn't really ready to talk to anyone, so I buried myself in paperwork, some of which was actually necessary.

Edie left me alone for the most part, except asking me to cover for her when she had to go to the ladies' room. Since she was just a few weeks from delivering a baby, though, her visits ended up being roughly five minutes apart. While she was gone, I fielded a few calls and played some solitaire on her computer, and I thought a lot about the cake for the Belle Lune Ball.

The ball would take place in January, so I wanted to avoid flavors too closely associated with the holidays, such as spice or chocolate-peppermint. Red velvet, though a traditional favorite in the South, would be both too ordinary and much too heavy for what I wanted. I wanted the flavor, filling, and icing to match well with the decorations, which meant they should be light and bright—but summery, citrusy flavors (like Aunt Margaret's pea-pickin' cake) would be out of place in the winter.

It may have looked like I was killing time, but I was actually very busy. This is why creative people often get a bum rap. We spend a lot of time in our heads thinking, planning, considering ideas, and tossing out the obviously bad ones before we ever take a step that someone else can see. Simone O'Neil had seemed enthusiastic about the cake design I'd sketched for her the day before, but until I had flavors in mind, I couldn't even begin to start planning in earnest.

During what was surely Edie's two-hundredth visit to the bathroom, while I was focused on a winning hand of solitaire, the front door opened and a large pot of Shasta daisies walked through it. We don't take walk-in clients at Zydeco, so seeing something walk through the door unannounced would have been unusual even if it hadn't been a pot of flowers.

The flowers settled on Edie's desk, and River appeared from behind them. He's a good-looking guy with short dark hair and a friendly smile. Sometimes he wears glasses. Sometimes he doesn't. He was wearing them today, and I thought they gave him a sincere look.

Upon first meeting, you'd never guess that he was Sparkle's brother. She's dark and goth and chronically annoyed by the world. He's the complete opposite. But then, to hear them talk about their childhood in the commune and their mother's utter lack of concern over details like the names of the men she'd slept with, there was a chance they weren't actually related by blood. Neither of them had any proof that the woman who'd raised them was actually their biological mother, and apparently, she'd been a bit vague on that point as well. Absent a rash of DNA tests, I didn't think anyone would ever know for sure.

River looked disappointed that I wasn't Edie. He nodded toward the megasized drink cup beside the computer and asked, "Is she in?"

I leaned over to get a better look at the flowers. The pot was ceramic and whimsical—pink with green polka dots and a handle that made it look like a giant teacup. I liked it, but I couldn't predict Edie's reaction. "She's here, just away from her desk for a minute. You're welcome to wait."

He glanced around nervously and then sat. "How's she doing?"

"You haven't talked to her?"

"I've tried. Believe me, I've tried. She won't answer my calls, won't reply to my texts, and won't respond to any of the messages I've left. I'm running out of ideas. If the flowers don't work, it may be the end of the road for me."

I gave him a noncommittal smile—one that I hoped conveyed, *I understand but I won't get involved*, then turned back toward the computer. "Well, let's hope the flowers work."

Full of nervous energy, River stood and took a couple of steps toward the front door. I pretended not to watch as he hesitated, pivoted on the balls of his feet, and strode back to the chair he'd just vacated. "She's driving me nuts, you know."

I wanted to welcome him to my world, but I thought that might sound rude so I stated the obvious instead. "She's eight months pregnant."

"It's more than that." He sat on the edge of his seat and leaned forward. "I thought she and I had a connection, you know? I mean, that night we met at the Dizzy Duke, we just . . . clicked. I had no idea about the baby until I came back to the States. If I'd known . . ."

He looked so miserable I decided to break my noninterference rule, just a little. "I know. She told me. Which means *she* knows that. Edie never expected you to come back at all, and she had absolutely no idea you were Sparkle's brother. I think it threw her for a major loop. She's still trying to absorb it."

"Yeah, well, that makes two of us. I had no idea she worked with my sister either, but I don't consider it a disaster. She does."

I abandoned my computer game and linked my hands together on the desk. "Would it have made a difference? If you had known who she was, I mean. Would you have done things differently?"

He rubbed his neck and hung his head. "Yes. No." His head came up again. "I don't know. Maybe. But I didn't know, and I didn't do things differently. And neither did she, by the way. So now this is the hand we've been dealt and we need to accept it. Why is she acting like I did something horrible to her?"

"I don't think that's what she's feeling," I said. I wondered how much to share, but I didn't have a lot to work with. Edie doesn't confide much. Also, I'm new at this BFF thing. So while I didn't want to cross the line, I wasn't even sure where the line here was.

"I don't think she blames you for getting her pregnant," I said. "That would be silly. It takes two. I think she's scared to death that you won't be there for her and the baby down the road when things get tough."

"I've told her a million times that I'll be there. That's my kid she's carrying."

"Not necessarily a slam-dunk argument," I said. "Sharing

DNA with a child doesn't automatically qualify someone for Father of the Year."

"You don't have to tell me," River said with a humorless laugh. "I know what it's like to grow up without a dad. I know what it's like to wonder who your dad is and whether he even knows you exist. There's no way in hell I want my kid to go through that."

"For what it's worth, I believe you. And I'm a pretty hard sell. But Edie's the one with the baby kicking her insides all hours of the night." I heard a door open down the hall so I lowered my voice and gave him my best counsel. "Just hang in there. It takes time to build trust. If you don't give up, eventually she'll realize that you mean what you say."

Edie waddled back into the reception area, saw River sitting there and the flowers on her desk, and burst into tears. "What are you doing here?" she demanded. "What is *this*?"

He stood uncertainly. "I came to see you. We need to talk."

That was my cue to vamoose, so I beat a hasty retreat into my office and closed the door to give them some privacy. I'd briefly considered leaving the door open a crack so I could hear what was going on, but decided that would be crass.

I went back to work, opening a new game of solitaire and trying to remember what I'd been thinking about when River arrived. Before I even found the first ace, the phone rang. Not wanting the call to give Edie an excuse to avoid talking to River, I snagged the phone myself.

"Ms. Lucero? That you? Deputy Georgie Tucker here. You remember me from the Terrebonne Parish Sheriff's Department?"

Even though I'd given her my number, she was still the last person I'd expected to hear from while I was at work. "Of course I remember. Are you calling with news about the case? Have you figured out who killed Silas Laroche?" I really hoped she would say yes, and that it was anyone except Bernice's cousin Eskil. I couldn't keep running back and forth to Baie Rebelle, and I had a feeling that's exactly what I'd be doing as long as Miss Frankie and Bernice were there.

Not that I was ready to see Miss Frankie. I was still working out how I felt about knowing she'd handpicked another woman to be Philippe's wife, and had apparently opposed Philippe's decision to choose me instead.

"Not yet, I'm afraid," Georgie said. "We're working on it, though."

"Do you have any leads? Were you able to identify any fingerprints on that toilet tank lid?"

"We have a few leads, but honestly not many. No usable prints on the murder weapon, but we're not letting that get us down. Listen, the reason I called is that I need to get an official statement from you. I should've taken care of that while you were here, but I thought I had what I needed. Turns out, I was wrong."

I do my best to cooperate with the police, especially when they're not accusing me of anything, and I was feeling especially cooperative that morning. "No problem. Do you want to do it now or make an appointment to talk later?" I was good either way. I mean, I did have an important solitaire game going, but I could put that off to do my civic duty.

"I wish I could do it over the phone," Georgie said, "but Sheriff Argyle is insisting that I get your statement in person, complete with original signature."

"Oh." My eagerness to cooperate evaporated, but I saw nothing wrong with negotiating. "Any chance you could come to New Orleans, or do I need to go all the way back to Baie Rebelle? Or could we split the difference and do this in Houma?"

"Baie Rebelle, if you don't mind. I'll be down there all day tomorrow so we could meet up whenever it's good for you."

I did mind, but what was the point of saying so? I didn't want to make a fuss about Georgie's request and look as if I had something to hide. "Okay. I'll drive down in the morning. Where should I meet you?"

"You know the Gator Pit? It's a bar in town."

"The one next to T-Rex's? Yeah, I know it."

"It opens at eleven for lunch. How about we meet then? Is that okay with you?"

I said I'd see her then and hung up the phone. This would be my third trip to Baie Rebelle in less than a week. Maybe I should think about starting a shuttle service. It might be a great way to supplement my income.

I pulled up in front of the Gator Pit right on time on Thursday morning. I didn't see Georgie's patrol car, but I trusted that she'd be there soon. With a few minutes to kill, I decided to wait inside so I could see how the locals lived. I almost changed my mind when I opened the door, but by then I'd already committed to the adventure and I like to follow through with what I start.

The Gator Pit was a small dark room with a short bar on one wall and six small round tables for customers. Cheap accordion-pleated paper jack-o'-lanterns and bats drooped on the tables, and a couple of dusty plastic ghosts bobbed on fishing line overhead. All the tables were empty, but a couple of bearded men sat at the bar. They were so dirty and hairy I thought they could have passed for the rougarou. The fact that they were sharing hunting stories with a long-haired bartender did little to reassure me.

Several dim lights hung from wooden ceiling beams, but

they barely chased away the gloom. The door shut behind me and I felt my way toward one of the tables.

As soon as I sat down, a middle-aged woman with long curly hair held back with a headband tossed a napkin on the table in front of me. A pair of new-looking jeans stretched across her broad hips, and a too-small T-shirt hugged every curve above her waist and showed an impressive cleavage. "What can I get you, hon?"

"Diet Pepsi?" I said hopefully.

"Diet Coke okay?"

"That's fine. Thanks."

"You're new around here, aren't you?"

I gave her a second look, wondering if I'd seen her before. She didn't look familiar, so I shrugged and shook my head. "Just visiting."

Both hunters glanced at me and the waitress asked, "Oh? You have folks around here?"

People in small towns can be friendly, but they can also be suspicious of strangers. Folks in the swamps of Louisiana are generally considered more suspicious than most. Under normal circumstances, establishing my tenuous connection to the Percifields might have been smart, but two things stopped me. First, I assumed that the murder of Silas Laroche was front and center in everyone's mind; and second, I wasn't sure I wanted these potential suspects to know that I was the one who'd found the body—at least not while I was alone.

I smiled and shook my head. "No relatives, I'm afraid."

They all waited expectantly, as if my next move was to offer my family history.

I tried not to look nervous and turned the tables on her. "Have you lived here long?"

"All my life." Her answer was cool and crisp. "Sure I can't get you anything else?"

I assured her that I would be fine with the soda and settled back to wait for Georgie. Five minutes later, I realized this was going to be a long wait. Two more customers wandered in. One of the originals at the bar wandered out. Those were the highlights.

The waitress was obviously friends with everyone there. She joked with customers about inconsequential things and argued mildly with the bartender about inventory and her schedule. She wanted Saturday off. He said their deal was one Saturday a month and reminded her she'd taken off the previous Saturday.

I swallowed a yawn and chided myself for forgetting to bring a book. Not that it mattered. It was so dark in there, I wouldn't have been able to see the words on a page. I briefly considered taking a nap, but I put my elbow in something sticky on the table and changed my mind.

I'm not sure how long I'd been sitting there when the door opened and Junior Laroche ambled inside. My day brightened considerably. At least now my eavesdropping had the potential to be interesting. Junior greeted his friends and neighbors and nodded to the waitress. He ordered a beer and perched on a bar stool.

Maybe I should strike up a friendly conversation with him. Or maybe I should just keep listening to see if he said something important. I contemplated the options for about three seconds, decided he'd probably say more to friends than he would to me, and scooted back into the shadows so I could implement Plan B.

For the first little while, the conversation was blindingly dull. The guys talked about hunting and fishing and debated the merits of different types of bait and the use of treble hooks when fishing alligators out in the open. Apparently the waitress also dipped her toe (figuratively) into the swamp now and then because she offered an opinion or two of her own between wiping down tables and sweeping the floor.

I found myself drifting off and trying to ignore the nudge from my conscience that told me I should check up on Miss Frankie and Bernice while I was in town. At some point the waitress stopped cleaning, and sat down beside Junior. I didn't notice until Junior raised his voice and thumped the bar with his fist, which pulled me rudely away from my daydreaming.

"You're not listening to me, Nettie. Kale needs boundaries. He's running around town like a loose cannon."

The waitress was Nettie? Silas Laroche's widow? Well, well, well. I made a real effort to pay attention.

Nettie tried to placate her brother-in-law. "He's upset, Junior. I know you don't care about Silas, but Kale always cared about his daddy, for all the good it did him."

"The boy's too damned soft," Junior complained. "It gets him into trouble. So his old man never cared about him. So what? My mama always liked my brother best. Did I let that bother me? Hell no. That kid's got to toughen up, Nettie. He's got to start doing what's expected of him. That's not going to happen if you keep coddling him."

Nettie left her seat and slipped behind the bar, where she started putting away a stack of clean glasses. I couldn't be sure, but I suspected she wanted to keep her hands busy so she wouldn't punch Junior in the face.

"I don't coddle him," she said in a low voice. "But I don't expect him to just shrug off all the crap life has heaped on him either. He's got a lot to work through. It wasn't his fault Silas took off the way he did."

"It wasn't my fault either," Junior said. All at once his voice lost its angry spark. He leaned up from his stool and touched her cheek. "Taking care of the two of you wasn't my responsibility, Nettie, but I did it anyway. Why do you think I did that? For the fun of it?"

Nettie looked too stunned by his touch for me to think they'd been having an affair. I wondered what he had up his sleeve. "You know I appreciate all you've done, Junior. You've been better to the both of us than Silas ever was."

"Then talk to Kale. Convince him to do the right thing."

Nettie looked like a deer caught in the headlights, but she nodded slowly. "I'll talk to him but I can't promise he'll do what I say."

Junior pulled his hand away from her face and smiled. "You can convince him, baby. I know you can. Just tell him how much it'll mean to you. And remind him that if he comes to work for me, he'll be building his future. He can help get things back on track for all of us. Isn't that what we both want?"

I don't know what Nettie's answer would have been because that was when Georgie arrived—thirty minutes late—and Junior beat a hasty retreat. He left so quickly I wondered if he was trying to avoid being in the same place with the sheriff's deputy. Maybe his rapid departure had nothing to do with Georgie's sudden arrival, but it looked that way to me. Gut instinct told me that Junior Laroche had more than one trick up his sleeve, and when my gut started speaking, I tried to listen.

Twenty

❧

Georgie didn't look twice at Junior. She just planted herself across from me and tossed a clipboard onto the table. With a heavy sigh, she tugged off her cap and dropped it beside the clipboard. I thought she looked tired. Even her freckles seemed faded.

"Sorry to keep you waiting. I got tied up on a call." She pulled a pen from her pocket and sat with it poised to write. "You ready to do this?"

"Sure." I glanced at the door. "But before we get started, did you see that?"

Georgie followed my gaze. The bartender was watching something on a small black-and-white TV behind the bar. Nettie was chatting with the two men still bellied up to it. "See what?"

"Did you notice how quickly Junior left when you walked

in? What do you know about him? Do you think he could have killed his brother?"

Georgie gave that a moment's thought and then shrugged it off. "Sure he *could* have, but why would he? Silas didn't have anything Junior wanted. Junior had it all. He had the money, the property. I mean, no, he doesn't have a wife or kids, but he has a good relationship with Silas's family. Way better than Silas did, that's for sure."

"I suppose you're right," I said reluctantly. There was something about the way Junior had touched Nettie's cheek—and her reaction to it—that made me uneasy. "You don't think he and Nettie are having an affair, do you?"

Georgie's eyes grew a little wider. "*You* think so?"

"Not really," I said quickly. "It's just they were discussing Kale, and Junior—" I broke off and shook my head. "He touched her face but I could swear she seemed surprised by it. Do you think it's possible that he's been waiting for his brother to die so he could make his move?"

Georgie snorted softly, "Would he really wait around for twenty years? Why wait all that time to make his move?"

"It does seem unlikely," I agreed. "Especially if it's true that their father cut Silas out of his will."

"That's pretty much common knowledge around here. The way I hear it, the old man was furious when Silas turned his back on his legacy."

"Junior said Silas did that because he doesn't believe that people can actually own property. Is that right?"

Georgie put down her pen and nodded. "Silas was a weird guy. In general, the people out here aren't too fond of rules and regulations, but most folks are real respectful of the rules when it comes to hunting and fishing. They know where they can go and they're careful not to encroach on each other's territory. But Silas didn't care. He had the idea that owning property was some kind of abomination against nature. He said that God made it for everyone to use. And he saw nothing wrong with taking the catch right off someone else's line or hunting out of season."

"He forgot that God wasn't happy about stealing?"

"Oh, Silas didn't consider that stealing," Georgie said. "In his mind, anyone who tried to claim ownership was taking away from everyone else. You know he and Eskil butted heads over that very thing, right?"

I nodded. "But Eskil says he's innocent, and I believe him. Was Silas ever arrested?"

Georgie put the pen down and pulled on her hair to tighten her ponytail. "He never took more than he needed to survive, so it's not like he was out there every day. We'd drive out to his place and make sure he knew we were watching, but it was hard to catch him at it. I tried for a while to pin him down on the other side, maybe selling hides or hauling a gator to the buyer, but I didn't have any luck. He lived off the land mostly, but you'd see him in town here from time to time picking up supplies from T-Rex. I don't know where he got the money to keep himself in chewing tobacco and coffee, but he always seemed to have a stash of cash."

It was a puzzle for sure. Silas didn't seem to have anything that anybody wanted. Not only that, it seemed he hadn't wanted anything from anybody. Yes, there was Silas's habit of poaching from his neighbors. But if he'd been doing that for two decades, why would anybody go off the deep end and kill him now?

There was only one other motive I could see. For twenty years Eskil had believed that Silas was responsible for Uncle Cooch's disappearance. There seemed to be no reason for Eskil to suddenly go crazy and take Silas out—unless he'd recently found evidence he wasn't telling anyone about. The chances of getting Eskil to 'fess up were remote, but maybe someone else in Baie Rebelle could fill in the pieces. Of course, to follow up on that possibility, I'd have to stay in Baie Rebelle and talk to everyone I could.

And that just wasn't going to happen.

About an hour later I finished giving my statement and left the bar. Georgie stayed behind to talk with Nettie, and while I was interested in hearing what Nettie had to say, I didn't want to spend even one more minute in that musty-smelling place. I popped the lock on the Mercedes and was about to get inside when a white Ford Ranger sped past me on the road. It reached the intersection leading to Aunt Margaret's house and drove straight through.

From where I stood, I couldn't see the driver, but I sure wanted to know who it was. The way I saw it, I could do one of three things: Go back to New Orleans and ignore everyone and everything else, drive over to Aunt Margaret's and check on Miss Frankie and Bernice, or follow the truck. It was a no-brainer really. I couldn't just drive off and ignore the truck, and I was in no hurry to look Miss Frankie in the eye.

I backed out as quickly as I could and gunned the engine as I pulled onto the road. My tires spun, then finally found traction. The Mercedes shot forward, spitting dirt and tiny rocks behind me. *Yee-haw!*

I'm no expert on tailing someone without getting caught, but how hard could it be? I'd just hang back a bit, but not so far that I lost sight of the truck. If the driver noticed me, I hoped he'd just think I was checking out the scenery.

Turns out tailing someone isn't as easy as it sounds. The Ranger and I were the only cars on the road, which made it difficult to disguise the fact that I was in hot pursuit. I held back as far as I dared but the truck barreled along at a fast clip, and that made it hard to keep up on unfamiliar roads.

We whipped past JL Charters and out into the country, where the houses were even fewer and farther between. The truck zipped over a narrow wooden bridge and I followed a few minutes later. On the other side of the bridge, the pavement ended and the road narrowed—a feat that I would have previously thought impossible. I wasn't convinced that the dirt road was even wide enough for all four tires to remain on the track at the same time.

I didn't want to slow down and lose the Ranger, but I wasn't confident enough in my driving skills to throw caution to the wind. And besides, the road dropped off sharply into deep ditches on both sides of the road. They reminded me of the terrain where I'd found Silas Laroche's body, and I did not want to end up in one of them.

Chewing on disappointment, I slowed down. That's when I realized that the Ranger was kicking up dust as it traveled on the unpaved road and the dust didn't settle immediately. That meant that I didn't have to keep the Ranger itself in sight. I just had to follow the cloud of dust.

That worked pretty well for a while, but eventually I dropped so far behind I was no longer eating the Ranger's dust and the trees were so thick I couldn't pick up the trail again. Hoping I'd spot the truck, I kept going for a few miles but the Ranger had disappeared.

I hate losing and I hate giving up, but even I knew it would be a waste of time and gas to keep going. Unfortunately, figuring out how to turn around and go back presented a problem. I'd passed a couple of narrow dirt cutoffs that I just knew headed straight into alligator country. It had been a long time since I'd seen an actual road. The Mercedes was too big to make a U-turn, and I was afraid I'd slide into a ditch if I tried to make a three-, four-, or even an eleven-point turn.

I wasn't all that familiar with the geography, but I knew that Baie Rebelle sat on a narrow piece of solid land in the middle of water and uninhabitable marshland. I didn't know how much farther the road would continue or what I'd find when I reached land's end.

After a while, I saw a slight widening in the road that I thought might indicate a path or a driveway. With a lot of concentration, I got myself turned around and headed back toward Baie Rebelle's version of civilization. I'd done my best. Now it was time to go home and do something productive. Instead of chasing trucks through the swamp, I should have been looking for recipes that would whet the appetites of New Orleans's elite.

Just over the bridge, where the road widened into almost two whole lanes again, something large and furry darted out of the trees and into my path. I slammed on the brakes, hit a patch of gravel, and careened out of control.

My parents died in a car when I was a girl, and I frequently have dreams of following them the same way. In a panic, I overcorrected and sent the Mercedes on a collision course with a stand of trees on the other side of the road. Time seemed to slow and my brain turned to sludge. Every thought in my head felt like it took half an hour to form.

I told myself over and over to stay calm, but it was a losing battle. I pumped the brakes and cranked the wheel as hard as I could toward the middle of the road, but my tires hit more gravel and I watched in horror as my worst nightmare played out in front of me.

The car slammed into a ditch, bounced from the impact, and hit the trees with a tooth-rattling jolt. The air bag deployed and the air around me filled with smoke and a strong sickly sweet smell. I reached for the car door, but I couldn't see well enough to find the latch. Disoriented, I felt around where I thought it *should* be, but either I was hopelessly confused or someone had moved it when I wasn't looking.

The air bag deflated a bit and the sweet odor gave way to the smell of burnt plastic. My lungs burned with every breath and my head buzzed. The seat belt strained to hold me in place and rubbed a spot on the side of my neck so that it felt raw. I desperately wanted out of that car, but from the angle of my body, I suspected that might not be possible without help.

A fresh wave of panic surged up inside and took over. I clawed at the door for what felt like eternity. I cursed and prayed and tried to rip off Mambo Odessa's beads, which I'd kept forgetting to take off when I had the chance. I didn't want to breathe, but holding my breath until help came wasn't an option. After a long time, my fingers brushed the automatic window panel and I felt a glimmer of hope.

I pressed, pulled, and hammered on the panel until one of the back windows eased down enough to let out some of that nasty chemical smoke. My vision cleared enough for me to see where I was. The good news was that my position wasn't as precarious as I'd first thought. The bad? I wouldn't be driving out of there.

I tried to open the door but it was jammed shut, making escape impossible, or at least more difficult. With effort, I got all four windows down at least partway before the engine coughed a couple of times and died. I mentally compared the partially open window with my hips and made a solemn vow to exercise more if I ever got out of there.

With no way out, I did my best to stay focused on the positive. I was alive. That was a big plus. I leaned my head out the window so I could gulp some air. It was cleaner than the air inside the car, but it was still filled with air bag powder. After a few minutes I regained enough presence of mind to check my cell phone. It took ages for me to make out what was on the screen, but when I did, I wasn't surprised. No service.

I did some more positive thinking, but it's not nearly as effective in a crisis as self-help gurus want us to believe. I didn't feel positive, only slightly less negative. Until, out of nowhere, I thought about Edie and the baby and my promise to be the kid's godmother. Sadness landed on my chest and pressed hard. I'd never had kids of my own, and now I might never even get the chance to see Edie's baby.

Tears burned my eyes and regret put a thick lump in my throat. I cried until my nose was too stuffed to breathe, which meant that I had to dig around until I found the stack of unused napkins I'd stockpiled from clandestine trips to fast-food restaurants. Yes, I'm a foodie but I'm not a snob.

Clearly feeling sorry for myself, I mopped up the tears and blew my nose, and then I decided to do something more productive than wallow in self-pity. I should take stock and list what I had on my side and what was working against me. Maybe that would help me find a way to escape.

Number one: I was stuck in the middle of nowhere in a car that wasn't going anywhere, holding a cell phone that didn't have a single bar of service. (I lumped them all together because I knew that separately they'd overwhelm me.) Either way, they landed firmly in the "against" column.

Number two: I was surrounded by wildlife that might or might not eat me for lunch. Definitely against.

Number three: I hadn't eaten anything since I left New Orleans hours earlier when I'd scarfed down an Asiago cheese bagel smeared with cream cheese. More against.

That brought me to my final conclusion: I was going to die.

The "for" column remained annoyingly empty, but if I didn't want to die (and I didn't), I would have to do something.

It took some work, but I finally got the seat belt unbuckled. Now that I was free, I slid down the seat toward the passenger's door, but dug my feet in and stopped myself from smashing into it.

Okay. That was good. Next step: Find food. I was almost positive I had a Halloween-sized Snickers in my purse. (Don't ask.) The candy wouldn't sustain me for long, so I scrounged in the glove box to see if I had anything else I could call food. There I found three linty breath mints, which I set aside in case the other supplies ran out. The best find of all was half a bottle of water, which apparently had been dislodged from under the seat during the crash. I didn't know how long it had been hanging around in the car. I hoped it was mine and not water left over from when this was Philippe's car, but beggars can't be choosers.

For a long time I sat there alternately contemplating my demise and the best way to remove lint from mints of indeterminate age. The sun had moved toward the west and shadows leaned across the road. A small flock of monarch butterflies flying south fluttered around for a while, and I tried to remember encouraging passages from the Bible. They always seemed to help Aunt Yolanda, but it had been a while. Besides, "Fear not," the only thing I could call up from memory, had to do with walking through the valley of death. Considering where I was, I didn't find that particularly comforting.

After a long time a strange noise caught my attention, but it took a little while to recognize it as a car's engine. I sat up as straight as I could and noticed dust floating up above the trees. A few minutes later the white Ford Ranger rattled over the bridge and came to a stop beside me.

Its driver, a young man with shaggy brown hair, leaned across the seat and called out to me. "You all right, ma'am?"

I blinked back fresh, hot tears and said, "I'm not seriously hurt, but I don't think I'm going anywhere and I can't get the door open."

He pulled off to the side of the road and came back to help me. My knees felt like rubber and my head felt as if someone had put it in a vise. My lungs and chest hurt like crazy, but at least I wasn't going to die in the car and turn into alligator bait. All things considered, I was a pretty lucky woman.

Twenty-one

❦

My rescuer wasn't carrying any spare toilet tank lids in the back of his truck. I know because I checked as he helped me up the road and into the front seat. There were three paint cans, though, and a number of other dangerous-looking implements he could have used to end my life if that's what he wanted to do.

In spite of my aching lungs and throbbing head, I pulled together enough logic to reason that if he wanted me dead, he would've only had to drive on by and leave me where I was. That made me feel a little better.

In the side mirror I saw him lean into my car. A minute later, he jogged up the road toward me and handed me my keys. "Figured you might need these."

"Oh. Yeah." I slipped them into my pocket and wondered if the fissures in my skull were obvious from the outside.

The kid started the truck and we lurched back onto the road. "I can take you back into town. That okay with you?"

I could call Aunt Margaret's house from there so I said that would be fine.

"You new around here?"

I tried to shake my head and quickly decided that any movement from the neck up was a bad idea. Also from the neck down. "No, I'm just passing through."

He looked surprised. "There ain't no through road out this way. Where'd you come from?"

Seriously? He hadn't noticed me tailing him before? "I, uh—I took the wrong road out of town, I guess. I realized my mistake and turned around, but then something ran in front of my car and I—" I waved a hand vaguely over my head. "Well, the rest is history, I guess. I'm Rita, by the way."

"Kale," he said with a grin. "You're lucky I came along when I did."

Double-lucky. Too bad I was so out of it—what were the odds that I'd be rescued by one of the people I most wanted to talk to? "I know how fortunate I am," I said. "I'd almost finished planning my funeral when you came along." Too late, I realized how callous my little joke had been. "I'm sorry," I said. "I didn't mean—you just lost your father and that was a really insensitive thing to say."

Kale's smile vanished. "You know who I am?"

Oops. Note to self: Never try to interrogate a suspect on the sly when your brain has just been put through a blender. "I assumed," I said. "You said your name was Kale, and I was here in Baie Rebelle when your father died." I mumbled an explanation that wrapped up my connections to Bernice, Miss Frankie, and Aunt Margaret without going into detail.

Kale didn't say anything for a while and I started wondering about all those tools in the back of the truck. "So are you the lady who found him?" he asked, finally breaking the silence.

"Yeah."

"I thought you went back to New Orleans."

"I did. But the sheriff's department needed my statement, so I came down today to give it to Georgie."

Kale's hands tightened on the steering wheel. "They said he was in the ditch. Is that right?"

My heart ached for him, even as my brain wondered if that was a real question or one designed to make himself sound innocent. I didn't know if he was a murderer, but I hoped he wasn't. I *did* know that he was a kid who'd just lost his father. I understood how confused and alone he must feel. I wanted to say something that would make it easier for him, but what would that be? I decided to give it to him straight. "Yeah. He was. In the ditch."

His eyes flickered toward me. "Was there blood?"

"Not that I could see, but it was dark. The sheriff's deputy said he'd been hit on the head and that's what killed him, so I'm guessing there must've been some."

Kale nodded and chewed on that information for a few minutes. "Do you think he suffered?"

"I don't know. I never saw his face."

Kale's expression turned to stone. "No? That's too bad. I hope the sonofabitch died a slow, painful death."

Maybe his response should have frightened me. At the very least, it should have made me nervous. But I'd been angry with God and everyone on the planet for a long time after my parents died. I wasn't going to take his reaction at face value.

"Were the two of you close?" I asked softly, knowing the answer.

Kale let out a sharp one-note laugh. "Close? Me and

Silas? No. Haven't you heard how he walked away from us when I was two?"

"I've heard," I admitted. "I know that your uncle Junior stepped in and did what he could to take Silas's place. But I also saw you talking to Silas on Saturday night outside the bar." Okay, so I hadn't actually seen Kale's face, but I'd seen his truck and I was taking a not-so-wild guess.

"So what? You think I killed him?"

I turned my head a fraction of an inch, thinking it might be smart to watch his face more closely. Pain zinged along my spine, and the pressure in my head made it feel as if it would explode any second. "No," I said. "No, I don't."

He shot a belligerent look at me. "I could have, you know. I should have. Most of my life I wanted to."

"I'm not surprised. I can't even say that I blame you. But you didn't do it, did you?"

He shook his head. "No."

"Who else knew where he lived? Who might have gone there to see him?"

"Everybody knew where the house was," Kale said. "That wasn't a secret. The still, though. That was different."

Thoughts were churning slowly inside my head so it took me a while to realize what he'd just said. "Silas had a still? Are you sure?"

"Yeah. I'm sure."

Was that a coincidence, or had Eskil been right about Uncle Cooch's disappearance? My heart fluttered with excitement. "Do you know where it is?"

"Naw. I tried following him a few times out of curiosity. Had the idea that if I could find the still, I'd show him I was better'n him. Every time I tried, he lost me, though." He tapped his fingers on the steering wheel and grinned. "Couple of times I thought I might be getting close, but both times he took a few shots at me to scare me. It worked, too. I backed off."

Wow. Shooting at his own son to protect his illegal—and possibly stolen—moonshine operation? I guess Silas's aversion to ownership didn't extend to property taken from others. I'm no psychiatrist, but I diagnosed Silas as a certified looney tune. "How long did he have the still? Was it a recent thing?"

"He had it all my life, I guess. I wasn't supposed to know about it at all."

"You overheard him talking about it?"

"Not Silas," Kale corrected me. "A couple of the men in town. They were customers of his, I guess."

"And you're sure they were talking about Silas's still?"

Kale nodded. "They mentioned him by name, which is why I paid attention. There's always talk if you know how to listen."

A kid after my own heart. "Did you ever ask Silas about it?"

"Nope." Kale spit something out his window and wiped his chin with the back of his hand. "Me and him never talked at all until a month or so ago. He came and found me after church one day. He said he had something important to tell me. I didn't want nothing to do with him and I told him so. But that didn't stop him from trying."

"You didn't actually speak to him?"

"Sure I did. I told him to get the hell away from me."

"How did he react to that?"

"Same way he did to everything else. He didn't care. He just did whatever he wanted."

"So he kept trying to talk to you, but you don't have any idea what he wanted to tell you?"

Kale shook his head. "I didn't want to know. I wanted him to go to hell. The way he ignored Ma and me wasn't right."

We bounced over a series of ruts, and pain shot through my head.

Kale asked, "You don't think that's why Silas got killed, do you?"

"Because of whatever he wanted to tell you? I don't know. It's possible, but it also might have been completely unrelated. Does your mother have any idea what he wanted?"

Kale looked sheepish. "I never told her about him coming around. It would've upset her too much."

"Are you sure it would have upset her? Is there any chance she was still in love with your dad?"

Kale actually laughed. "Oh, *hell* no. I think she liked Junior better'n she liked Silas—and she don't like Junior all that much."

"Well, then why did she stay married to him? And why did she let Junior take care of her all these years?" The questions popped out before I could stop them. I winced at my own audacity.

"What is this? Freaking *CSI* or something?"

"No," I said quickly. "I'm not with the police or anything. I'm just curious. You have to admit, it's a strange situation. Your father walked out on your mother twenty years ago but he lived just a few miles away the whole time. She knew where to find him, but she never filed for divorce and she let her brother-in-law take care of her and help raise her son. Anybody would be curious."

"Yeah, but not everybody would be rude enough to ask about it," Kale shot back.

I dipped my head in agreement. "You're right. I'm sorry. I'm not feeling so good after the accident and I'm just trying to keep myself distracted." I told myself to let it drop, but Kale's assessment of Nettie's relationships with the Laroche brothers had piqued my curiosity.

"I only asked because I saw her talking to Junior earlier today. I'm pretty sure they were talking about you."

Kale curled his lip and cut a glance at me. "Let me guess. It was about me going to work for Junior?"

"Yeah. I take it you don't want to do that."

"Nope," he said, and fell silent. I was afraid I'd lost him, but finally he said, "I know that Eskil hated Silas."

"So I hear. Do you know why?"

Kale shrugged and this time he didn't answer.

"I heard that maybe Silas helped Cooch Percifield disappear years ago. Do you think he could have done that?"

Our friendship was cooling rapidly. "What's it to you?"

He'd been pretty honest with me—at least I thought he had—so I gave him a straight-ish answer. "Eskil's cousin Bernice is a friend of mine. She's worried about him. There are some people in town who think Eskil killed Silas, and if it's true that Silas helped Cooch disappear, Bernice might have good reason to worry. It would give Eskil a pretty solid motive, wouldn't it? So what do you think? Could Silas have done something to Cooch?"

"Sure. My old man was mean as a snake. But *why* would he?"

"The family still disappeared when Cooch did. Maybe Silas took over the operation."

Kale looked intrigued, but he didn't say anything. Junior's place loomed into view but Kale didn't even glance at it as we passed. "He used to give Eskil a rough time about Cooch disappearing the way he did," he said at last, "but I never thought it meant anything. Silas was mean, but he wasn't stupid. You can't be dumb and survive in a place like this. I think he knew what Eskil thought, and he got a charge out of acting like it was true."

Somewhere inside my head a bass drum of painful

throbbing began to beat a steady rhythm. The thought of arranging for a tow truck and waiting inside T-Rex's or the Gator Pit for someone to pick me up made me want to cry. I sighed, but it came out sounding more like a whimper.

"You okay?"

I offered up a weak smile. "Yeah. Just tired."

"Tell you what," he said. "I'll take you on up to Miss Margaret's if you want, but I've gotta stop by and take something to Ma first. You mind a quick detour?"

My smile gained a little strength. "I don't mind at all."

Twenty-two

Nettie Laroche lived in a small yellow house set back from the road behind a yard full of weeds and wild grass. If there had ever been a lawn, it had disappeared a while ago.

"This may take a few minutes," Kale warned. "Come on inside so you don't have to wait in the heat."

I didn't want to move, but I wasn't in the mood to bake either so I followed him up an uneven sidewalk to the back door. We stepped into a tiny kitchen with cluttered counters and dirty dishes strewn over the table. I thought there might be chairs around the table, but it was hard to be sure. All I could really see were empty plastic bags and stacks of paper. A small window unit blew cool air into the room, and I could hear a television playing somewhere in another part of the house. The scents of sausage and old coffee hung heavily in the air.

Kale wiped his feet on a mat and I followed his example. "Ma?" he shouted. "We got a visitor."

The television went silent and Nettie appeared in the doorway wearing a curious expression. She'd changed out of her jeans and T-shirt into a faded floral muumuu and a pair of pink fuzzy slippers, and she carried what looked like a whiskey and soda in her hand. She waved the glass in my direction. "I know you. Weren't you in the Pit earlier?"

"I was. My name's Rita Lucero."

"You were talking to Georgie."

"I was," I said again. "She needed a statement from me."

Nettie's eyes narrowed. "What kind of statement?"

"She's staying with the Percifields," Kale explained to his mother. "She's the one who found Silas."

I watched Nettie's reaction to the mention of her late husband's name, but her face gave nothing away. "Okay," she said slowly. "What are you doing with Kale?"

That was a perfectly legitimate question. I'd have wondered the same thing in her place. "I had an accident out there . . . somewhere. Your son was good enough to rescue me."

"I'm taking her to Miss Margaret's," Kale said as he clomped through the kitchen and looked inside the fridge. "I've got that paint you wanted in the back of the truck. Where do you want me to put it?"

Nettie leaned against the door frame and smiled at her son. "In the garage. I won't need it today."

Kale turned away from the fridge and filled a glass with water from the sink. My mouth was dry and my chest still hurt from breathing the air bag smoke. I willed him to offer me a glass, but apparently the domestic variety of Southern hospitality wasn't his thing.

"I hear you and Junior were talking about me today," he said to Nettie when he'd emptied the glass.

Her expression sobered. "Where'd you hear that?"

I thought the answer to that question was obvious, but

there *had* been other people in the bar, so maybe she wouldn't know it had come from me. Just in case, I kept my mouth shut and tried not to look guilty.

Kale put the glass next to the sink and leaned against the counter. "What does it matter? What did he want? The usual?"

"Of course. It's always the same old thing." Nettie let out a heavy sigh and her shoulders sagged. "Why are you being so stubborn? He only wants to make sure you have what's rightfully yours."

"Yeah. I'm sure that's why he's doing it." Kale rummaged in a cupboard near his head and found a box of crackers. He shook a few into his hand and dropped them one by one from his fist into his mouth. "Junior's all about the other guy."

"You're not the 'other guy,'" Nettie said with a scowl. "You're his nephew."

"Whatever." Kale shoved another handful of crackers into his mouth.

I was uncomfortable listening to their conversation, but it wasn't as if I was eavesdropping, so I tried not to feel guilty.

"Look," Nettie said, "I know Junior and I have had our arguments, but at least he cares. That's more than Silas ever did."

Pain flashed across Kale's face.

His mother didn't seem to notice. "All I'm asking is that you try the job. If Junior pushes too hard or asks you to do anything that makes you uncomfortable, then quit."

I wondered what kinds of things might fall into that category but I didn't ask. Mostly because I didn't want them to get nervous and stop talking. But also because my head was pounding and my face felt hot.

"I already don't like what he's doing," Kale told her. "And it's not like he wants me around. He just thinks I'm the best way to get to you."

Nettie did the same deer-in-the-headlights thing she'd done when Junior caressed her cheek at the Gator Pit. "That's crazy talk," she said when she'd gathered her wits.

I stopped dwelling on my throbbing head so I could use my energy to file away details of their conversation. All at once Kale seemed to remember I was there and held out the box to me. "Crackers?"

I was almost hungry enough to accept his offer, but I managed to resist. "No. Thanks. I'd appreciate some water, though. And if you have a phone, I'd like to make a call. It's long-distance, but I'll pay the charges. And if you know the number of a local towing service, I need to arrange for someone to pick up my car."

"Oh Lord. Where are my manners?" Nettie brushed past her son and fixed me some ice water. Kale went outside, probably to put the paint in the garage, and she handed me the glass with a smile and an apology. "Phone's in there," she said, nodding toward the living room. "Help yourself. There's no towing service out here, but Kale can help you get the car back to town. No need to pay for the calls."

When she left me alone, I dialed Sullivan's cell number but the call went straight to voice mail. Strike one. I left a brief message explaining that I needed a ride from Baie Rebelle to New Orleans and told him I'd call again when I had the chance. I repeated the process, this time with Gabriel's cell. He didn't answer either, so I left the same message for him.

I briefly considered calling Zydeco, but I didn't want to ask Ox for help. I shoved that idea on the "last resort" shelf in my head and slipped a ten under the phone just in case Nettie didn't make a fortune at the Gator Pit and her phone plan didn't include unlimited long-distance.

Kale had returned to the kitchen by the time I was

finished, and the two of them were talking quietly when I rejoined them.

"Sorry to talk about family stuff in front of you," Nettie said. "This kid of mine doesn't know a good thing when he sees it. He makes me crazy sometimes."

I don't like to weigh in on other people's problems, but since she'd pulled me into the conversation . . . "You think that his uncle's offer is a good one but Kale doesn't agree with you?"

She brushed some magazines and empty plastic bags from a chair and offered me a seat. "You don't know Junior, but he's a hard man. Tough. Unbending. And he's been worse than usual lately, so I understand why Kale doesn't want to work with him." She glanced at her son and went on. "But half of what Junior has belongs to Kale by rights. It's not Kale's fault his idiot daddy threw it all away. I know Junior will do right by Kale, but Kale's gotta give a little, too. He's gotta cooperate with Junior."

Kale's face turned to stone. "I'm not going to hang around hoping that someday he'll take pity on me. The land's his. The money's his. Just let it go, Ma. I'll make it on my own."

"You don't *have* to make it on your own," she said. "That's the point. I can bring Junior around. I just need time." She sighed with resignation and shook her head. "We'll talk about this later. We've got company."

"Yeah, and we're leaving." Kale opened the door and looked back at me. "You ready?"

Did I have a choice? I gulped down the rest of my water and followed him out to the truck. My head was still spinning from the wreck, and I felt more confused than ever. I couldn't see any reason for Nettie or Kale to have wanted Silas dead. It seemed far more likely that if one of them had been wandering around with an extra toilet tank lid and nothing to do on a Saturday night, they'd have paid Junior a visit. And yet Silas was the one lying in the morgue.

Factoring in what Kale had told me about Silas having a still, the only person with a solid reason for wanting Silas dead was the person whose name I wanted to clear. Poor Bernice. Poor Aunt Margaret. They wanted so badly for Eskil to be innocent, but it was looking less likely all the time.

Twenty-three

❦

Kale didn't say anything as we trudged back to the truck and I didn't pressure him to. Questions were zipping in and out of my head, but I'd already asked a lot and I didn't want to spook him. If I came on too strong, he might shut me out completely.

I listened to the hum of tires on the pavement and watched greenery turn into a blur as we sped along the road. And I realized that in this maze of trees and swamp, I had no idea where Silas Laroche had lived. Was it near Aunt Margaret's house? Was that why his killer had chosen to dump his body there? But why move the body in the first place? Why not just leave it where it fell?

Sullivan's theory that the killer wanted the body found was the only thing that made sense, but why? I stewed on that question for a while but I couldn't come up with an answer. I needed to know more about Silas before I could understand what had happened to him.

It wasn't that I didn't trust Georgie and the sheriff's department to do the job right. I kept thinking about Bernice and remembering the look on Aunt Margaret's face when she'd asked for my help. Which was why I finally broke the silence. "Out of curiosity, where did Silas live?"

Kale looked startled by the sound of my voice. "Down this road a bit."

"Close to the Percifields' place?"

He lifted one shoulder. "I guess. It's about ten miles on past Miss Margaret's house."

"So if you were going to Silas's house, you'd have to drive past Aunt Margaret's to get there? Is there any other way to get to and from Baie Rebelle?"

"Not by car. You could get there and back on the water, though. You can get anywhere on the water."

Yeah, that's what I was afraid of. "How many houses are there between the Percifields' and Silas's?"

"None," Kale said. "Why? What are you thinking?" Far from being put off by my questions, Kale seemed intrigued.

"I'm just wondering how easy it would be for someone to get to Silas's place without being noticed."

"Easy enough," Kale said. "You've seen how far back Miss Margaret's house is from the road. It's surrounded by trees. They might hear a car driving past but they probably wouldn't see it."

Which meant that although Eskil had (relatively) easy access to Silas's property, he wasn't alone. Almost anyone could have gone there and back without being seen. And that brought me right back to the question that seemed to have no logical answer: If Eskil had killed Silas, why would he cart the body home and dump it in his own ditch? It simply didn't make sense, and that was the only thing that kept me hoping the police would eventually be able to clear him.

We were drawing close to Aunt Margaret's house by that time and Kale surprised me by asking, "You want to see it?"

"See . . . what?"

"The old man's place. You want me to show you?"

Seriously? I'd have preferred to wait until I felt better, but I might not get another chance. "Why not?" I said, hoping I didn't seem too eager. It was a long shot, but maybe we'd come across something important. Something the sheriff's department had missed when they went over the crime scene. Even if we didn't, at least I'd know that I'd done my best to help Bernice's family.

Kale talked about the country as he drove, telling me about how life used to be in the swamp before the oil companies moved in and the Army Corps of Engineers began draining swampland and diverting the water. He was probably too young to have known the old ways personally, but obviously someone had educated him.

He pointed out things of interest, naming trees and types of birds in case I was curious. I wasn't really. I forgot most of what he said as soon as he said it, but I was surprised by the variety. If someone was interested in living off the land, the swamp seemed to be the right place for it.

"And over there?" Kale said as we crested a small hill. "See? Between the trees? That's Junior's property. That's where he's planning to build his new and improved charter company."

I leaned up to get a better look. I saw a broad expanse of water rimmed by cypress on one side and choked with lilies on the other. The one thing I didn't see was land. "It's water," I said in case Kale hadn't noticed.

"It's swamp. My grandpa bought it years ago. Junior's planning to drain it and build."

That surprised me. "Can he do that?"

"There's some red tape to jump through, but yeah. He's

been working on it for a few years now. He wants me in on it with him, but I don't like the idea. We're already losing something like twenty miles of swamp every year. We don't need to get rid of more."

I frowned thoughtfully. Okay, so I'm not a fan of the swamp, but it seemed like a big mistake to drain it and turn it into just another business district. "How soon will he start working on it?"

"I'm not sure. He was going great guns for a while, but about a month ago he slowed down. Maybe he's looking for money or something."

I glanced out over the water again and mumbled, "If that's the case, I hope he doesn't find it."

Kale shot an odd look at me and a slow smile curved his lips. "Yeah? Well, don't say that to him."

I laughed and pretended to zip my mouth shut. I wasn't sure what to make of Junior but I had no intention of antagonizing him.

We reached our destination a few minutes later. Access to Silas's house was by way of a trail just wide enough for a single vehicle. A double track had been matted down by tires over time, but the wild grass growing between the tracks made it clear that this path wasn't used often. At the end of the trail, a wooden shack leaned to one side and a ramshackle outhouse sat in tall grass behind it.

Junk dotted every inch of the clearing. Rusty farm implements, old tires, and spare wheels shared space with broken furniture, at least three toilets (I wondered if one had a missing lid), and a couple of stoves. A few monarch butterflies fluttered around the refuse, a touch of elegance and grace amid the clutter.

"Is this it?" I asked, sweeping my gaze across a porch heaped with refuse. "He lived here?"

Kale nodded. "Sad, huh?"

"For a man who didn't believe in owning anything, he sure had a lot of stuff."

"He didn't believe in owning anything God made," Kale corrected me. "At least that's what Ma told me. Like I said, I never actually talked to him except to tell him to leave me alone."

"Well, your mom should know."

Kale stopped in front of the shack and we both got out of the truck. "There's no crime scene tape," I said. "I guess that means the sheriff's department is finished out here."

Kale hooked his thumbs in his back pockets and looked around for a moment. "Yeah. I guess. Where do you think it happened?"

"I don't know, but Georgie said something about a stream. My first guess would be by the toilet closest to the water." I let him think about that for a moment. In spite of his brave claims that he felt nothing for his father, I knew he must feel something.

He toed the ground and made a face. "Bunch of worthless junk."

"One man's trash is another man's treasure," I said. "Why did he have the toilets if he didn't even have indoor plumbing?"

"How would I know?" Kale said. "He didn't talk to me for twenty years. I can't tell you why he did anything."

I stared around the clearing for a while. "You're sure he didn't give you any indication about why he wanted to talk to you? None at all?"

Kale shook his head. "He just said that he had something important to tell me. I was so pissed I wouldn't let him say anything else."

That was too bad. I had a feeling Silas might have been able to provide a few clues to his final days on earth. "Did he have any friends? Is there anybody who might know what he wanted to tell you?"

Kale's laughter bounced around the clearing. "No ma'am. Not that I know of anyway. Silas screwed everybody over at one time or another."

We fell silent for a moment and the sounds of frogs, lizards, and insects filled the air. A deep roar somewhere in the distance made me shudder. Even the insects stopped buzzing. It must have been an alligator, but it was easy to see how tales of mystical creatures like the rougarou got started.

"So who inherits all this?" I asked. "Is this your problem now?"

Kale snorted. "I don't want it. It's probably Ma's anyway."

"She's his widow now, so you might be right about that. He didn't own the land, did he?"

"Nope. This land belongs to the Dudley family."

That brought my head up fast. "Bernice's family?"

"I guess so. Those her husband's people? I don't know which one of 'em owns it legal, but they let Silas stay. I guess it was easier than trying to run him off." Kale brushed something from his shoulder. "You want to look inside the house?"

The idea of stepping into that ratty-looking shack made me shrink back. The whole place gave me the heebie-jeebies. I imagined all kinds of creepy-crawly things inside. Maybe there was also evidence in there, but somebody else would have to find it.

"No. I—I . . . no. I'm sure the sheriff has checked it out thoroughly. Have you ever been inside?"

Kale shook his head. "I told you, I've never been here before." He was visiting his father's house for the first time ever, and here I was turning up my nose.

I felt like a jerk. "Do you want to look inside?"

"Nope."

"You aren't curious about it?"

"Nope."

"Not even a little? Or did you sneak out here to see it for yourself when you thought you wouldn't get caught? Because I would have."

Kale ran a hand across his face. "Never. I was afraid of him, okay? He had a temper. A bad one. All my life I heard horror stories about the things he'd done and what kind of man he was. Everybody in town hated him. His own brother hated him, and I was scared spitless that I'd turn out just like him. So I thought that if I could stay far enough away from him, he wouldn't rub off on me."

His candid answer surprised me, but I was glad he was finally releasing some emotion. "And your mother? Did she hate him, too?"

"What do you think? He walked out on her. She had a hard life without him."

I glanced around and pointed out, "I think she might have had a harder life if he'd stayed."

Kale heaved a sigh and his head drooped. "Yeah. Probably."

"Why *did* she stay married to him, Kale? Most women would have cut their losses under those circumstances."

"She doesn't believe in divorce, I guess. And she wanted to make sure the family treated me right. Around here, family's important. Real important. But the Laroches aren't like most people. Except for Silas, things are more important to them than people. Junior has always been around when we needed something, but he only did it so he'd look good to his old daddy."

It was warm in the clearing. A trickle of sweat snaked down my back, encouraging me to cut the visit short. "This would be the daddy who cut Silas out of his will? Why would he care how Junior treated you?"

"He cut Silas out of his will because Silas threw away everything the old man worked for. I was okay with him because I didn't. That's all there is to it."

I wasn't so sure, but I only had gut instinct to go on. I dropped the subject and jerked my chin toward the garbage dump in front of us. "Do you want to go look out there?"

"Not really."

"Would you mind waiting for a minute while I do?"

Kale shook his head. "Go for it. Just watch out for snakes."

"Snakes?" I shuddered and froze mid-step. "What kind of snakes? Poisonous ones?"

"Some."

"Change of plans," I announced, and turned toward the truck instead. "Another time maybe."

Kale chuckled and walked past me toward the truck. I followed more slowly, checking the ground for anything that slithered. Just a few feet from the truck my reconnaissance turned up results in the form of a tube of lip gloss pressed into the sandy mud. I might not have given it a second thought but it looked new. Plus, I was pretty sure it hadn't belonged to Silas.

I picked it up and gave it a once-over. Cherry flavored. Interesting. I slipped the tube into my pocket, hoping Kale hadn't noticed. I didn't think it was his either. He didn't seem like the cherry lip gloss type. I wanted to make sure it didn't belong to Georgie before I let myself jump to conclusions, but despite Kale's claims that everyone had hated Silas, I was convinced a woman had been here recently.

I could think of only two possibilities: Nettie or Adele. Now I wondered whether the mystery woman had been here before, during, or after Silas's murder.

Twenty-four

❧

Miss Frankie and Bernice seemed surprised but pleased to find me knocking on Aunt Margaret's front door. Aunt Margaret and Bitty welcomed me with open arms. Tallulah and Eskil didn't exactly seem happy to see me, but they each treated me civilly.

Kale and I had been at Silas's place for a while, but not long enough for either Sullivan or Gabriel to call Aunt Margaret's looking for me. Miss Frankie made noises about getting me some medical attention, and Aunt Margaret offered to call a neighbor who was a *traiteur*, the local faith healer, but considering how effective Mambo Odessa's beads had been against obstacles, I put my faith in a dose of ibuprofen.

Since I was stuck in Baie Rebelle for the foreseeable future, Aunt Margaret said that of course I must spend the night—and as many nights as I needed to. She'd put a sleeping bag on the floor of the guest room for me. She was a bit distressed that it wouldn't be the most comfortable sleeping arrangements. I was more concerned that I'd be rooming with Miss Frankie and Bernice because sharing a bedroom would make it much more difficult to avoid my mother-in-law.

Everyone seemed eager to hear about my day. Well, everyone but Tallulah, who didn't seem eager at all, but joined us anyway. I shared a few of the highlights and watched Miss Frankie carefully for her reactions. I didn't notice any unusual vibes coming from her, but when it came to sensing undercurrents, I didn't have the best track record. I'd thought my marriage was on solid ground until the day Philippe walked out on me.

Now that I was safe, exhaustion hit me like a ton of bricks. I managed to stay awake through an amazing supper of fried chicken that was crispy on the outside, moist and tender on the inside, roasted parmesan-crusted sweet potatoes, green beans and tomatoes from the garden, and summer squash sliced, sipped in egg wash and flour, and then fried until the outside was lightly browned and the inside still slightly al dente. Eskil added a dish of Cajun-spiced alligator tenderloin, which, for the record, did *not* taste like chicken. With its chewy texture, I can't say it was my favorite part of the meal, but I enjoyed the experience and made a few notes for ways to make it more palatable.

Aunt Margaret followed the masterpiece supper with banana pudding. Since moving to the South, I'd been surprised and a little confused by the love affair some people have with that particular dessert. I just didn't understand its appeal. But after just one bite of Aunt Margaret's rich, creamy pudding, the mystery was solved and I became a banana pudding convert.

I tried again to reach Sullivan with no luck, which probably meant that he was on a case. I called the Dizzy Duke, but Gabriel wasn't at work so I called his cell phone, which went straight to voice mail again. I left another message, this time including Aunt Margaret's number so he could return the call, then I helped with the cleanup after dinner. I was just about to offer my excuses so I could crawl into my sleeping bag when Miss Frankie suggested that we go out onto the porch to talk.

This wasn't how I wanted our first conversation to play out; namely, in someone else's home when I was achy and bone tired. But I couldn't come up with an excuse I thought she'd listen to. Steeling myself, I grabbed a glass of Aunt Margaret's peach tea and trailed Miss Frankie outside.

Bernice came outside with us and patted my shoulder as she moved past me to claim a rocking chair. We spent a few minutes arranging ourselves and commenting on the weather, and then my mother-in-law got down to business.

"Did you get a chance to talk to Kale about his father's death?" Miss Frankie said when we'd all made ourselves comfortable.

I let out a thin laugh and nodded. "Yes, a little. You're not wasting any time getting right to it, are you?"

Miss Frankie waved a hand and regarded me expectantly. "Why should I? We all know what this is about, don't we?"

Yes, I suppose we did. I didn't want to let my conversation with Ox creep into my head while I was sitting here with Miss Frankie, but doubts are insidious things. They find even the smallest chink in the armor and worm their way in. Had I detected censure in Miss Frankie's voice or had I imagined it? Was there disapproval in her expression? In the dark it was hard to tell.

Bernice linked her hands together on her lap. "It's just that we're all so concerned about Eskil. The sheriff was out here this afternoon trying to question him. Eskil still isn't talking, and I'm afraid it's making him look bad."

"So what did Kale have to say?" Miss Frankie prodded.

"Not much. He says that Silas started trying to talk to him about a month ago. Kale didn't want anything to do with the guy, so he has no idea what Silas wanted."

Bernice took that in with an almost imperceptible nod. "Do you believe him?"

"I think so, but also I think he's confused and hurt. He's spent his whole life knowing that his father was just a few miles away, but also aware that his father wanted nothing to do with him. I don't think he knows what he feels right now."

"That could be reason enough for the boy to kill his father," Miss Frankie said. "Silas ignored him for most of his life and then suddenly wanted to see him? The boy would naturally get angry. Maybe he snapped."

"Yeah," I said. "Except for that scenario to work, Kale would have had to visit Silas and he claims he never did. He said that he was afraid of his father and terrified that he'd turn out like him. He tried to stay away so Silas wouldn't rub off on him."

Bernice put a hand to her chest. "Oh, that poor boy. What a burden to carry."

"Of course," Miss Frankie said. "If he's telling the truth."

"Even if he's not, it would be hard to prove that he's lying. Silas lived out in the middle of nowhere. There are no neighbors and no eyewitnesses." I stifled a yawn and thought longingly of the sleeping bag waiting for me inside. "Kale told me that Silas was squatting on land owned by your late-husband's family, Bernice. Do you know if that's true?"

Bernice's eyes flew wide open. "Dudley family land? I have no idea. Where was his cabin? Do you know?"

I pointed down the road. "That way about ten miles, I think. And I wouldn't exactly call it a cabin. It's more like some boards leaning against each other. I wish I could be more exact but that's about all I know—except that it's in some trees and he has a pretty impressive garbage dump going on."

Miss Frankie shook her head. "What about Silas's wife? When you met her, did she say anything interesting?"

"Nettie wants Kale to work for his uncle, but I don't understand why. Kale says that his mom doesn't like Junior, but she seems to be pushing Kale to accept the job offer."

"But everyone says that Junior has been good to her," Bernice said. "Why doesn't she like him?"

"She says he's a difficult man," I told them, "and from what I've seen of him I believe her. To be honest, I've found more reasons somebody might want to kill Junior than Silas. Silas didn't have anything. He squatted on land and poached whatever he wanted when he wanted it. From what I've learned, Silas didn't want anything except to be left alone."

"And apparently to talk to his son," Miss Frankie reminded me.

"True. And he also kept the locals supplied with moonshine."

Bernice gasped. "Eskil was right? He had Uncle Cooch's still?"

"He had *a* still," I said. "I don't know if it was Uncle Cooch's or not. I wish I had better news for you, Bernice, but the only person who seems to have had a real motive to want Silas dead was Eskil."

Bernice's hand fluttered to her mouth and she caught back a sob. "But he didn't do it," she insisted. "He couldn't have."

"I hope you're right," I said. I wished I could give her more reassurance than that, but that was the best I could do.

We stopped talking, and for a while our silence was interrupted only by the creaking of rocking chairs and the brush of a light wind over the undergrowth. In spite of my certainty that man-eating critters were lurking out there just waiting for someone to drop a careless foot on the ground, it was oddly peaceful.

Right up until the moment Miss Frankie decided to change the subject. "You haven't told me how your meeting with Simone O'Neil went," she said. "You did meet with her, didn't you?"

I kept my gaze straight ahead so I wouldn't inadvertently shoot her the stink eye. "Yes."

"She's a lovely girl, don't you think?"

"She's hardly a girl," I said. My voice came out tighter than I'd intended so I tried to temper it with a laugh. "But yes, she's lovely."

From the corner of my eye I saw Miss Frankie turn her head to look at me. "Are you all right, sugar? You seem tense."

"I'm fine," I said in a voice that even I knew sounded terse and defensive. "I'm just tired. It's been a long week and today wasn't exactly a walk in the park."

"Of course." Miss Frankie looked out over the yard again. "When we get back home, we'll need to get busy on our Christmas plans. Have you had a chance to think about what you'd like to add to the menu?"

"No. I haven't." *Tell her about Albuquerque*, my conscience whispered. I was so tired of its constant nagging, I decided to take its advice so it would leave me alone. And maybe I wanted to drop a bombshell so I could gauge her reaction. "The thing is, I'm not going to be here for Christmas. I'm going to Albuquerque."

The rhythm of her chair changed slightly, but she didn't look at me. "Oh? When did you decide to go there?"

Bernice leaned back into the shadows. Was she anticipating trouble from Miss Frankie?

"I made the decision a couple of weeks ago," I said. "My

uncle Nestor already bought the ticket. I haven't been home in a year and a half. I miss my family, and it means a lot to Aunt Yolanda and Uncle Nestor."

"You didn't mention it last time we talked."

"I didn't want to hurt your feelings."

She slid a sidelong glance in my direction. "And you think that letting me believe you'd help me and *then* announcing your plans would hurt less?"

It had been a long day. My head hurt. My lungs hurt. During supper I'd noticed a new ache in my neck. Plus, I'd been nursing hurt feelings over Miss Frankie and Simone for a couple of days. Add the fact that neither Sullivan nor Gabriel had tracked me down at Aunt Margaret's house to see why I'd called, and I was feeling pretty low. Which may or may not have made my temper slightly more volatile than usual.

I stopped rocking completely and gaped at her. "First of all, you blindsided me—*again*—with the Belle Lune job, which you didn't even bother to discuss with me. *And* you blindsided me with the whole Christmas deal, as if you think I exist only to take care of your whim of the moment. Christmas at your house was Pearl Lee's idea. She can help you. I'm going home."

Miss Frankie's expression turned to ice. "What is wrong with you, Rita?"

"Wrong? Nothing." Too agitated to sit any longer, I stood and walked to the edge of the porch. "I take that back. Something *is* wrong. You set me up, Miss Frankie, and I don't appreciate it."

"How did I do that?"

"You lied to me," I went on. "You told me that Philippe tried to get the Belle Lune Ball contract, and that wasn't true. He'd turned down the offer because he didn't want to work with Evangeline Delahunt."

"Who told you that?" Miss Frankie asked softly.

I might have been angry with Ox, but I wasn't going to throw him under the bus. "Does it matter? It's true, isn't it?"

"There's a lot of history there," she said. "You don't understand."

"I understand that you and Evangeline wanted Philippe to marry Simone Delahunt and that the two of you did everything you could to get them together. I understand that you were planning their wedding when Philippe left for pastry school. And I understand that you didn't want Philippe to marry me. Do you know how much hearing that hurt me?"

"I wanted Philippe to find a woman who loved him. One who wasn't after his money. I didn't know you, Rita. All I knew was that you came from a very different background. I didn't know what you wanted from him. So yes, at first I was skeptical. I feel differently now."

My knees were shaking and I could take only shallow breaths. I heard what she said, but I didn't know if I could believe her. I'd battled the feeling of not belonging my whole life—at least from the summer I turned twelve and I went to live with Aunt Yolanda and Uncle Nestor. They'd loved me as much as anyone could. They'd treated me like one of their own. I could never find fault with anything they'd done, but I'd still felt as if I was standing on the outside looking in.

Miss Frankie stood and smoothed the legs of her pants. "I'm sorry you don't want to believe me. Now if you'll excuse me, I'm tired and I'm going to bed."

I dropped into my chair as soon as she went inside.

"You're so wrong about her," Bernice said from the shadows.

I'd forgotten she was still sitting there. The sound of her voice made me jump. "Excuse me?"

Bernice got up and came to stand in front of me. "You're wrong about her. She loves you deeply."

I desperately wanted to believe her, but the old doubts were just too strong. I thought I should say something, but the words wouldn't come.

"If she didn't love you," Bernice went on, "she could have fought you for everything you inherited when Philippe died, and she would have won. You were in the process of divorcing him. Any court would have taken one look at those divorce papers and handed everything to Frances Mae." She sat in the chair Miss Frankie had vacated and put a gentle hand on my arm. "She didn't fight you, Rita. In fact, she went to great lengths to make sure you stayed in her life. So whatever it is you think she once felt for Simone Delahunt has nothing to do with how she feels about you."

Tears filled my eyes and I still couldn't speak. Bernice touched my cheek and smiled down at me. "One of these days, I hope you'll learn to let her love you. It would mean so much to her."

I felt small and petty, embarrassed that I'd let all my old junk get the best of me again. I wasn't completely wrong. Miss Frankie really had to stop committing me to things without asking. But getting her to change would be a long, slow process. We weren't in a TV sitcom where one conversation could bring about a lasting life change. If it could, I'd be a changed woman every week.

Twenty-five

✦

Thinking about everything that had happened that day ramped up the exhaustion I'd been feeling, but I wasn't ready to go inside and settle in for a sleepover, so I tried to map out a plan for fixing the Mercedes and getting back to New Orleans.

I wasn't going to wait for Gabriel indefinitely, but I still didn't want to call Ox, which meant I also couldn't call Isabeau. She might be keeping secrets from him, but I wouldn't ask her to drive to Baie Rebelle and not tell him where she was going. I could ask Dwight or Estelle, but I was almost certain that either of them would tell Ox where they were going, and if Ox thought I was in trouble, he'd come along for the ride. I liked knowing that about him, but that's what makes our relationship so complicated. Edie was out in her condition, and I didn't want to drag Sparkle too far away either when her niece or nephew might be born at any time.

I'd just have to wait until morning and hope that sleep would clear my head so I could figure out what to do.

Stars filled the night sky, and every so often something would rustle one of the nearby bushes. I tried not to think about what was out there. After a few minutes I caught the distinctive aroma of cigarette smoke and saw Eskil walk to the edge of the porch at the far end of the house. He looked tired. Maybe even a little sad. I wondered if I was looking at a killer. Had he finally found proof that Silas's moonshine business should have been his? Had he had enough of Silas's taunts? Had he flipped out? Spotted a toilet tank lid and lost control?

He turned and caught me watching him. I held my breath and tried to look . . . I don't know, maybe invisible.

"What you doin' out here all by yourself?" he asked.

Apparently my invisibility cloak wasn't working. "Just looking at the stars. It's a beautiful night."

"It is that." He crushed his cigarette under the toe of his boot and moved closer to where I was sitting. "What are you going to do about your car?"

I shrugged. "I haven't figured that out yet. The first thing will be to get it towed to a mechanic so I can find out what the damage is."

Eskil sat, groaning like an old man as his knees bent. "I hear those airbags can be expensive to replace." He lit another cigarette and held it up as an afterthought. "This gonna bother you?"

"Not really." I could have just kept my mouth shut and looked at the stars, but I thought about Bernice and the promise I'd made the other night to help clear Eskil. And I remembered the disappointment on her face just a few minutes earlier. Most of all, I thought about all the times she'd been there for Miss Frankie in the short time I'd known her, and I knew that I couldn't let the moment pass. It seemed that Eskil was feeling talkative. I couldn't just walk away.

"Aunt Margaret told me why you disliked Silas. She said you think Silas had something to do with your father's disappearance."

Eskil stared out at the clearing and smoked in silence. Just when I'd decided he was no longer in the mood to share, he dropped his head and looked at me from the corners of his eyes. "I don't think it. I know it."

My heart skipped a beat. "You know that for a fact? How?"

"Sonofabitch told me, that's how. He was always hinting around. Throwing it in my face. Every time I got on him for cutting one of my lines or poaching something I trapped, he'd tell me how he outsmarted my daddy and he'd outsmart me, too." Eskil rested his arms on his thighs and looked down at his boots. "Silas was crazy. No doubt about that. And he deserved to die if anyone did. But I didn't kill him if that's what you're thinking."

I believed him. At least I wanted to. "Can you prove it?"

He laughed through his nose. "Well, now, how can you prove you didn't do something you didn't do?"

"I don't know. Maybe you could provide an alibi."

"By admitting I went to New Orleans and scared the bejesus out of Bernice?"

"That might be a start," I said. "It was you, wasn't it?"

"Of course it was. How many people you know as ugly as me?"

I laughed and let myself relax a little. "I don't think you're ugly at all. But you do have a distinctive look. So why all the secrecy? Will you tell me?"

"Mama said she told you about Daddy's still."

I nodded. "She mentioned it."

"Well, that's why I went. That morning Silas stopped

hinting around. He came right out and told me that he slit my daddy's throat and threw him into the swamp. Somehow he'd tracked Daddy to the still. Daddy caught him spying and they got into it."

I shuddered at the image. "Silas told you this? Why? I mean . . . *Why*? After all this time?"

Eskil shrugged. "I don't know. He'd been acting weird for a while, but even weirder since his own mama died last month. Far as I know, he hadn't seen her in years. He never stopped by. Sure as hell never called her. Didn't act like he gave a damn. Didn't even show up for his own daddy's funeral. Or hers either. But I guess losing her made him go crazy."

"You don't know why?"

"I don't have a clue, but it's not as if the folks in that family tell me their secrets."

"This is a small town," I said. "I thought everyone knew everybody else's business. I thought that was the law or something."

Eskil chuckled. "Don't believe everything you read."

"Okay. I won't. But what does any of that have to do with you going to Bernice's house?"

"Silas told me he'd killed my daddy. He told me he'd stolen a still that had been in my family for a hundred years. Daddy died before he could give me the location of the still and nobody else would've known it."

"And you thought Bernice might?"

He grinned and shook his head. "Not exactly. But her daddy got our granddaddy's things when Granny died. I thought she might still have them tucked away somewhere."

"Why all the sneaking around?" I asked. "Why not just ring the bell and ask for what you wanted?"

Eskil shrugged. "If she didn't know what she had, I didn't want her to know. It was a matter of pride. I didn't want to be the first Percifield man to let the secret out. I'm pretty good at getting in and out without being spotted. I figured I could just look around without her knowing I was there."

Epic fail. "She was completely convinced that she saw Cooch's ghost," I said. "And after she found out that you were supposedly lost in the swamp, she thought Cooch had come to warn her."

Eskil looked sheepish, which I thought was the least he could do.

"What was it you thought Bernice might have?"

"I thought there might have been a message of some kind. A clue. Something that might give me an idea where to look for the still. It was a crazy idea, I know. I was pissed. I got drunk. I wasn't thinking straight."

"You drove to New Orleans drunk? Are you out of your mind? You could have killed somebody!"

Since he was under suspicion of doing just that, I was embarrassed by my reaction. Eskil seemed to feel worse than I did. He wagged his head and took a long drag from his cigarette. "Yeah. I know. It was a stupid thing to do. I was so angry I *would* have killed Silas if I'd seen him again that night. It's pure dumb luck I didn't."

"Where were you when he confessed to killing Uncle Cooch?"

"At the dock. He'd been up to his old tricks. He'd cleaned off a few of my lines. I saw him and confronted him about it."

"And out of nowhere he confessed?"

Eskil's beard twitched. "No. We had a talk. Then he told me that I'd never prove what he was doing, and then he confessed."

"And you just let him go."

"I took a couple of swings. Got in a solid punch or two. But I needed him alive to find what he stole."

"The family still."

"That's right."

Parts of his story had the ring of truth, but I wasn't completely convinced. "You expect me to believe that Silas admitting to killing your father and you just let him walk away? You got drunk and drove to New Orleans, knowing what Silas had done?"

"How else was I going to prove it?"

"You could have called the sheriff's department. You could have told them what Silas said and let them investigate." The irony of me giving him that particular piece of advice wasn't lost on me, but we weren't talking about me. And besides, the circumstances were completely different. "I take it you didn't find a clue at Bernice's house?"

"Didn't even look. She started screaming and I took off. I thought maybe everything would blow over and she'd forget."

I laughed softly. "Yeah. Good plan. Why did you tell everyone you'd been lost in the swamp?"

"After I left Bernice's, I found a parking lot and spent the night in my truck. Next morning I had breakfast at the Waffle House and killed some time in the city. I wanted to make sure I'd sobered up before I hit the road again. That afternoon I stopped to fill my truck with gas a couple of towns up the road from home. Heard people talking and realized all of Baie Rebelle was out looking for me. If I'd pulled up in my truck like nothing had happened, I'd never have heard the end of it. I didn't figure on anybody realizing I wasn't out on the water all night."

Unbelievable. Something dark darted from one bush to another and I gasped. "What was that?"

"What was what?"

I pointed. "That. There. Something is out there."

Eskil watched for a moment and then shrugged off the question. "Maybe a possum. Maybe a rabbit. Maybe the rougarou comin' to get me."

"Funny." I watched for a little while longer and then returned to the conversation we'd been having. "So you went to New Orleans intending to break into Bernice's house and rifle through her things. That plan failed, so you came home and perpetrated a giant fraud on the whole town to keep from being embarrassed? Is that about right?"

"I've got my pride."

I still had questions, but that one statement seemed to sum it all up in his mind. He looked up at the sky and stood. "It's getting late and I want to be out on the water by sunrise. If you need anything, just let Mama know."

He strolled away, whistling softly, and I went inside right away. Not because I believed the rougarou was lurking in the trees, but because I didn't think I could stay awake another minute.

Miss Frankie and Bernice were already asleep by the time I crept down the hall and into the guest room, but I found one of my mother-in-law's nightgowns folded on top of my pillow. It had been a long, hard day and my emotions were raw. My car was stuck in the middle of nowhere, and I was stuck in Baie Rebelle with no way out. There was no other reason why seeing that nightgown waiting would reduce me to tears.

Twenty-six

❧

Friday morning I was up with the sun, but I was still the last one out of bed. My chest still hurt and my neck was still sore from yesterday's crash. The smell of air bag chemicals clung to my hair and skin, but otherwise I felt almost good. I was alive, and that counted for something.

Miss Frankie and Bernice had somehow gotten past and out the door without disturbing me, but they'd left a pair of jeans, a plaid shirt, and a pair of granny panties on the foot of my sleeping bag. The jeans were too short and the shirt too large, but everything was clean so I wasn't going to complain.

The kitchen was empty but I found coffee and bread for toast. After wolfing down a slice (or two), I made a couple of calls. First, I left Ox a message that I wouldn't be in that morning and then I tried Sullivan's number again. I didn't expect to reach him, but he answered and apologized for being unable to help. I had just enough time to tell him not to worry about me before he had to go. After we hung up, I tried to decide who to call next, but the phone rang while I was still running through the possibilities. I answered before I could think about the fact that I was in someone else's house and using their phone. Which turned out to be a good thing.

"You're up!" Gabriel said when he heard my voice. "I was looking forward to waking you up myself."

I was so glad to hear his voice, I giggled. "You got my message?"

"I heard it after work last night. I didn't want to call this number and wake everyone up, so I waited. Are you okay?" He sounded far away and I picked up a strange interference on the line, but I was just thrilled that we had any connection at all.

"A little stiff and sore, and if I never have an air bag go off around me again, I'll die happy. Is there any chance you can come and get me? There's no way I'm driving out of here in the Mercedes—and if by some miracle I find someone who can fix it, I won't be on the road anytime soon."

"I'm nearly there," he said. "I just stopped for gas and I'm about to get back on the road."

"You're coming to Baie Rebelle?"

"You said you needed help, didn't you?"

My eyes filled with tears. "Yeah, I did."

"So help is on the way. I'm maybe half an hour away, but my cell signal's been in and out for miles, so I decided to call while I had a few bars. Is there anything I need to know to find the house?"

I gave him directions to Aunt Margaret's and told him what to watch for along the road that would help him find me.

I hung up a few minutes later wearing a smile that stretched from ear to ear. I couldn't expect Gabriel to tow the Mercedes back to civilization, so I got busy trying to arrange a rescue for my poor car. Unfortunately, Nettie had been right. I couldn't find a towing service locally, and the cost of getting an actual tow truck way out to the back of beyond to haul the Mercedes to a certified mechanic was astronomical.

I tried three different companies and did my best to negotiate a reasonable fee, but nobody was willing to budge. So when Kale Laroche showed up on the doorstep with a friend and an offer to pull the Mercedes out of the ditch for me, I accepted the help gratefully. I handed over my keys and jotted down directions to a place called Ed's, where Kale and his friend planned to take the Mercedes. Could this Ed repair my car? I could only hope.

After Kale and his friend left, I spent some time pretending to work on sketches for the Belle Lune Ball, but I was too antsy to sit still so I decided to look around outside. I thought I was alone, but to my surprise, I came across Tallulah digging in a flowerbed in the backyard.

She looked up as I walked toward her and used the back of her wrist to brush the straight brown hair away from her forehead. "So. You're awake." I guess she wanted to make sure I'd noticed.

"I've been up for a while," I told her. "I've been making phone calls."

"Humph." At least I think that's what she said. It was hard to tell. She sat back on her heels and the frown on her face turned into the stony glare of a challenge. "I hope you're not expecting breakfast."

What was wrong with her? I knew I wasn't her favorite, but she seemed even more hostile than usual. I did my best not to give attitude back. "I've already eaten. Where is everyone else? The house seems deserted."

"Ladies' Bible study," Tallulah said. "Down at the church. They waited around for you, but you never got out of bed so they gave up."

If she was trying to make me feel guilty, she'd have to do better than that. My aunt Yolanda could out-guilt anyone I'd ever met. Plus, I remembered Bitty saying that Tallulah didn't participate with the good ladies of the church, so she had no room to talk. She could try to make me feel bad, but I was determined to be gracious. "That was nice of them," I said with a saccharine smile. "Another time, I guess."

She answered that with a second *humph* and started digging again. "Clothes fit you, I see."

I glanced down at my ankles protruding from the pants and the shirt hanging to my knees. I hadn't worn clothes this ill fitting since I was a kid and Aunt Yolanda took me school shopping at the thrift store. "Yes. Do I have you to thank?"

Tallulah jerked her chin. "Frances was going to find you something from her suitcase, but I said she's too tall for you." She went back to digging. "Those are fine, yes?"

I wasn't sure she expected an answer but I gave her one anyway. After all, I wouldn't want to seem rude. "Yes. They're fine."

She flicked her eyes over me and tossed a spade full of sandy dirt at my feet. "I heard your phone call this morning. Does Liam know you've got another man on the side?"

Aha! So that's what had put her in such a cheerful mood. It would have been amusing if it hadn't been so annoying. "You listened in on my personal phone call?"

"I answered a call on my own phone," Tallulah said with a sniff. She wagged a cordless handset in my face. "How was I to know you'd pick up the phone when it rang?"

"I had no idea anyone was here," I said. "I thought you were all out somewhere and I'd given this number to a few people."

Another flick of disapproving eyes. Another spade full of dirt aimed at my feet.

"A friend of mine is on his way to drive me back to New Orleans since my car isn't working. But thanks for jumping to conclusions."

Tallulah tugged off a thick gardening glove and raked her fingers through her hair. "You think you can play fast and loose with men, but you can't. Sooner or later it'll catch up with you."

Was she for real? "I appreciate your concern," I lied, "but you really don't have to worry. Liam knows all about Gabriel and vice versa."

"Men don't like to be lied to," Tallulah went on, as if I hadn't said a word. "You can't play with their feelings."

"I'm not," I assured her. "And at the risk of sounding rude, it's really none of your business."

"If you don't believe me, ask Bitty. She could tell you a thing or two. Me? I got a man and settled down. One man was good enough for me."

I refrained from telling her that I knew that man had walked out on her, and instead I squeaked out a surprised, "Bitty?"

Tallulah brushed dirt from her knee and dug around a bit more. "You know what she's like. She has trouble making decisions, and she's always been that way. She had two men dangling on a string, and in the end she lost them both." She shook the spade at me, sending dirt flying. "You mark my words. You keep playing around the way you are, you'll be the one who loses in the end."

Half a dozen hot retorts rose to my tongue, but for Bernice's sake, I swallowed them all. Tallulah and her family had taken me in on a moment's notice. They'd fed me, housed me, and even clothed me. I wouldn't repay their generosity with an argument, no matter how wrong Tallulah was.

And she was wrong, even though deep down, far beneath my outrage, I wondered if I could be making a mistake. How long would both Sullivan and Gabriel wait around for me? Should I pick one and let the other go? I didn't think I was playing around with their affections. I'd been up front with both of them and as honest as I knew how to be. But were they really okay with the status quo or was I simply justifying my behavior?

I heard a car door shut and my heart gave a leap. I left Tallulah to her digging and hurried back to the house. To be honest, I just wanted to escape the look in Tallulah's eyes and the questions she'd raised. I wasn't sure whether I was more upset with Tallulah because she was wrong about me—or because she was right.

Gabriel took one look at my too-short pants and baggy plaid shirt and let out a low whistle. I'd pulled my hair into a messy bun and I had no makeup with me so my face was scrubbed clean. "Looks like I got here just in time. I had no idea you were in this much trouble."

I've looked better, but he'd also seen me looking worse, so I grabbed his arm and tugged him inside. "Not another word about the way I look. You have no idea what the past couple of days have been like."

He sobered and ran another look over my face, this one filled with concern. "I'm just glad you're in one piece," he said and leaned in for a gentle kiss.

My heart flipped when his lips touched mine, but it didn't

flop the way it usually did. Probably because Tallulah had stirred up all those nasty feelings of guilt.

He must have sensed a difference in me because he pulled back slowly, his eyes narrowed slightly. "I didn't hurt you, did I?"

"Of course not. I'm just . . . ready to get out of here." Which was true. It just wasn't the whole truth. I waved him toward the couch and headed toward the bedroom. "Give me two minutes to grab my things. Then we can hit the road."

"What about your car?" he called after me.

"A couple of local guys are towing it to a place called Ed's. It should be safe enough there until I can figure out how to get it back to the city." I ducked into the bedroom, stuffed my dirty clothes into a pillowcase I'd return later, and rolled up the sleeping bag. I thought about leaving a note for Miss Frankie and Bernice, but after our conversations last night, I thought it might be better to speak to them in person.

Back in the living room, I jerked my head toward the door. "I'm ready if you are. I just need to make one stop before we leave town. It shouldn't take long."

"You're calling the shots," Gabriel said as he followed me outside. "Where do you need to go?"

"Ladies' Bible study. The church is right next to the bar. You passed both on your way through town."

Gabriel didn't even bat an eye.

"I need to tell Miss Frankie that I'm leaving," I explained. "And I'm hoping she'll let me use her car for a few days while I'm trying to figure out what to do about mine."

"Gotcha." Gabriel held the door and I quick-stepped across the front yard to his car.

Tallulah came around the house as Gabriel and I climbed

into his car. She kept her distance, but I could feel her watching us and passing judgment on every move I made.

"Who's that?" Gabriel asked.

I kept the answer simple. "She's Bernice's cousin Tallulah."

"She seems to be waiting for something. Do you think you should say something to her?"

"No, I don't." I knew that I sounded impatient and maybe even nervous, but the last thing I wanted was for Tallulah to share her opinions with Gabriel. Bad enough that she'd shared them with me. I buckled up and pulled down the visor. "Can we just *go*?"

Gabriel started the car and took off. I watched Tallulah grow smaller and smaller in the side mirror, and then finally disappear.

"Are you going to tell me what's going on?" Gabriel asked as he turned onto the highway.

"It's nothing," I said. "She was in a mood this morning, and so was I. It wasn't a good combination." I made myself more comfortable and put Tallulah out of my mind. "Thanks for coming all this way to get me. I hope it wasn't too much trouble."

"No trouble at all," he said with a grin. "I'm just glad I could help. Are you going to tell me what happened to your car?"

I gave him the short version of the story, leaving out unnecessary details like the fact that I had been tailing Kale through some deserted swampland at the time. Gabriel tends to get overly protective of me in certain circumstances, and I already knew that tailing murder suspects was one of them.

If he suspected that I was holding back, he gave no sign of it, and by the time I finished my story, we'd reached the Baie Rebelle Church single-wide. Bible study was breaking up, so I made arrangements with Miss Frankie to use her car, and promised to collect the mail at both their houses while they were away. A few minutes later, we were driving away from Baie Rebelle and its hidden stills and murder by toilet tank lids, and toward the real-life world of cake, feuding staff members, and babies on the way. I'd been in Baie Rebelle for just twenty-four hours, but it felt as if I'd been away for weeks.

Twenty-seven

❧

I found several messages waiting for me when I walked into my office on Friday morning. Evangeline Delahunt wanted to see me on Monday to discuss the menu for the Belle Lune Ball, Edie had scheduled two wedding consults for the following week, and Simone O'Neil had left three messages for me to call her as soon as possible. Concerned about what could be so urgent, I decided to follow up on that right away.

"Change of plans," she said when I returned her call. "Evangeline has decided to take the ball in another direction, and I thought I should let you know before you go too far down the road we talked about at our last meeting."

I held back a groan. Not that I'd already done a lot of work on my ideas, but I had done a lot of thinking. I couldn't believe that Evangeline expected me to abruptly shift gears with only a few days before my next command appearance.

I glanced at my cluttered desk and the few sketches I'd

completed before my most recent visit to Baie Rebelle. "Can she do that?"

"Technically? No. It's for the board of directors to decide, but they tend to give my mother whatever she wants. And she's decided that she wants to do something different."

Maybe I was getting paranoid, but I wondered if she was going in a new direction purposely to throw me off. Evangeline Delahunt seemed to delight in setting others up for failure. She'd apparently already steamrolled over Dmitri Wolff and Gâteaux. Now it was my turn.

"What does she want to do?" I asked.

Simone didn't answer immediately. "It might be better if I showed you. Are you free for lunch? It would be my treat."

Uh-oh. Something that couldn't be described didn't sound good. "When and where?" I asked. The sooner I knew what Evangeline was up to, the better my chances of beating her at whatever game she was playing. We arranged to meet at Galatoire's on Bourbon Street. A convenient choice for Simone. A lot less convenient for me, but she was the client so it was her call.

I arrived ten minutes early, which was a good thing since the streets were crowded and it took a while to find a parking place. I hustled inside three minutes late, hot, sweaty, and frazzled. Simone was waiting for me just inside the doors looking remarkably cool and collected. She took my hands and air-kissed my cheeks, which seemed entirely normal for her but made me a bit uncomfortable, considering. Oblivious to my discomfort, she signaled the maître d' that we were ready.

Dozens of tables packed a long, narrow dining room. It could easily have felt crowded, especially with diners leaving their own tables to visit friends, but a bank of full-length mirrors running along the wall made the room look larger than it actually was. Rows of ceiling fans turned slowly overhead, and light from each of them reflected from the mirrors, making the whole room sparkle.

We slipped into seats at a table for two set with crystal and silver, and I tried not to feel gauche and out of place. "It's beautiful in here," I said, my voice hushed.

Surprise lit Simone's dark eyes. "You haven't been here before?"

I shook my head slowly. "It's been on my list of places to visit but it's hard to get away from work. This is my first time here." I'd added Galatoire's to my culinary bucket list for several reasons, the first of which was that it was a New Orleans tradition dating back more than a century. In all that time, little about the restaurant's look and seating had changed. I knew that reservations were accepted for the second-floor dining room, but here on the first floor seating was first come, first served.

Simone watched me take in the ambience with a smile and eventually nodded toward the menu in front of me. "Everything here is wonderful," Simone said, "but if you'd like, I can make a few suggestions."

When it came to dining out, I'd long ago learned to always let someone in the know offer suggestions before making any decisions. Uncle Nestor had taught me that, and Philippe had echoed the advice when the two of us got together. Experienced servers knew what was especially good, which ingredients were fresh, and maybe more important, what to avoid on any particular night. Other diners could direct you to dishes that were consistently delicious. I'd experienced some amazing food by following my *tío*'s advice, and I had no doubt that Simone would steer me in the right direction.

After some discussion, we decided on Galatoire Goute,

an appetizer plate consisting of shrimp *remoulade*, oysters *en brochette*, and crabmeat *maison*. Simone suggested we follow that with fresh fish topped with crabmeat and shrimp and tie up the meal with *café brûlot*, a strong, hot coffee flavored with citrus peel, sugar, cinnamon, and cloves.

Once our choices had been relayed to our server, Simone linked her hands together on the table and got down to business. "I'm sorry about these changes. I know this is going to make things more difficult for you. They've certainly thrown a monkey wrench into my plans."

"I may be in a better position than you are," I said with a sympathetic smile. "You've been working on this for months. I've only had a few days." I didn't admit that most of my time had been spent in Baie Rebelle or that I only had a few sketches on paper, none of which had even come close to knocking my socks off, so I held out little hope that Evangeline would have been impressed. "Which part of the theme does she want to change?"

"All of it," Simone said. "She had a dream the other night and woke up convinced she's been going in the wrong direction. It's still going to be a twentieth anniversary celebration, but now she wants a more rustic theme. She wants to concentrate on the fashions that people tend to ignore from our time period. Less *The Great Gatsby* and more *The Grapes of Wrath*."

Our server arrived with our first course, but I was so stunned by Simone's news, I barely even noticed. "She wants to design the whole event around the styles from the Great Depression?" Could those clothes even be considered fashion? Maybe people with too much money would find it entertaining to see how the other half had lived. Having come from the other half, I struggled not to find it insulting. "And the board of directors is going to let her do that?"

"According to Mama, the idea originated with one of the board members. They had a conversation. Mama went home and had a dream, and—*voilà!*—change is afoot."

Simone was certainly taking it well, which made me nervous. Were she and Evangeline working together? Was I being set up? Or was I just being paranoid? "Have you had time to decide how you're going to decorate?" I asked.

"Not entirely, but I'll figure something out. And I have all the faith in the world that you'll do something amazing with the food. I just wanted you to have a heads-up before your meeting with Mama next week." She picked up her knife and fork and held them poised over her *maison*, a crab salad dressed with mayonnaise, olive oil, vinegar, capers, and scallions, seasoned with just the right amount of salt and pepper, and served on fresh butter lettuce leaves with a tomato garnish. "Honestly, the change is a bit annoying, but in the history of the society, we've never done anything remotely like this. I think that together we can make this an event that will be remembered for years to come."

Her expression seemed free of guile, so I laughed and picked up my own silverware. Based on looks and aroma alone, the *maison* rated a ten. After my first taste, I upped my rating by several points. "I hate to break it to you, but this year's event might be remembered even if we fail."

"The two of us working together? How could that possibly happen?" She sobered slightly and held my gaze. "Really, Rita, I have a good feeling about this. I know it will mean big changes for the menu and for the cake, but I really think we could blow everybody away."

Her enthusiasm was infectious. The idea was beginning to grow on me, and for the first time since Miss Frankie had volunteered Zydeco to work with the Vintage Clothing Society, ideas began to race through my head. "What would you think about an untraditional menu for the banquet?" I asked. "I'm talking about the kind of food you don't usually see at high-society events."

Simone's smile bloomed. "Such as?"

"Down-home food. Beef roasted in garlic. Chunks of sweet potato crusted in parmesan. Corn casserole. Turkey-cranberry Monte Cristo sandwiches. Banana pudding that would make you swoon—and I mean that literally."

Simone's smile grew even broader. "I love it."

"And Evangeline? Do you think she'll approve?"

"We'll make sure she does," Simone said firmly. "We'll call in reinforcements if we have to. In fact, if you have time after we're finished here, we can talk to a friend of Mama's. If we can get her on board with our idea, we'll have it made."

I had a hard time imagining that anyone could influence Evangeline's decisions, but I had to trust that Simone knew what she was talking about. "I have time," I said. "And I think I can pull together a menu by Monday."

We chatted as we ate, each of us tossing ideas about food and decorations into the mix so by the time we'd finished our meal and paid the bill (with some minor argument from me about paying my fair share), we were both almost giddy with excitement. I followed Simone out of the restaurant into the bright autumn sunlight and dug Miss Frankie's keys out of my purse. "You paid for lunch, so let me drive. Where are we going?"

She waved away the offer and started walking toward the corner. "It's just on the next block over. We don't need to drive."

I trotted after her, eager to meet whoever it was who possessed the ability to influence Evangeline Delahunt. I pictured someone wealthy, with impeccable breeding and the right social standing. I didn't expect Simone to lead me into a narrow building on Dauphine Street with peeling white paint and bright blue shutters . . . which I recognized with shock as Mambo Odessa's shop.

The overpowering scent of potpourri almost knocked me over as we stepped inside, and I felt myself bracing for a room full of shrunken heads and human bones. To my surprise, the tiny shop seemed almost normal. A number of gris-gris bags filled with herbs, roots, and oils made up a display along one wall. Another section contained a tasteful variety of dolls dressed in bright colors and feathers, a selection of educational books and DVDs, jujus, and jewelry.

Opposite those I saw a selection of bath oils, soaps, and candles. According to the signs posted here and there, everything inside was designed to enhance love, fortune, health, or good luck.

Mambo Odessa wore a bright orange caftan decorated in shades of yellows, browns, and rusts. She wore her tiny round sunglasses even inside the dimly lit store, but they didn't seem to impact her ability to see and recognize us. She embraced Simone warmly and beamed a friendly smile at me.

"This," Simone said to me with a flourish of her hand toward Mambo Odessa, "is one of my favorite people in the world. She's the only person I know who can get my mother to do anything."

What were the odds?

"Come in, come in." Mambo Odessa ushered us toward a collection of comfortable chairs in the far corner, smiling at me as if she'd known I'd show up here on this exact day, at this precise moment, in the company of Simone O'Neil. And maybe she had. But if so, I'm not going to lie, the whole idea left me feeling skittish.

I took a few shallow breaths and tried to talk myself down. Of course Mambo Odessa knew Simone and

Evangeline. She was Ox's aunt, after all. I already knew that Ox and Simone were friends. It just hadn't occurred to me that Mambo Odessa and Evangeline Delahunt ran in the same circles. They seemed so . . . different.

Then again, this was New Orleans, where a high-powered politician and a parish priest could sit down to dinner with a female impersonator and a jazz musician and nobody thought a thing about it. It was disconcerting and reassuring at the same time.

Mambo Odessa sat beside me and touched my wrist. "You're still wearing your Brazilian wish bracelet, I see."

Only because I kept forgetting to take it off, but I didn't admit this to her. "Yes. I guess I am."

"And has it helped?"

"Maybe. I'm not really sure."

Simone watched the exchange with a little scowl of curiosity. It seemed I wasn't the only one who needed a few minutes to connect all the dots. "I should have realized the two of you would know each other," Simone said when the pieces finally clicked for her. She shook her head and laughed at herself. "Okay, so here we are. Mambo Odessa is the board member who got Mama started down this whole Depression Era path."

Somehow, in spite of everything, that piece of information still had the power to surprise me. I gaped at Mambo Odessa. "You're on the Vintage Clothing Society board of directors?"

"Yes, child. I sure am."

"And it was your idea to change the theme for the Belle Lune Ball?" I don't believe in coincidence, but in that moment I wanted to. I didn't like thinking that Evangeline Delahunt, Mambo Odessa, and Miss Frankie were connected, or that Evangeline's sudden change of heart had been set in motion to somehow benefit me. There was no doubt in my mind that this new theme would make life easier for me, but that suspicion killed some of the excitement I'd been feeling. I wanted to succeed on my own. If I failed, I wanted to fail on my own.

"Not my idea," Mambo Odessa said. "I merely passed along an idea that was shared with me."

Yeah. Right. Okay then. I glanced at Simone, whose eyes were alight with anticipation. Maybe this wasn't all a setup, I told myself. I wanted that to be true. I liked Simone and I thought she and I could be friends long after the Belle Lune Ball was over. And I actually liked Mambo Odessa, too.

So I gave them both the benefit of the doubt. Because after all, that's what friends do.

Twenty-eight

❧

I stayed busy over the weekend putting together a menu for the Belle Lune Ball and sketching cakes I thought might appeal to Evangeline Delahunt. Both Simone and Mambo Odessa attended the meeting on Monday. I can't say that Evangeline was friendly toward me, but she was civil and she actually approved both the menu I'd proposed and my idea to highlight several classic cake flavors, including banana layer cake with fresh banana buttercream icing; a country-style blueberry cake drizzled with crème Anglaise and dolloped with sweet whipped cream; spice cake loaded with nutmeg, cinnamon, cloves and ginger and topped with buttercream; an orange almond breadcrumb cake with orange custard icing; and of course, the ultimate vintage cake, devil's food with chocolate custard.

That afternoon I helped the staff bake and decorate six-teen dozen candy corn cupcakes while Ox and Dwight built a cupcake display shaped like a giant haunted house for the school party. Tensions were still running a bit high between Edie and the rest of the staff, but they were almost back to normal and discussing the costumes they planned to wear. Frankly, hearing them chatter about Halloween plans was the best thing I'd heard in days. I had to admit that Ox had done a great job while I was gone. I didn't notice any cracks between Ox and Isabeau either, which made me happy. Maybe Mambo Odessa had been right about them. I hoped so. But I was still a bit nervous since it appeared that we'd all be thrown together over the next few months. The more Ox saw of his aunt and Isabeau together, the more likely he was to pick up on their secret meetings.

It was none of my business, of course, unless their relationship imploded right in the middle of preparations for the Belle Lune Ball. Only time would tell whether I needed to worry about that. Right then I had other things to worry about, like how to get my car fixed and how long Miss Frankie and Bernice planned to stay in Baie Rebelle.

And, of course, the issue of Christmas. My nonrefundable airline ticket had arrived in my e-mail, putting pressure on me to resolve the new question hanging over my head: Could I really leave Zydeco that close to the Vintage Clothing Society's anniversary banquet? The answer, of course, was no—but admitting that broke my heart. I hated letting my family down, especially after disappointing Miss Frankie, but I couldn't see any way around it.

That afternoon, I went with Ox, Dwight, and Isabeau to deliver the cupcakes, which kept us busy for several hours as we set up the display and loaded it with almost two hundred orange and yellow cupcakes. Most of them made the journey undamaged, but we were kept busy fixing the ones that hadn't.

By the time I got home that evening, I was bone-tired and ready for bed. Too exhausted to cook, I'd picked up a pretzel burger and fries and I planned to eat them in bed so I could roll over and fall asleep after the last slurp of Diet Pepsi crossed my lips.

Before I could even unwrap the burger, I got a call from Miss Frankie telling me that she and Bernice were ready to come home (good news) and that Ed was going to start charging me a daily storage fee for the Mercedes (not so good).

I was up bright and early the next morning, hoping to take care of everything in Baie Rebelle and get back to New Orleans before lunchtime. If Ed couldn't repair the Mercedes, I'd have no choice but to pay for towing even if the fee I'd been quoted made my stomach tie itself in knots.

I'd be glad to have Miss Frankie and Bernice home where they belonged and was relieved that I wouldn't have to keep racing off to Baie Rebelle every few days. I felt guilty for not getting Eskil out of the woods (so to speak), but I had to believe that Georgie and the sheriff would do their jobs and clear him. After all, my job was to make cake, not catch killers.

I found Ed's after driving around Baie Rebelle for at least an hour, and only after asking the clerks at T-Rex's for help. I'd been looking for a business. Ed's turned out to be a double-wide trailer where a guy named Ed lived.

Ed was around thirty, a tall guy with a husky build and a full black beard. He acted as the town's mechanic whenever someone encountered a problem they couldn't fix on their own. I didn't ask how often that happened. Nor did I ask if Ed had worked on a Mercedes before. I didn't really expect him to fix it. I just counted it a victory that the car wasn't out in the middle of nowhere turning into a nesting area for local wildlife.

The guys had pushed the Mercedes around back where,

apparently, Ed's "shop" was. I'd assumed that Ed had already checked out the Mercedes and could give me an opinion, but despite his down-home digs and laid-back appearance, Ed didn't lift a finger if he wasn't getting paid.

He told me to make myself comfortable and promised to be back in a little while. I guessed he was performing diagnostics so I found a metal chair in front of the trailer and made a mental note to keep something to read in my purse at all times. A book or magazine would have come in handy.

Since I didn't have anything to read and my cell phone had no service, I kept myself busy by pulling the lint off the breath mints I'd found in the glove box the day of the accident. I'd almost finished that task when a maroon pickup pulled into the driveway and Adele Pattiere got out.

Sensing the opportunity for something more interesting than lint removal, I said hello. She returned my friendly greeting after a slight hesitation, and I took that as a sign that she might be up for some conversation. I was convinced that Kale was the young man she'd been talking to the night of Eskil's dramatic "rescue" and I was curious about why she kept denying it.

She didn't owe me an explanation, but I left the comfort of the metal chair and walked toward her. She looked better than she had the last time I saw her. Her eyes weren't red and puffy, but they still looked haunted.

"Are you looking for Ed?" I asked.

"Yeah. Is he around?"

I jerked my head toward the trailer. "He's in back looking at my car. I had an accident a few days ago."

"Oh, yeah? You're okay, right?"

Her concern was touching. At least it might have been if she'd looked at me. Since she didn't, I had to assume she didn't actually care. "I'm fine," I said in case I'd read her wrong. "I met a friend of yours, I think. Kale Laroche found me out there and came to my rescue."

That got her to look at me but she didn't say anything.

"You know Kale, right?" I said. "I saw the two of you talking that night at Margaret Percifield's house."

Adele nodded slowly. "Of course I know Kale. But like I told you before, you didn't see us talking."

I'd be leaving town soon, so I called her on it. "Actually, I did. It doesn't seem like it should be a big deal, but you keep denying it so I guess it is. And you're the only person in town who seems to care that Silas is dead, including his son Kale. What gives?" I caught a flash of misery on her face and decided to take it down a notch. "Plus, I hate to see anyone grieving. I know what it feels like to lose someone."

Adele shushed me and looked around quickly. "You're not from around here. You don't know how people felt about Silas."

"I know that most everybody hated him," I said. "But I don't think you hated him at all. I think his death has been tough on you."

She blinked a couple of times and swallowed hard. "He was a friend. But you can't tell anybody that. If it got out, nobody around here would work with me again. It's rough enough trying to make a living as a woman in the swamp."

"Why wouldn't they work with you?"

"Because no one trusted Silas, and so they wouldn't trust me. Around here trust is everything. You don't survive without the help from other people. You have to know that they're willing to do whatever needs to be done, and they have to know that about you."

"And people wouldn't know that about you if they found out you and Silas were friends?"

She shook her head. "I don't run my own boat, and I need

the work I get helping others with their tags. I had a rough
go last year and Silas helped me out. But we kept it quiet.
Silas was different. People didn't trust him. If word gets out
now, I might be able to regain trust, but it would take a long
time."

"How close were the two of you?"

Adele's gaze skimmed across my face. "Close enough."
She toed the ground. "We had something, but I don't even
know what it was. It had only been a few months."

"It didn't bother you that he was married?"

"That was just a technicality. He didn't consider himself
married."

Oh. Well. In that case . . .

"They would have been divorced if Nettie wasn't such a
gold digger."

I laughed. I couldn't help myself. "What was she digging
for? I thought Silas didn't have anything."

"It wasn't what he had that Nettie wanted. It was what
he was going to get."

I stopped laughing. "What was he going to get? I was
told that his father wrote him out of his will when Silas
deserted his family and moved to the swamp."

"He did," Adele said, "but his mother didn't agree with
what her husband did." She leaned against the hood of her
truck and crossed one foot over the other. "When Tommy
Laroche changed his will, he gave everything to Suzette,
his wife. Before that, he'd given Suzette the house and some
money and divided the rest between Junior and Silas. I guess
he believed that Suzette would honor his wishes and give
everything to Junior when she died."

My fingers began to tingle. I thought I could see where
Adele was going with her story, and I jumped ahead. "But
she didn't, right? She left half the estate to Silas."

Adele nodded. "At first, Nettie stayed in the marriage because she thought Silas might change his mind and come home."

"But he didn't."

"No, but by the time she realized that he wasn't coming back, she was used to living alone and doing stuff on her own, and Junior had stepped in to help out so they weren't suffering."

"When did she find out that Silas was going to get the property?"

Adele shrugged. "I don't know for sure. Suzette must have told her. Maybe as a reward for being a faithful daughter-in-law. All I know is that Suzette never said a word to Silas or to Junior. Silas only knew because Nettie told him."

"How did Silas react to that?"

"He didn't. He didn't think that something written on a piece of paper meant anything. So old Tommy died, and eventually Suzette died, and then one day about a month ago a letter came from an attorney notifying Silas that half of everything was his."

The tingle spread up to my elbows. "Half of everything that for years Junior thought was his alone."

Adele nodded. "And exactly what Nettie had been waiting for. Silas didn't pay any attention to it, but Junior started coming around, trying to get Silas to sign it all over to him. And then Nettie started dropping by. At first I thought she was going to try to interest Silas in coming back to her, but I think all she really wanted was to make sure Junior didn't influence Silas. She wanted the inheritance for Kale."

I wondered how far Junior and Nettie would have gone to get what they wanted. "What about Kale? Did he know about his grandmother's will?"

"I don't think so."

"Did he know about you and Silas?"

Adele looked miserable. "He found out. Nettie told him. She came by one night while I was there."

"I take it he wasn't happy?"

"No and neither was Nettie."

"She thought you might cause friction in her marriage?" It was meant to be a joke, and Adele's lips curved slightly on the edges.

"It's probably more like she thought I'd create a block on the road to her becoming a wealthy woman."

That gave Nettie a motive for killing Silas. As Silas's widow, she was walking away with his half of everything. But to collect from the estate, she would have needed the body discovered quickly so legal wheels could start turning. And she'd seemed so nice. "Do you think Nettie killed Silas?"

Adele ducked her head and lifted a shoulder. "I don't know. Maybe. Nettie went to see Silas that morning. She was worried that Junior was making headway and she wanted to make sure Silas didn't sign everything over to his brother. Her visit upset Silas. He'd been trying to talk to Kale for weeks but Kale wanted nothing to do with him. That night I begged Kale to talk to his dad, but he refused."

I wondered if she was telling the truth about that. Silas was probably already dead when I saw her and Kale together. If she really was trying to convince Kale to talk to his dad, she must not have known he was dead. "Do you know what Silas wanted to tell him?"

"No, but I wish I did. He wouldn't tell me a thing. All I know is that he was getting tired of all the visitors. He liked his privacy."

From what I'd heard about Silas, I thought that was an understatement. "Out of curiosity, how much land are we talking about?"

"I don't know exactly," Adele said. "Silas never said. It's a lot, though, and I do know that the part Silas inherited cuts right through where Junior plans to expand his charter business. He's been talking about draining the swamp in that area so he can build guest cabins and whatnot."

That would explain why Junior had suddenly stopped working on the project. It also sounded like a motive for murder—except that if he killed Silas, Nettie would inherit. I wanted Junior to be the bad guy, but getting his brother out of the way wouldn't help him or his planned expansion. It would just throw up another roadblock. It seemed far more likely that Nettie or Kale had wanted Silas dead.

The tingling sensation rushed to my shoulders as pieces began to click into place. "If Junior knew that Silas got that land after their mother died, he'd know that Kale will eventually inherit from Nettie. Is that why he's so fired up to get Kale on his payroll, and was that why he'd suddenly started coming on to his sister-in-law?"

The crunch of footsteps on gravel distracted Adele for a moment. Ed came around the trailer, and I watched her close up right in front of my eyes. "I don't know," she whispered. "You'd have to ask him." She turned toward Ed with a wave and a smile. "There you are. You got some time to look at my starter?"

"You bet." Ed stopped in front of us and wiped his greasy hands on a rag. "I got bad news for you, Miss Lucero. There's no way I can fix that Mercedes of yours. The front axle is cracked, one door is a goner, and those air bags will cost a fortune to replace. There's a whole long list of what's wrong, but bottom line? The thing's totaled."

Twenty-nine

I didn't care about the Mercedes right then. I knew I'd care eventually but it was just a car. A really great car, but just a car. I'd inherited it when Philippe died, so it had never really felt like mine. All I could think about was who'd killed Silas, and how to get that information to the right people. Instinctively, I checked my cell phone, but the earth hadn't shifted on its axis and cell towers hadn't magically migrated to new locations. I still had no service.

After paying the storage fee I'd already racked up and promising to let Ed know my plans for the Mercedes, I drove back to T-Rex's and went inside. The clerks were happy to let me use the phone so I placed a call to Georgie Tucker.

"I know what happened," I said when she answered her phone. I heard a gasp behind me and realized I shouldn't say too much where the T-Rex staff could hear me. I didn't want anybody to let Nettie and Kale know that I was on to them before Georgie could arrest them. I cupped my hand around the receiver and whispered, "We need to meet. How soon can you get here?"

"You know who killed Silas?"

"Yes."

"I'm about an hour away," Georgie said. "Why don't you just tell me who you think it was?"

"I can't do that," I said. "I'm calling from the general store."

"You don't want anyone to overhear?"

"That's right."

"Stay where you are," Georgie ordered. "I'll be there as soon as I can."

"I'll be in the parking lot," I told her. I figured she'd find me without any trouble. Miss Frankie's car was bound to stand out.

Both clerks looked curious when I hung up. I think they expected me to explain myself. That might be what everyone in Baie Rebelle did when they made a public phone call, but sometimes you just have to buck tradition.

I smiled and thanked them for the use of the phone, and then let myself outside.

I chafed at every second I had to wait. A couple of times, I had the urge to play hero and drive out to Nettie's just to make sure she and Kale didn't get away. But I wasn't stupid. If Nettie Laroche saw me at her house, she'd probably realize the jig was up. I couldn't outrun her in Miss Frankie's car. I'd be too nervous about wrecking it to try. Besides, Nettie and Kale had immediate access to (and familiarity with) hundreds of miles of remote swampland. I can't stress enough how much I did not want to end up a statistic on somebody's death-by-alligator list.

I waited for about twenty minutes before three things

happened simultaneously: I got too antsy to sit still; I realized my mouth was dry as dirt; and I remembered that Nettie was probably at work. I could get a table at the Gator Pit and order a Diet Coke. That way I could easily keep an eye on Nettie until Georgie arrived.

Great plan—except that the Gator Pit was empty save the long-haired bartender who'd been on duty last time. Long Hair looked up from the small TV behind the bar and gave me a chin-jerk greeting. "Getcha anything?"

"A Diet Coke, please." I sat on a barstool and glanced around. "Is Nettie here?"

"You know Nettie?"

"We've met a couple of times. I thought I'd say hello."

Long Hair put a glass in front of me and almost got it on the coaster. "Nettie ain't here. She didn't show up this morning."

I tried not to jump to conclusions. She could have been sick. Missing a shift at work didn't necessarily mean that she was a coldblooded killer on the lam. "Have you called her?"

"Tried three times. She ain't answering her phone. A possum or a raccoon maybe chewed through the phone line."

Okay. It looked bad. But again I told myself that Nettie's failure to show up wasn't necessarily a reason to worry. "Is that usual? Does she skip shifts often?"

Long Hair wiped down a spot on the bar and shook his head. "Not since I've been here. She's usually right where she's supposed to be." He tossed the rag into the sink and jerked his chin toward the empty room. "I woulda gone to check on her but I'm the only one here. She's probably sick. Kale will come by and let me know."

I did my best to believe that Nettie was under the weather and that animals had taken out her only means of communication, but the uneasy feeling wouldn't go away. If Nettie and Kale were on the run, I should let Georgie know right away.

"Why don't I go check on her," I said to the bartender. "If Georgie Tucker comes looking for me, would you tell her I've gone out to Nettie's house?"

"Sure thing. You'll let me know what's going on after you talk to her?"

"I'll make sure of it."

I drove as fast as I dared on those narrow, winding roads to Nettie's tiny yellow house. I kept telling myself that I was just being overly cautious. That I shouldn't jump to conclusions. That Nettie and Kale couldn't know that I'd figured out everything they'd done to get Silas's inheritance and ensure Kale's future. They wouldn't disappear now.

I picked up the scent of burning wood before I actually saw the smoke curling up over the trees. Sick with fear, I pressed the accelerator and shot around those curves faster than I felt safe. It seemed to take forever, but I finally rounded the last turn.

Thick gray smoke billowed from the rooftop and my heart plummeted. Had Nettie and Kale torched the house? As I pulled into the driveway and saw the white Ford Ranger near the back of the house, my breath left my lungs in a *whoosh!* I hadn't wanted Kale to be in on his mother's scheme, but that thought was better than the alternative. I couldn't bear to think that Nettie had left Kale behind.

Back in the city I could have dialed 911 and emergency crews would have been on their way within minutes. Here in Baie Rebelle that wasn't an option. The closest phone was inside the burning house. I'd never get to a neighbor in time to save him. I was his only chance of survival.

I shouted for Kale at the top of my lungs, but I couldn't hear any response. The idea of going into a burning building terrified me, but I couldn't just sit back and do nothing. I'd never be able to live with myself, especially after the way Kale had saved me when I was stranded on the side of the road. I might already be too late, but if I were the one inside, I'd like to think someone would at least try to get me out.

I ran around to the back of the house, where towels hung on a makeshift clothesline. That laundry drying innocently in the sun seemed incongruous to me. Would Nettie have hung out the laundry if she planned to set fire to the house?

While my brain pondered that question, I checked the door and window. I couldn't see flames, but it looked like the whole house was filled with smoke. Drawing on every speck of courage I could find, I carefully put my hand on the door to feel for heat. It was warm, not hot, but I grabbed a towel off the line and wrapped my hand before I tried the knob.

It turned easily so I pushed the door open and stepped back in case flames shot out at me. Smoke poured out the door, temporarily blinding me. My eyes burned and my lungs, still sore from the air bag incident, seized up on me. I gasped shallow breaths and pushed inside. Smoke filled my lungs immediately. I dropped to the floor, somehow remembering that smoke rises, and coughed out Kale's name again.

The reality of being inside that burning house was even more horrific than I could have imagined. Boards creaked and groaned beneath me, making noises that sounded almost human. I couldn't go in much farther. I'd never make it out alive.

Carefully, I inched forward and called out again. My voice came out on a cough that felt as if it had shredded my lungs. I had to get outside.

Just then I saw something move in the smoke ahead of me. The shape turned into a person, and Kale backed into the room, dragging his mother behind him.

Without thinking, I crawled forward to help. Kale was disoriented and terrified. He swatted me away and kept tugging his mother toward the door. My head was spinning and I could barely see. My lungs were ready to explode, but I scooted around so I could grab Nettie's feet.

After what felt like an eternity, Kale and I made it out the door and into the fresh air. We took a few seconds to suck in some oxygen and orient ourselves, but we were far from free of danger. "We have to get away from the house," I said to Kale. My voice sounded like I'd swallowed gravel. Even those few words hurt.

Together, we picked Nettie up and started moving toward Kale's truck. I had no idea where the nearest hospital was, and the only medical help in Baie Rebelle was the faith healer Aunt Margaret had mentioned to me, but I thought a *traiteur* would be better than nothing. We had to get help for Nettie.

We were halfway to the truck when I heard something zing past my ear, followed by a *ping* that sounded like rock hitting metal.

Kale slammed into me and knocked me to the ground, shouting, "Take cover!"

My mind was working in slow motion. I had difficulty understanding him. While I was still trying to arrange his warning into words I could comprehend, another *ping* came and my mind suddenly clicked into working order.

Someone was shooting at us.

Thirty

❧

I was in full fight-or-flight mode by the time the third shot came, and I wasn't seriously considering the "fight" option. Kale threw Nettie over his shoulder and ducked behind the Ranger. I followed Kale, throwing myself on the ground a split second before shot number four pierced the truck bed.

Nettie coughed a couple of times, so I knew she was alive. At least for now. Kale threw an arm over her and warned her to stay down but I thought she looked too weak to get up anyway. I smelled gasoline and realized the gunman must have hit the gas tank. Which meant we couldn't use the Ranger to get away. Until that moment, I'd been counting us lucky that he'd missed his targets. Now I realized he—or she—was a better shot than I'd thought.

"Is there any place we can hide?" I asked.

Kale tipped his head toward the garage. It was detached from the house, but only a few feet from the truck. "That's it unless we can get to a neighbor's," he said. "And I don't think we'd make it with Ma."

I inched up so I could see over the Ranger's hood and scanned the area. "I think the shots came from that hill," I said, pointing across the highway.

"He won't stay there," Kale said, crouching beside me. "He knows where we are. He'll move to get a better shot at us."

His assessment made sense to me. "How long do you think we have?"

"Couple of minutes, maybe."

That wasn't nearly long enough. We couldn't get to safety but we couldn't just stay there and turn ourselves into sitting ducks. "Is it Junior?" I asked.

Kale nodded. "Has to be. If Mom dies, all that land comes to me. If I'm gone, Junior's the only one left to inherit."

So he staged a house fire to kill off the competition? Apparently, Silas wasn't the only deranged nut on the family tree. "We have to find a way to beat him at his own game," I said. "What are his weaknesses?"

"Out here? He doesn't have any."

"Everybody has weaknesses," I insisted. "What are his?"

Kale's temper snapped and he turned on me. "He doesn't *have* any. He's one of the best. He can pick off an alligator swimming in the open with a single shot. Do you know how small the kill-spot is on a gator? It's the size of a quarter."

"I don't care," I shouted back. "I know we're being hunted, and I know he's good enough to take us out, but we have to do *something*. We can't just sit here and wait for him to pick us off. What pushes his buttons, Kale? You have to know."

Nettie coughed again and this time she tried to speak. "Too . . . smart."

They were making *me* crazy. Junior had been there for

them so long they'd started thinking of him as invincible. But if they held on to that way of thinking, we were all doomed. "He's not that smart," I snapped. "Come on. We can do this if we put our heads together."

Kale stood up before I could stop him. "You stay with Ma. I'll see what I can do."

Worried that he'd just put a bull's-eye on his chest, I grabbed his arm and jerked him down toward the ground. He let out an *oooph!* and crashed onto me hard enough to knock the air out of my lungs. Hot, sticky blood hit my face and neck.

I screamed and tried to shove him off me. I was certain he'd been killed and I didn't want to lie there beneath a dead guy. Besides, I couldn't save Nettie or myself if I couldn't get up.

It took some effort, but Kale finally rolled to one side with a deep groan. I leaned over him and searched for the bullet wound. Blood covered his shirt, but he was alive. I couldn't see anything with all that blood on him so I tore his shirt open. I spotted the wound on his left shoulder. His shoulder, not his heart. Thank God.

I ripped a piece of fabric from his shirt and used it to stanch the flow of blood. It wasn't much of a bandage and it wasn't nearly good enough, but it was all I had. I was pretty sure that Kale would survive the wound if he didn't lose too much blood or get shot again. Junior wouldn't miss a second time.

I couldn't think. I had no idea what to do. I had two seriously injured people with me. Both of them needed medical attention, but I wasn't strong enough or fast enough to get it for them. I would have given anything for a miracle. A few bars of service on my cell phone. The help of a random stranger who had either medical training or a high-powered rifle. I wasn't picky.

I sat in the dirt watching gasoline creep across the driveway and feeling utterly helpless. Other than decorating cakes and making a mean *chili verde*, I didn't have many useful skills. I should learn how to shoot. Or go to medical school. I should study covert undercover operations and practice moves that would let me get across that road and up the hill without being detected.

I should be able to do *something*.

I knew we'd already been sitting there too long. Junior would reach a new location any second. I strained to hear any sound or see any movement that might tell me his location, but he was good at what he did. Nothing gave him away.

But I did pick up a low hum that seemed to grow louder all the time. The hum of wheels on pavement. Someone was coming toward us, but I didn't know whether to be relieved or frightened. Maybe we were about to be rescued. Maybe Junior had decided to finish the job up close and personal.

My breath caught in my throat and my heart slammed against my ribs. I inched forward carefully and watched for the vehicle to come into view, and I prayed that Georgie had figured out where I was and was now riding in like the cavalry.

After a very long time a truck came into view. I couldn't tell who was driving, but it didn't look like Junior's truck and I was able to let out the breath I'd been holding. Two more trucks rounded the curve in the road right behind the first one. In a blur of motion all three trucks pulled to the side of the road and people began to pour out.

I didn't know if Junior would try to finish what he'd started with so many witnesses around, but I thought I should warn them that they could be in danger. I jumped up and raced toward them, shouting for them to get back and take cover.

Eskil stepped out of the tangle of people and grabbed my

arms. "Slow down there, Rita. Don't worry. We came to put out the fire."

I tried to explain but the words kept getting stuck. Whole sentences turned into single words by the time they reached my mouth. "Nettie," I said insistently. "Kale. Shot."

Eskil gently pressed me toward someone else. "Don't worry, little girl. It'll be okay."

I grabbed his arm, desperate to make him understand. "Junior. Out there," I said and did my best to pinpoint his location. "He shot Kale."

One of the other men seemed to understand what I was saying. I directed him toward the Ranger and turned back to find that Eskil's face—what I could see of it between his eyebrows and beard—was tight with anger. "You're sure it's Junior?"

Was I? I shook my head and managed to connect a few words at a time. "No, but Kale said. Tell Georgie. Have to stop him."

Eskil led me along the caravan of rescue pickups and put me inside the cab of the last one in line. He grabbed a rifle from the rack behind my head and growled, "You stay right here. I'll take care of this."

"No! Don't. Let the sheriff do it."

My plea fell on deaf ears. I watched in horror as Eskil trotted across the road and disappeared into the undergrowth. I sank down in the seat and tried to take a couple of deep breaths, but I was too worried to sit still. If anything happened to Eskil, I knew Bernice would never forgive me. I had no idea what I could do to help him, but that useless feeling filled me with desperation. Still not sure what I could do to prevent a tragedy, I opened the door.

I heard a clatter and a metallic click followed by a deep

male voice. "Stop right there, ma'am. I can't let you get out of the truck."

I whipped around to see who was talking and ready to argue with whoever Eskil had told to keep an eye on me, but the face I saw in the driver's side window chilled me to the bone.

Pointing some massive handgun at my head, Junior slid into the truck with me and turned the key. I knew that wasn't the gun he'd used to shoot at us from the hill, but I caught a glimpse of a rifle with a scope as he tossed it into the truck bed.

Before anyone noticed what was happening, Junior executed a perfect three-point turn and took off toward town. I hadn't buckled my seat belt, and I didn't buckle it now. I had to look for an opportunity to jump out of the truck, and I didn't want anything to slow me down when I found it.

Junior drove like a madman, which, of course, he was. The truck bounced over ruts in the road and swerved dangerously around curves. And the only thing I could do was hang on for dear life.

Facing your own mortality is not as much fun as it looks in the movies. A million thoughts raced through my head as Junior and I barreled toward Baie Rebelle. Most of them were completely inane. I noticed the color of the sky, the way the butterflies swarmed up from the bushes, and how those bushes swayed as we roared past.

I knew I should be looking for a way to escape, but I couldn't seem to order my thoughts. I gripped the armrest and told myself over and over that I would be able to jump when Junior slowed to go through town. It seemed logical, but I felt an almost overwhelming pressure to do something now.

Maybe he wouldn't take me into town. Maybe he had a secret hiding place along the way. Maybe he'd shoot me, or throw me into the water. Maybe nobody would ever know what happened to me.

Nervous energy mixed with the fear. My foot began to tap in an erratic rhythm that only made me feel worse. More to calm myself than to get Junior to confess, I decided to get him talking. Even hearing him rant and rave would be preferable to sitting there in silence, imagining all kinds of horrible things.

I said the first thing that popped into my head: "You're not going to get away with this, you know."

"Shut up."

"Everybody knows you set that fire. Nobody will believe it was an accident. But your plan failed. Nettie's still alive and so is Kale."

"Shut. Up!"

"All this has been for nothing. You wanted your father's property all for yourself, but you'll never get it now. You'll spend the rest of your miserable life in prison."

I didn't see his hand move in time to duck. He backhanded me across the cheek. Pain seared my face and the taste of blood filled my mouth.

"I said *shut the hell up.*"

A rational woman would have taken his advice, but I was a long way from rational. "When did you decide to frame Eskil? Before you killed your brother, or after?"

He glowered at me. "You're a pain in the ass."

"And you've just added kidnapping to your long list of felonies. Did you really think nobody would figure out it was you? Because that's just crazy, you know."

He sneered at me. His eyes were ice cold and empty. "Who's the crazy one?" he said in an ominous voice. "Who's the stupid one? Huh? Tell me, which one of us is driving the truck?"

Junior had a point, but it had been pure dumb luck, not superior genius, that had put him behind the wheel. Plus the fact that he was carrying a loaded gun. And the whole homicidal maniac thing.

I experienced a moment of crushing despair before I remembered what Nettie had said when she started regaining consciousness back at the house. "Too smart," she'd said right after I'd asked about Junior's weaknesses. Junior was too smart for his own good. She'd tried to give me the answer but I'd misunderstood her.

If that's what she meant, I had two choices: Try to placate Junior and hope he'd calm down enough to have second thoughts about turning me into alligator bait; or push his buttons and hope anger made him careless.

Since I didn't think I could convincingly pull off calm and soothing, I went with Plan B. Besides, I'd been doing a pretty good job of pissing him off already.

"You didn't know what your mother was going to do until she died, did you? She didn't tell you that she was giving half of the property to Silas."

Junior's jaw clenched but he didn't say a word.

"You thought you were going to get everything. You really thought your mother was going to cut Silas out just because your father had?"

"She was stupid," Junior said through clenched teeth. "She couldn't see what a worthless piece of shit he was. He threw it all away. All of it. And why? Because of some crazy-ass idea that owning property was wrong."

We zoomed past a house that was nestled in a grove of

trees. It was there and gone too quickly for me to think about escaping.

I tried to keep him talking. "You didn't mind that at the time, though. In fact, I'll bet you encouraged Silas to think that way. I'll bet you fed into his crazy idea so you could have it all. You knew how he was."

"He didn't know how to listen to anybody else," Junior said. "He didn't know how to compromise. He didn't know how to change his mind. Once he made a decision, he stuck with it."

"Except his marriage and family," I said. "He changed his mind about them."

Junior laughed. "Shows what you know. He didn't change his mind about them, it just never occurred to him that going off and living in the swamp for twenty years was abandoning his family." He shot a look at me and his smile slipped off his face.

"Did you plan to kill him, or did you just see an opportunity and go for it?"

"I went there to talk sense into him," Junior said. "I told him we could do great things together. I told him we could put the land together and make the biggest charter company in the state. We could have made money hand over fist. But he wouldn't listen. Silas *never* listened."

"He told you no?"

"He told me to leave and never come back. He told me he'd been watching me with Kale and he was angry that I'd stepped up to take his place." Junior snorted a harsh laugh. "Like *he* was any kind of a father to the kid."

"He'd been trying to talk to Kale since your mother died. Did you know that?"

"Oh, yeah. I saw the two of them together that night. But that kid's a chip off the old block. He won't listen to anybody either."

"Silas was trying to tell Kale about your mother's will?"

"Silas was trying to warn him not to work with me. He thought I was using Kale. I gave my life to that kid, and Silas tried to ruin everything!"

"And that's why you killed him?"

"I killed him because he deserved to die. Somebody had to do it."

"I know he did a lot of damage," I said. "He hurt people. He abandoned his family. He broke his mother's heart. He stole from his neighbors, taking the fish they caught and the animals they trapped right under their noses. I never even met him and I know he did bad stuff. But we don't get to decide who lives and dies."

Junior didn't give me a direct answer. "My father worked himself to death trying to make this family one that other people would respect. I've broken my back to do the same. Silas? He didn't give a rip. He killed a man we all considered a friend. He stole a family secret."

"The still?"

"That's not what we do out here," Junior ranted. "We watch out for each other. We help each other."

And apparently kill each other, but I kept that observation to myself.

"He called me stupid," Junior said. "He. Called *me*. Stupid! He lived like a damn pauper out there. He gave up everything and turned his back on everybody, and my mother still loved him best."

I didn't know if that was true or not, but that didn't matter. Junior believed it, and it had become his reality. It would take someone with greater skills than mine to make him see the world differently.

We were close to town by then so I started watching for my chance to get away. Moving surreptitiously, I put my hand on the car door and felt around for the handle. We reached the junction and I planted my feet, prepared for Junior to slow down so I could jump.

He rounded the corner so fast we rocked up on two wheels. I thought we were going to flip, but the truck righted itself and the two airborne tires slammed onto the pavement. My teeth snapped together and I bit my tongue. It hurt, but I was more upset at the realization that Junior wasn't going to slow down.

He stomped on the gas and the truck shot forward again. He was focused on the road in front of us and I knew it was now or never. A few miles to the north he'd run into a patchwork of roads that spiraled off in a dozen different directions. If I let him get that far, nobody would ever find him—or me.

I didn't let myself think about what I was doing or how risky it was. Bringing my feet up, I twisted in my seat and kicked his arms as hard as I could. He lost his grip on the pistol and it clattered to the floor. I kicked again and the steering wheel jerked to the left. The truck careened dangerously as Junior tried to regain control. I didn't dare change tactics. Even a few seconds could make a difference between living and dying.

While I tried to keep him off balance, Junior struggled to get control of the truck. He lashed out at me with his fist, but I didn't let the pain distract me. He didn't have the gun, and that's what mattered.

I leaned against the door for leverage and tried to kick harder. I aimed for his shoulder, his hands, and his legs, always going for a different body part to keep him from anticipating my next move. Several times, I almost fell off the seat, but I managed to hold on until we rounded a sharp curve a little north of town.

Junior swore and stomped on the brakes, and this time I

did lose my balance. I landed on the gun and scrambled to pick it up as the truck screeched to a halt. Junior fumbled to shift into reverse as I climbed back on the seat and put the gun right up against his head. "If this truck moves another inch," I warned, "I swear to God I'll shoot you."

Beneath the sound of blood rushing through my veins, I thought I heard voices. Dimly, I became aware of someone outside the window. I blinked to clear my vision and realized that red and blue lights were swirling on the edge of my peripheral vision.

Georgie threw open the truck door and yanked Junior out of his seat. Two other deputies shouted for him to get down on the ground and put his hands over his head. At least I think that's what they were saying. My teeth began to chatter and my hands to shake. And very gently, Georgie took the gun from my hand and put it somewhere out of my reach.

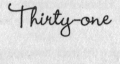

I didn't get the whole story for days, but Eskil had realized almost immediately that the truck he'd put me in had disappeared. I don't know where he went to make the call, but somehow he'd alerted Georgie to the danger I was in.

She was only a few miles from Baie Rebelle at the time, and based on my claim that I'd solved the murder, she'd brought backup. They'd set up a roadblock and the rest was history.

We stayed with Aunt Margaret that night and drove back to New Orleans the next day. On the way back, I finally talked to Miss Frankie about Christmas. She was shocked that I'd been so nervous to bring it up with her. And since *she* hadn't been pulled in a dozen different directions for days in a row, she was able to come up with a solution so logical it had eluded me: I'd be far too busy to go away in December anyway, so why not go home for Thanksgiving week?

Duh!

I thought even Uncle Nestor would be okay with that. (Especially since it turned out that the fee to change the ticket wasn't too steep, thank goodness.)

To my surprise, Miss Frankie even agreed to have Pearl Lee help her host the family dinner at Christmas. The only thing she asked was that I show up. With Pearl Lee on the organizing committee, I'd be there with bells on.

Aunt Yolanda was beside herself with joy at the prospect of having me home even sooner than expected, and for a whole week. She really didn't care when I came. So now that the decision was made and the new airline ticket bought and paid for, I could finally let myself get excited.

I'll never know whether or not I would have pulled the trigger that day. Sometimes I want to think I would have, and other times I assure myself that I could never take a life. What I do know is that there's no absolute right or wrong when you're in a life-and-death situation. Fight or flee. Cooperate or get in the way. Scream or stay quiet. You do what you have to do. Nobody else gets to judge your decision.

I'd taken one look at Miss Frankie's face after my brush with death and realized all over again how foolish I'd been to doubt her feelings for me. She'd told me more than once that she considered me family. She'd assured me over and over again that she loved me. It was my own insecurities that had taken over and made me doubt the evidence right in front of my eyes. I needed to do a better job of getting my personal demons under control. If my time in Baie Rebelle had taught me nothing else, it had taught me that.

Two days and one trip to the doctor later, I walked into the design room at Zydeco and found everyone sitting around a couple of silver tables. I'd been looking for Edie for several minutes, but I hadn't been able to find her anywhere. Mystery solved. She was there, wearing a pumpkin costume over her bulging belly, and glaring at me from a stool at Ox's table. Ox and Isabeau were dressed as Batman and Robin, Estelle had turned herself into Lucille Ball for the day, Dwight wore camouflage and had let his beard grow so that he resembled one of the locals from Baie Rebelle, although I was pretty sure he was aiming for one of the Robertson boys from *Duck Dynasty*. Sparkle wore a vampire costume that I think came out of her own closet.

I stood in the doorway for a minute, pleased with the cheerleader costume I'd thrown together at the last minute and half expecting them all to leap out of their seats and shout, "Surprise!" It took a while for me to realize that wasn't going to happen.

"What's going on?" I asked when nobody spoke. "What's everybody doing back here? We have work to do. Ox, you and I are meeting with Evangeline Delahunt tomorrow and we have a lot to get ready before then. Dwight, aren't you supposed to be working on the Holt retirement cake?"

Someone in the back of the room stood up and moved toward me. He was tall. Solid. Six feet or so of good ol' boy charm, dressed as a plainclothes police officer—only that was no costume. What was Sullivan doing here?

"Sit down, Rita," he said. "Your friends asked me to come here today because they're concerned about you."

I laughed uncomfortably and held out my arms so they could all get a good look. "I'm *fine*, okay? I barely got a scratch. Junior Laroche is in jail facing so many charges he'll probably never go free." This was only about the hundredth time I'd said the same thing since I came back from Baie Rebelle, but they all seemed determined to doubt me.

Sullivan kept walking, and for the first time I noticed

that Gabriel was also there, sitting in the corner. His face was solemn, his eyes a cloudy brown.

"You're not fine," Sullivan said. "In the space of a few days you were in an accident that totaled your Mercedes, almost got caught in a house fire, got shot at, and were kidnapped. Have I left anything out?"

A few mumbles rose up from my so-called friends (and I use that term loosely). I laughed and looked around the room in disbelief. "Cut it out, you guys! You all look so serious, but you can't stage an intervention wearing Halloween costumes! Gabriel, quit glaring at me. And you, Sullivan. You're just being creepy."

"This isn't a joke," Estelle said. Her round cheeks turned pink and her full red-lipped mouth curved into a frown so deep it touched one of her chins. "You have to stop doing this. One of these days you're going to come back dead."

I grinned at her phrasing. "Well, actually—"

"You know what she means," Dwight said, cutting me off. "You're not a cop. You're not a private investigator. You can't keep putting yourself in danger."

"Hey, look. I didn't want to get involved," I told them. "I tried *not* to get involved. I would have been right here at work if I hadn't been in that accident."

"Which you got into because you were following a murder suspect," Isabeau pointed out.

"A minor point since he turned out to be innocent." I turned away. "You all go ahead and have your fun. It was hilarious. But now I'm going back to work."

Sullivan stepped in front of me. "It's not a joke," he said softly. "They really are staging an intervention."

"Well, that's just silly," I said. "Will you all knock it off? We have too much work to waste time like this."

Ox stood and started to say something, but at that very

moment Edie let out a yowl and cut him off. She stared down at the pumpkin costume and tried to get a look at the floor. "My water just broke!"

"Nice try," I told her. "It's not going to work this time."

"No! I'm serious! Look!"

Isabeau was the only one who took the bait, but the look on her face after she checked the floor spurred everyone else to action. For the moment all of my transgressions were forgotten. If I was lucky, they'd all be so wrapped up in the baby once it got here, it would be a while before they remembered.

"Call River," I told Sparkle when I realized that the baby was really and truly on its way. "Now!"

The baby came into the world that night at nine fifteen. I don't know if anyone else was surprised when River came out of the delivery room to tell us he had a son, but I sure was. I'd been almost certain the baby was a girl.

Maybe that's because I was still freaking out about the god-mother thing. I knew nothing about babies, but I stood a remote chance of getting it right with a girl child. You could fit what I knew about boys on the head of a pin. A very small pin.

The hospital staff kept us all away until Edie had recovered enough for visitors. Sparkle was half crazy by the time they let her in to see her nephew. She and I went into Edie's room first, Sparkle as the baby's vampire aunt and me as his cheerleader godmother. I guess there were some perks.

Edie, relieved of her pumpkin costume, looked weak but happy and River just looked overwhelmed, but in a good way. He held the baby, but it was obvious that the baby already had his daddy wrapped around his little finger.

I kissed Edie's cheek and gave River a quick but awkward

hug so I wouldn't hurt his little bundle of joy. "I can't believe he's really here," I whispered. "Do you have a name yet?"

Edie shook her head and leaned back on her pillow. "Not yet. We haven't really talked about it."

"John David," River whispered.

Edie gave him a bleary one-eyed look. "What?"

"I'd like his name to be John David."

"I love it," Sparkle said. "It's perfect."

Edie opened the other eye. "Don't I get a say in this?"

"Of course," River assured her. "I just said that I'd like his name to be John David. If you don't like it, we'll find another one."

Edie gave up a weary smile. "I never said I don't like it. It just came out of the blue, that's all. What's so special about John David?"

River kissed the baby's forehead and traced a finger along his cheek. "Nothing really. It's just the name I wanted for myself when I was a kid."

I thought it was a nice name. I tried sending Edie a subliminal message not to turn this perfect moment into an argument. It must have worked, because she let out a soft sigh and said, "Sounds good to me. You're his father."

After a while, River put John David in Sparkle's arms, and that's when I found out that the baby had miracle-working powers. The instant Sparkle touched her new nephew, she went through a remarkable transformation.

With one breath that baby tore off the bored goth mask Sparkle wore every day and exposed her for who she really was: a real live girl. I'd been privileged to catch glimpses of her in the past, beneath the pale makeup, the leather, and the spikes, but John David brought her out into the open. She laughed and cooed and even sang—which wasn't really her strong suit but John David didn't seem to mind.

And then it was my turn. River showed me what to do with my arms and explained about supporting the newborn's neck, then carefully settled the baby—my godson—in the crook of my arm and took a step back. The baby was heavier than I'd expected, but I thought I adjusted quickly. Then he stirred and I looked up at River in a panic. "I think you should take him back."

"You're okay."

"But what if I drop him?"

"You won't," Edie said.

"I could," I warned. "I could lose my grip on him. He could roll right out of my arms and land on the floor and get hurt."

"You'll be fine," River said and took another step away.

"But—"

John David made a mewling sound and I looked down at his perfect little face. And just like *that* I fell hopelessly in love. I'd just been blindsided again, but this time I didn't mind at all.

Recipes

❧

Cajun Boudin Sausage

Makes 4 to 4 ½ pounds sausage

1½ pounds pork steak
½ pound fresh pork liver, rinsed (Use the freshest liver
   possible, and for best results, don't use frozen.)
1 medium onion, coarsely chopped
3 garlic cloves
1 sprig fresh thyme
2 bay leaves
cold water as needed
4 feet of 1½-inch sausage casings (Can be found at many
   grocery stores and specialty markets or even
   ordered.)
kosher salt and black pepper to taste

> 2 cups uncooked long-grain rice
> 1 bunch green onions, thinly sliced
> ½ cup Italian parsley, finely chopped
> cayenne pepper to taste

Cut the pork steak and liver into 2-inch pieces and place in a large saucepan. Add the onion, garlic, thyme, and bay leaves. Cover with water (1 to 1½ inches over the contents of the pan). Season to taste with salt and black pepper.

Bring to a boil then lower the heat to a simmer; skim off any foam that rises to the surface. Simmer for about 1 hour or until the meat is very tender. Remove the bay leaves and thyme, then strain the solids from the broth. (Be sure to reserve the broth.)

Grind the meats and cooked onion and garlic while they're still hot. If you don't have a meat grinder, you can chop the meat into small pieces by hand.

To make the rice: In a saucepan with a lid, combine the rice with 3 cups of the reserved broth. (You can make the rice with water, but using the broth adds a lot of wonderful flavor.)

Taste the broth for seasoning. If necessary, season with salt and black pepper. Bring to a boil, then turn down to very low heat and cover. Cook until the rice is tender and the liquid is absorbed, about 20 minutes. Do not remove the lid from the pot during cooking time.

When the rice is cooked, combine it with the ground meat mixture, green onions, and parsley. Mix thoroughly and season to taste with salt, black pepper, and cayenne.

Stuff into prepared hog (sausage) casings or form into patties or balls for pan frying.

Boudin also makes a great stuffing.

To heat the stuffed boudin sausages, either poach them in water between 165°F and 185°F, or brush the casings with a little oil and bake in a 400°F oven until heated through and the skins are crispy. If poaching, take the boudin out of the casings to eat it because the casings can become rubbery.

* * *

Aunt Margaret's Pea-Picking Cake
(aka Pig-Picking Cake)

Makes one three-layer cake using 8- or 9-inch round cake pans

> 1 (18-ounce) "moist"-type yellow cake mix (Regular
>   cake mixes will work as well, but the layers may be
>   shorter and denser.)
> 1 (11-ounce) can mandarin oranges with juice
> 4 eggs
> ½ cup vegetable oil
> 1 (8-ounce) carton frozen whipped topping, thawed
> 1 (8-ounce) can crushed pineapple, with juice
> 1 (3.4-ounce, 4-serving) box instant vanilla pudding

Preheat the oven to 350°F. Grease and flour three 8- or 9-inch cake pans.

In a mixing bowl, combine the cake mix, mandarin oranges and juice, eggs, and oil. Beat for 2 minutes with an electric mixer.

Pour into the pans and bake for 20 to 25 minutes or until the cake tester comes out clean.

Cool in the pans for 5 minutes, turn out of the pans, and finish cooling on wire racks.

To make the frosting: In a mixing bowl, combine the whipped topping, pineapple and juice, and vanilla pudding mix. Frost between the layers and on the top of the cake. (The frosting will be too light to stick to the sides of the cake.)

*　　*　　*

Homemade Banana Pudding

This recipe has been passed down for a few generations and, like so many recipes of its kind, information on serving sizes has been lost (if it ever existed). I'm going to say this recipe will serve 12, but if you have a table full of folks who really love their banana pudding, it may only serve 6.

> *1 box vanilla wafer cookies*
> *5 bananas*
> *½ cup sugar*
> *⅓ cup flour*
> *3 egg yolks*
> *2 cups milk*
> *dash salt*
> *½ teaspoon vanilla*
> *whipped cream (You can use a prepared whipped*
> *topping if desired.)*

Place a layer of vanilla wafer cookies in the bottom of a medium-sized mixing bowl. Slice a banana over the top.

Repeat two more times with another layer of wafers and the remaining bananas.

In a saucepan (or double boiler) on medium-low heat, combine the rest of the ingredients except the vanilla. Stir well with a wire whisk.

Allow to cook until thickened, stirring constantly to prevent scorching (about 15 minutes). Add the vanilla and stir.

Immediately pour over the wafers and bananas. Let sit for about 5 minutes or so before serving, to allow the wafers time to absorb the pudding. Top with whipped cream.

* * *

Alligator in Garlic Wine Sauce

Serves 8

> 2 pounds alligator meat, cut into cubes
> 3 tablespoons fresh lime juice
> salt and pepper to taste
> approximately 1 cup flour
> 2 tablespoons olive oil
> 1 tablespoon minced garlic
> ½ cup white wine (Use a wine you would drink at the
>   table for best results.)

Toss the alligator cubes with the lime juice, cover, and refrigerate for 1 hour to marinate.

Squeeze any excess liquid from the alligator and place into a large bowl. Season with salt and pepper, then toss with enough flour to coat.

Remove the alligator, shake off the excess flour, and set aside.

Heat the olive oil in a large skillet over medium-high heat. Add the garlic; cook and stir until fragrant, about 30 seconds. Add the alligator, and cook until firm and opaque, 5 to 6 minutes.

Remove and place the alligator in a serving dish, then pour the wine into the skillet and simmer until thickened, about 2 minutes. Pour the sauce over the alligator to serve.

* * *

Cousin Eskil's Barbecue Sauce

Makes about a pint

4 tablespoons cornstarch, mixed with water
2 cloves garlic, minced
½ to 1 cup distilled vinegar
½ to 1 cup ketchup
1½ cups brown sugar
1 teaspoon seasoned salt
1 teaspoon soy sauce (up to 1 tablespoon, to taste)

Cook all the ingredients together, stirring constantly until thickened. Pour into a bottle and store in the refrigerator.

* * *

Roasted Parmesan Sweet Potatoes

Serves 3 to 4

2 large sweet potatoes, peeled and cubed
2 large cloves garlic, minced
2 tablespoons extra virgin olive oil
2 to 3 tablespoons Parmesan cheese, finely grated
½ teaspoon dried thyme
salt and pepper to taste

Preheat the oven to 400°F, and put the oven rack in the middle position. Line the bottom of a large baking sheet with aluminum foil.

In a medium-sized bowl, place the cubed sweet potatoes, garlic, olive oil, Parmesan cheese, and dried thyme. Distribute the ingredients evenly to cover the sweet potatoes. Sprinkle with salt and pepper to taste. Transfer the sweet potato mixture to the prepared baking sheet and spread out so that the cubes are in a single layer.

Roast in the oven for about 40 minutes, *or* until the potatoes can be easily pierced with a sharp knife. Set the oven to broil, and broil until the tops of the potatoes start to brown, about 8 to 10 minutes (keep an eye on them when broiling, as your time may differ and you want to take care not to burn them).

Serve immediately.

* * *

Candy Corn Cupcakes

Makes 18 cupcakes

CUPCAKES

> 1 (18-ounce) white cake mix
> 2 eggs
> 1 cup sour cream
> ½ cup milk
> ⅓ cup vegetable oil (I prefer canola, but use what you
>   like best.)
> orange and yellow food coloring

FROSTING

> 1 cup butter
> 4 cups powdered sugar
> ¼ teaspoon salt
> 1 teaspoon vanilla extract
> ⅓ cup heavy whipping cream

GARNISH

> candy corns
> orange sprinkles

Preheat the oven to 350°F, and line cupcake pan with paper liners. If you use white liners, the colors of the cupcakes will show through beautifully.

Combine all the cupcake ingredients in a large bowl and mix just until incorporated. Scrape the sides of the bowl and then beat on medium-high speed for 3 minutes.

Divide the batter in half. Color one half orange and the other half yellow.

Fill the paper liners with about 1 to 2 tablespoons of yellow batter. Top with 1 to 2 tablespoons of orange batter. Bake according to cake mix package directions—about 15 to 18 minutes.

Cool the cupcakes.

To make the buttercream frosting: In a mixing bowl, cream the butter until fluffy. Add the powdered sugar and continue creaming until the frosting is well blended. Add the salt, vanilla, and whipping cream. Blend on low speed until moistened. Beat at high speed until the frosting is fluffy.

Frost cooled cupcakes and add garnish.

Note: You can use this technique for fun confetti cupcakes using any color combinations you'd like; e.g., pink and blue for a baby shower or primary colors for a child's birthday.

Berkley Prime Crime titles by Jacklyn Brady

A SHEETCAKE NAMED DESIRE
CAKE ON A HOT TIN ROOF
ARSENIC AND OLD CAKE
THE CAKES OF WRATH
REBEL WITHOUT A CAKE